ENTER THE SAINT

On the side of the law and yet outside it, here the Saint at his ebullient best – and his ruthless enemies... The Soho vice king who couldn't help winning – until he crossed swords with the Saint; the murderous 'Spider' and his horde of diamonds, buried for seven years on Dartmoor; 'Straight' Audrey alias the Countess Marova – and the yachtload of millionaires she planned to fleece off the coast of Corsica. Three expert thrillers in one volume, all featuring the inimitable Simon Templar, the man who is always one step ahead of 'the Yard'.

ENTER THE SAINT

ENTER THE SAINT

by

Leslie Charteris

Dales Large Print Books
Long Preston, North Yorkshire,
BD23 4ND, England.

British Library Cataloguing in Publication Data.

Charteris, Leslie
Enter the Saint.

A catalogue record of this book is
available from the British Library

ISBN 1-84262-132-7 pbk

First published in Great Britain in 1971
by Hodder & Stoughton Ltd.

Published in Large Print 2002 by arrangement with
Hodder & Stoughton Ltd.

Dales Large Print is an imprint of Library Magna Books Ltd.

Printed and bound in Great Britain by
T.J. (International) Ltd., Cornwall, PL28 8RW

The characters and situations in this book are entirely imaginary and bear no relation to any real person or actual happening

Contents

FOREWORD

When a character has had as long a run as the Saint, the author must eventually be overtaken by problems which he never foresaw when he began his creation. For the world moves on, not even steadily, but with what often seems to be an inexorable acceleration; and the writer himself grows older, and wiser, and a better master of his craft. As with all ageing, the changes are gradual, almost imperceptible from year to year, until one day it becomes possible to see this whole accumulation in one startling glance, as by placing a man of 50 beside a photograph of him taken 30 years before.

This book, which contains the first novelets I ever wrote about the Saint, was first published in 1930, at which time about one-third of the potential readers of this edition were not even born. And only those in the oldest bracket will have personal memories of the era in which the stories were laid.

In those days I had no idea that the first Saint book would be followed by at least 35 others, and I might well have been appalled by the prospect if it had occurred to me, as

I would have been by seriously contemplating a vision of myself as a grandfather. And I would certainly have been somewhat indignant at the suggestion that this book was not nearly the best thing of its kind ever written, let alone that I would ever wish that it might survive only in mellowing reminiscence like an old silent movie.

But all these things have happened; and here we are with something which is rapidly becoming a period piece, if it isn't one already, yet which the publishers insist on keeping alive over my own protests, because, they say, too many people who have become Saint addicts recently would complain if they were arbitrarily cut off from tracing his career backwards to the earliest records of it.

My first thought in this situation was to revise these older stories, polishing the crudities of style which I am now conscious of, toning down the uncouth juvenilities which now embarrass me, changing outdated topical allusions, modernizing the mechanics of the action to conform with the timetables and technologies of today. But after some reflection and experiment I realized that that was no solution.

The polishing and toning down I might do – but was it worth devoting to it the time and effort which could be better employed in writing something entirely new? The dated topicalities could be replaced by new and current allusions – but how long would it be before those were no less dated? And basically, can a story honestly constructed within the framework of the conditions and attitudes and limitations of a bygone generation be displaced into another age without creating a new complex of unrealities and inconsistencies?

And where would this modernizing ever end, once it was started? Wouldn't it have to be done over again every five or ten years? And would the Sherlock Holmes stories be as durable if they had been translated from the idiom of hansom cabs to taxis to helicopters to a jet-powered anti-gravity belt?

Regretfully, I have decided that if the Saint Saga must remain permanently in print in its entirety, then it can only do so in its original form. That I can only ask readers to keep in mind the dates to which the first stories belong, and that I must hope they can adjust themselves not only to slightly archaic means of locomotion and telecommunication but also to the fact that all of the exuberances and philosophies expressed are not necessarily the same as those which I, or Simon Templar, would defend today.

This does not mean that we have renounced our zest for adventure. It only means that our taste may have become more subtle as our panoramas became larger. It is thrilling enough for a boy to skirmish with imaginary savages in a stalk through the woods. Later he will discover much quieter and deadlier monsters, while at the same time he is reaching towards the stars.

LESLIE CHARTERIS

THE MAN WHO WAS CLEVER

1

Mr 'Snake' Ganning was neither a great criminal nor a pleasant character, but he is interesting because he was the first victim of the organization led by the man known as the Saint, which was destined in the course of a few months to spread terror through the underworld of London – that ruthless association of reckless young men, brilliantly led, who worked on the side of the Law and who were yet outside the Law. There was to come a time when the mere mention of the Saint was sufficient to fill the most unimaginative malefactor with uneasy fears, when a man returning home late one night to find the sign of the Saint – a childish sketch of a little man with straight-line body and limbs, and an absurd halo over his round blank head – chalked upon his door, would be sent instinctively spinning round with his back to the nearest wall and his hand flying to his hip pocket, and an icy tingle of dread prickling up his spine; but at the date of the Ganning episode the Saint had only just commenced operations, and his name had not yet come to be surrounded with the aura of almost supernatural infallibility which it was to earn for itself later.

Mr Ganning was a tall, incredibly thin man, with sallow features and black hair that was invariably oiled and brushed to a shiny sleekness. His head was small and round, and he carried it thrust forward to the full stretch of his long neck. Taking into the combination of physical characteristics the sinuous carriage of his body, the glittering beadiness of his expressionless black eyes, and the silent litheness with which he moved, it was easy to appreciate the aptness of his nickname. He was the leader of a particularly tough racecourse gang generally known as 'The Snake's Boys', which subsisted in unmerited luxury on the proceeds of blackmailing bookmakers under threat of doing them grievous bodily harm; there were also a number of other unsavoury things about him which may be revealed in due course.

The actual motive for the interference of the Saint in the affairs of the Snake and his Boys was their treatment of Tommy Mitre on the occasion of his first venture into Turf finance. Tommy had always wanted to be a jockey, for horses were in his blood; but quite early in his apprenticeship he had been thrown and injured so severely that he had never been able to ride again, and he had had to content himself with the humble position of stable boy in a big training establishment. Then an uncle of Tommy's, who had been a publican, died, leaving his nephew the tremendous fortune of two hundred pounds, and Tommy decided to try his luck in the Silver Ring. He took out a licence, had a board painted ('Tommy Mitre – The Old Firm – Established 1822') and enlisted a clerk. One day he went down to Brighton with this paraphernalia and the remains of his two hundred pounds, and it was not long before the Snake's Boys spotted the stranger and made the usual demands. Tommy refused to pay. He ought to have known better, for the methods of the Snake had never been a secret in racing circles; but Tommy was like that – stubborn. He told the Snake exactly where he could go, and as a result Tommy Mitre was soundly beaten up by the Snake's Boys when he was leaving the course, and his capital and his day's profits were taken. And it so happened that Simon Templar had elected to enjoy a day's racing at Brighton, and had observed the beating-up from a distance.

Snake Ganning and a select committee of the Boys spent the evening in Brighton celebrating, and left for London by a late train. So also did Simon Templar.

Thus it came to pass that the said Simon Templar wandered up the platform a couple of minutes before the train left, espied the Snake and three of the Boys comfortably ensconced in a first-class carriage, and promptly joined them.

The Saint, it should be understood, was a vision that gave plenty of excuse for the glances of pleased anticipation which were exchanged by the Snake and his favourite Boys as soon as they had summed him up. In what he called his 'fighting kit' – which consisted of disreputable grey flannel bags and a tweed shooting-jacket of almost legendary age – the Saint had the unique gift of appearing so immaculate that the least absent-minded commissionaire might have been pardoned for mistaking him for a millionaire duke. It may be imagined what a radiant spectacle he was in what he called his 'gentleman disguise'.

His grey flannel suit fitted him with a staggering perfection, the whiteness of his shirt was dazzling, his tie shamed the rainbow. His soft felt hat appeared to be having its first outing since it left Bond Street. His chamois gloves were clearly being shown to the world for the first time. On his left wrist was a gold watch, and he carried a gold-mounted ebony walking-stick.

Everything, you understand, quietly but

unmistakably of the very best, and worn with that unique air of careless elegance which others might attempt to emulate, but which only the Saint could achieve in all its glory…

As for the man – well, the Snake's Boys had never had any occasion to doubt that their reputation for toughness was founded on more substantial demonstrations than displays of their skill at hunt-the-slipper at the YMCA on Saturday afternoons. The man was tall – about six feet two inches of him – but they didn't take much count of that. Their combined heights totted up to twenty-four feet three inches. And although he wasn't at all hefty, he was broad enough, and there was a certain solidity about his shoulders that would have made a cautious man think carefully before starting any unpleasantness – but that didn't bother the Snake and his Boys. Their combined widths summed up to a shade over six feet. And the Saint had a clear tanned skin and a very clear blue eye – but even that failed to worry them. They weren't running a beauty competition, anyway.

The important point was that the Saint had a gold cigarette-case and a large wad of banknotes. In his innocent way, he counted over his pile before their very eyes, announced the total at two hundred and fifty pounds odd, and invited them to congratulate him on his luck. They congratulated him, politely. They remarked on the slowness of the train, and the Saint agreed that it was a boring journey. He said he wished there was some sort of entertainment provided by the railway company for the diversion of passengers on boring journeys. Somebody promised a pack of cards…

It can be said for them that they gave him the credit for having been warned by his grandmother about the danger of trying to find the Lady. The game selected was poker. The Saint apologetically warned them that he had only played poker once before in his life, but they said kindly that that didn't matter a bit.

The fight started just five minutes before the train reached Victoria, and the porters who helped the Snake and his Boys out of the compartment were not thanked. They gave the Boys a bucket of water with which to revive the Snake himself, but they couldn't do anything about his two black eyes or his missing front teeth.

Inspector Teal, who was waiting on the platform in the hope of seeing a much-wanted con-man, saw the injured warriors and was not sympathetic.

'You've been fighting, Snake,' he said brightly.

Ganning's reply was unprintable, but Mr

Teal was not easily shocked.

'But I can describe him to you,' said the Snake, becoming less profane. 'Robbery with violence, that's what it was. He set on us–'

'"Sat" is the past tense of "sit",' said Teal, shifting his gum to the other side of his mouth.

'He's got away with over three hundred quid that we made today–'

Teal was interested.

'Where d'you make it?' he enquired. 'Have you got a real printing press, or do you make it by hand? I didn't know you were in the "slush" game, Snake?'

'Look here, Teal,' said Ganning, becoming more coherent. 'You can say what you like about me, but I've got my rights, the same as anybody else. You've got to get after that man. Maybe you know things about him already. He's either on a lay, or he's just starting on one, you mark my words. See this!'

Mr Teal examined the envelope sleepily.

'What is it?' he asked. 'A letter of introduction to me?'

'He gave it to Ted when he got out. "That's my receipt," he said. Didn't he, Ted? You look inside, Teal!'

The envelope was not sealed. Teal turned it over, and remarked on the flap the crest of the hotel which had provided it. Then, in his lethargic way, he drew out the contents – a single sheet of paper.

'Portrait by Epstein,' he drawled. 'Quite a nice drawing, but it don't mean anything to me outside of that. You boys have been reading too many detective stories lately, that's the trouble with you.'

2

The Saint, being a man of decidedly luxurious tastes, was the tenant of a flat in Brook Street, Mayfair, which was so far beyond his means that he had long since given up worrying about the imminence of bankruptcy. One might as well be hung for a sheep, the Saint reflected, in his cheerfully reckless way, as for a foot-and-mouth-diseased lamb. He considered that the world owed him a good time, in return for services rendered and general presentability and good-fellowship, and, since the world hitherto had been close-fistedly reluctant to recognize the obligation and meet it, the Saint had decided that the time had come for him to assert himself. His invasion of Brook Street had been one of the first moves in the campaign.

But the locality had one distinct advantage

that had nothing to do with the prestige of its address; and this advantage was the fact that it possessed a mews, a very small and exclusive mews, situated at a distance of less than the throw of a small stone from the Saint's front door. In this mews were a number of very expensive garages, large, small, and of Austin Seven size. And the Saint owned two of these large garages. In one he kept his own car; the other had been empty for a week, until he had begun smuggling an assortment of curious objects into it at dead of night – objects which only by the most frantic stretch of imagination could have been associated with cars.

If the Saint had been observed on any of these surreptitious trips, it is highly probable that his sanity would have been doubted. Not that he would have cared; for he had his own reasons for his apparent eccentricity. But as it was, no one noticed his goings-out or his comings-in, and there was no comment.

And even if he had been noticed, it is very doubtful if he would have been recognized. It was the immaculate Saint who left Brook Street and drove to Chelsea and garaged his car near Fulham Road. Then, by a very subtle change of carriage, it was a not-nearly-so-immaculate Saint who walked through a maze of dingy back streets to a house in which one Bertie Marks, a bird of passage, had a stuffy and microscopical apartment. And it was a shabby, slouching, down-at-heel Bertie Marks who left the apartment and returned to the West End on the plebeian bus, laden with the packages that he had purchased on his way; and who shambled inconspicuously into the mews off Brook Street and into the garage which he held in his own name. The Saint did not believe in being unnecessarily careless about details.

And all these elaborate preparations – the taking of the second garage and the Chelsea apartment, and the creation of the character of Bertie Marks – had been made for one single purpose, which was put into execution on a certain day.

A few hours after dawn on that day (an unearthly hour for the Saint to be abroad) a small van bearing the name of Carter Paterson turned into the mews and stopped there. Bertie Marks climbed down from the driver's seat, wiping grimy hands on his corduroys, and fished out a key, with which he opened the door of his garage. Then he went back to his van, drove it into the garage, and closed the doors behind him.

He knew that his action must have excited the curiosity of the car-washing parade of chauffeurs congregated in the mews, but he wasn't bothering about that. With the consummation of his plan, the necessity for the continued existence of Bertie Marks was rapidly nearing its end.

'Let 'em wonder!' thought the Saint carelessly, as he peeled off his grubby jacket.

He switched on the light, and went and peeped out into the mews. The car-washing parade had resumed its labours, being for the moment too preoccupied to bother about the strange phenomenon of a Carter Paterson van being driven into a garage that once housed a Rolls.

The Saint gently slid a bar across the door to shut out any inquisitive explorers, and got to work.

The van, on being opened, disclosed a number of large, wooden packing-cases which the Saint proceeded to unload on to the floor of the garage. This done, he fetched from a corner a mallet and chisel, and began to prise open the cases and extract their contents. In each case, packed in with wood shavings, were two dozen china jars.

As each case was emptied, the Saint carried the jars over to the light and inspected them minutely. He was not at all surprised to find that, whereas the majority of the jars were perfectly plain, all the jars in one case were marked with a tiny cross in the glazing. These jars the Saint set aside, for they were the only ones in which he was interested. They were exactly what he had expected to find, and they provided his entire motive for the temporary and occasional sinking of his own personality in the alias of Mr Marks. The other jars he replaced in their respective cases, and carefully closed and roped them to look as they had been before he tampered with them.

Then he opened the marked jars and poured out their contents into a bucket. In another corner of the garage was a pile of little tins, and in each jar the Saint placed one of these tins, padding the space that was left with cotton wool to prevent rattling. The jars so treated were replaced one by one and the case in its turn was also nailed up again and roped as before – after the Saint, with a little smile plucking at the corners of his mouth, had carefully laid a souvenir of his intervention on the top of the last layer of wood shavings.

He had worked quickly. Only an hour and a half had elapsed from the time when he drove into the garage to the time when he lifted the last case back into the van; and when that had been done he unbarred the garage doors and opened them wide.

The remains of the car-washing parade looked up puzzledly as the van came backing out of the garage; it registered an even greater perplexity when the van proceeded to drive out of the mews and vanish in the direction of Bond Street. It yelled to the driver that he had forgotten to close his garage after him, but Mr Marks either did not hear or did not care. And when the parade perceived that Mr Marks had gone for good, it went and pried into the garage, and scratched its heads over the litter of wood shavings on the floor, the mallet and chisel and nails and hammer, and the two or three tins which the Saint had found no space for, and which he had accordingly left behind. But the bucket of white powder was gone, riding beside Mr Marks in the front of the van; and very few people ever saw Mr Marks again.

The van drove to an address in the West End, and there Mr Marks delivered the cases, secured a signature to a receipt, and departed, heading further west. On his way, he stopped at St George's Hospital, where he left his bucket. The man who took charge of it was puzzled, but Mr Marks was in a hurry and had neither time nor the inclination to enlighten him.

'Take great care of it, because it's worth more money than you'll ever have,' he directed. 'See that it gets to one of the doctors, and give him this note with it.'

And the Saint went back to the wheel of his van and drove away, feeling that he was nearing the end of an excellent day's work.

He drove to the Great West Road, and out

of London towards Maidenhead. Somewhere along that road he turned off into a side lane, and there he stopped for a few minutes out of sight of the main traffic. Inside the van was a large pot of paint, and the Saint used it energetically. He had never considered himself an artist, but he manhandled that van with the broad sweeping touch of a master. Under his vigorous wielding of the brush, the sign of Carter Paterson, which he had been at some pains to execute artistically the night before, vanished entirely; and the van became plain. Satisfied with the obliteration of the handiwork which only a few hours before he had admired so much, the Saint resumed the wheel and drove back to London. The paint he had used was guaranteed quick-drying, and it lived up to the word of its guarantee. It collected a good deal of dust on the return voyage, and duly dried with a somewhat soiled aspect which was a very fair imitation of the condition in which Mr Marks had received it.

He delivered it to its home garage at Shepherd's Bush and paid twenty-four hours' hire. Some time later Mr Marks returned to Chelsea. A little later still, the not-so-immaculate Simon Templar turned into another garage and collected his trim blue Furillac speedster, in which he drove to his club in Dover Street. And the Simon

Templar who sauntered through to the bar and called for a pint of beer must have been one of the most impeccably immaculate young men that that haunt of impeccably immaculate young men had ever sheltered.

'We don't often see you as early as this, sir,' remarked the barman.

'May it be as many years before you see me as early as this again, son,' answered the Saint piously. 'But this morning I felt I just had to get up and go for a drive. It was such a beautiful morning.'

3

Mr Edgar Hayn was a man of many interests. He was the proud proprietor of 'Danny's' – a night club in a squalid street off Shaftesbury Avenue – and he also controlled the destinies of the firm of Laserre, which was a small but expensive shop in Regent Street that retailed perfumes, powders, rouges, creams, and all the other preparations essential to modern feminine face-repair. These two establishments were Mr Hayn's especial pets, and from them he derived the greater part of his substantial income. Yet it might be mentioned that the profits of 'Danny's' were not entirely earned by the sale of champagne, and the adornment of fashionable beauty was not the principal source of the prosperity of the house of Laserre. Mr Hayn was a clever organizer, and what he did not know about the art of covering his tracks wouldn't have been missed from one of the microscopical two-guinea alabaster jars in which he sold the celebrated Crême Laserre.

He was a big, heavy-featured man, clean-shaven, pink complexioned, and faintly bald. His name had not always been Hayn, but a process of naturalization followed by a Deed Poll had given him an indisputable legal right to forget the cognomen of his father – and, incidentally, had eliminated for ever the unpleasant possibility of a deportation order, an exercise of forethought for which Mr Hayn was more than once moved to give his sagacity a pat on the back. The police knew certain things about him which made them inclined to regard him with disfavour, and they suspected a lot more, but there had never been any evidence.

He was writing letters at the big knee-hole desk in his private office at 'Danny's' when Ganning arrived. The knock on the door did not make him look up. He said, 'Come in!' – but the sound of the opening and closing of the door was, to him, sufficient indication that the order had been obeyed; and he went on to finish the letter he had been drafting.

Only when that was done did he condescend to notice the presence of his visitor.

'You're late, Snake,' he said, blotting the sheet carefully.

'Sorry, boss.'

Mr Hayn screwed the cap on his fountain-pen, replaced it in his pocket, and raised his eyes from the desk for the first time. What he saw made him sag back with astonishment.

'Who on earth have you been picking a quarrel with?' he demanded.

The Snake certainly looked the worse for wear. A bandage round his head covered one eye, and the eye that was visible was nearly closed up. His lips were bruised and swollen, and a distinct lack of teeth made him speak with a painful lisp.

'Was it Harrigan's crowd?' suggested Hayn.

Ganning shook his head.

'A bloke we met on the train coming back from Brighton last night.'

'Were you alone?'

'Nope; Ted and Bill were with me. And Mario.'

'And what was this man trooping round? A regiment?'

'He was alone.'

Hayn blinked.

'How did it happen?'

'We thought he was a sucker,' explained Snake disgustedly. 'Smart clothes, gold cigarette-case, gold-mounted stick, gold watch – and a wad. He showed us the wad. Two-fifty, he said it was. We couldn't let that go, so we got him into a game of cards. Poker. He said he didn't know anything about the game, so it looked safe enough – he struck us as being that sort of mug. We were geeing him along nicely right up to ten minutes or so before Victoria, and we'd let him take fifty off us. He was thinking himself the greatest poker player in the world by then, you'd have said. Then we asked him to be a sport and give us a chance of getting our money back on a couple of big jackpots with a five-pound ante. He agreed, and we let him win the first one. We all threw in after the first rise. "What about making it a tenner ante for the last deal?" I said, tipping the wink to the boys. He wasn't too keen on that, but we jollied him along, and at last he fell for it. It was his deal, but I shuffled the broads for him.'

'And your hand slipped?'

Ganning snorted.

'Slipped nothin'! My hand doesn't slip. I'd got that deck stacked better than any conjurer could have done it. And I picked up a straight flush, just as I'd fixed it. Mario chucked in right away, and Ted and Bill dropped out after the first round. That left the Mug and me, and we went on raising each other till every cent the boys and I could find between us was in the kitty. We even turned in our links and Mario's diamond pin to account for as much of the Mug's wad as possible. When we hadn't another bean to stake, he saw me. I showed down my straight flush, and I was just getting set to scoop in the pool when he stopped me. "I thought you told me this was next to unbeatable," he says, and then he shows down five kings.'

'Five?' repeated Mr Hayn frowning.

'We were playing deuces wild, and a joker. He'd got the joker.'

'Well, didn't you know what he was holding?'

'It wasn't the hand I fixed for him to deal himself!'

Mr Hayn controlled his features.

'And then you cut up rough, and got the worst of it?'

'I accused him of cheating. He didn't deny it. He had the nerve to say: "Well, you were supposed to be teaching me the game, and I saw you were cheating all the time, so I thought it was allowed by the rules!" And he started putting away our pile. Of course we cut up rough!'

'And he cut up rougher?' suggested Mr Hayn.

'He didn't fight fair,' said Ganning aggrievedly. 'First thing I knew, he'd jabbed the point of his stick into Ted's neck before Ted had a chance to pull his cosh, so Ted was out of it. Bill was all ready for a fair stand-up fight with the knuckle-dusters, but this man kicked him in the stomach, so *he* took the count. Mario and me had to tackle him alone.'

The Snake seemed disinclined to proceed further with the description of the battle, and Hayn tactfully refrained from pressing him. He allowed the Snake to brood blackly over the memory for a few moments.

'He wasn't an amateur,' said Ganning. 'But none of us could place him. I'd give the hell of a lot to find out who he was. One of these fly mobsmen you read about, I shouldn't wonder. He'd got all the dope. Look at this,' said the Snake, producing the envelope. 'He shoved that at Ted when he got out. Said it was his receipt. I tried to get Teal to take it up – he was at the station – but he wouldn't take it seriously.'

Hayn slipped the sheet of paper out of the envelope and spread it out on his desk. Probably he had not fully grasped the purport of Ganning's description, for the effect the sight had on him was amazing.

If Ganning had been disappointed with Inspector Teal's unemotional reception of the Saint's receipt, he was fully compensated by the reaction of Mr Edgar Hayn. Hayn's pink face suddenly turned white, and he jerked away from the paper that lay on the blotter in front of him as if it had spat poison at him.

'What's it mean to you, boss?' asked the bewildered Ganning.

'This morning we got a consignment over from Germany,' Hayn said, speaking almost in a whisper. 'When Braddon opened the case, there was the same picture on top of the packing. We couldn't figure out how it came there.'

'Have you looked the stuff over yet?' demanded the Snake, instantly alert.

Hayn shook his head. He was still staring, as though hypnotized, at the scrap of paper.

'We didn't think anything of it. There's never been a hitch yet. Braddon thought the men who packed the case must have been playing some game. We just put the marked jars away in the usual place.'

'You haven't had to touch them yet?'

Hayn made a negative gesture. He reached out a shaky hand for the telephone, while Ganning sat silently chewing over the startling possibilities that were revealed by this information.

'Hullo ... Regent nine double-o four seven ... please.' Hayn fidgeted nervously as he waited for the call to be put through. It came after what seemed an eternity.

'Hullo... That you, Braddon?... I want you to get out the marked jars that came over in the case with the paper in – you remember?... Never mind why!'

A minute ticked away, while Hayn kept the receiver glued to his ear and tapped out an impatient tattoo on the desk.

'Yes?... What's that?... How d'you know?... I see. Well, I'll be right round!'

Hayn clicked the receiver back and slewed his swivel-chair round so that he faced Snake Ganning.

'What's he say?' asked the Snake.

'There's just a tin of Keating's powder in each,' Hayn replied. 'I asked him how he knew what it was, and he said the whole tin was there, label and all, packed in with cotton wool to make it fit. There was ten thousand pounds' worth of snow in that shipping, and this guy has lifted the lot!'

4

'You may decant some beer, son,' said Simon Templar, stretched out in the armchair. 'And then you may start right in and tell me the story of your life. I can spare you about two minutes.'

Jerry Stannard travelled obediently over to

a side table where bottles and glasses were already set out, accomplished his task with a practised hand, and travelled back again with the results.

'Your health,' said the Saint, and two foaming glasses were half-emptied in an appreciative silence.

Stannard was then encouraged to proceed. He put down his glass with a sigh and settled back at his ease, while the Saint made a long arm for the cigarette-box.

'I can't make out yet why you should have interested yourself in me,' said Stannard.

'That's my affair,' said the Saint bluntly. 'And if it comes to that, son, I'm not a philanthropic institution. I happen to want an assistant, and I propose to make use of you. Not that you won't get anything out of it. I'm sufficiently interested in you to want to help you, but you're going to pay your way.'

Stannard nodded.

'It's decent of you to think I'm worth it,' he said.

He had not forgotten – it would have been impossible to forget such an incident in two days – the occasion of his first meeting with the Saint. Stannard had been entrusted with a small packet which he had been told to take to an address in Piccadilly; and even if he had not been told what the packet contained, he could not have helped having a very shrewd idea. And therefore, when a heavy hand had fallen suddenly on his shoulder only a few minutes after he had left Mr Hayn, he had had no hope…

And then the miracle had happened, although he did not realize at the time that it was a miracle. A man had brushed against him as the detective turned to hail a taxi, and the man had turned to apologize. In that crisis, all Stannard's faculties had been keyed up to the vivid supersensitiveness which comes just before breaking-point; and that abnormal acuteness had combined with the peculiarly keen stare which had accompanied the stranger's apology, so that the stranger's face was indelibly engraved on Stannard's memory…

The Saint took a little package from his pocket, and weighed it reflectively in his hand.

'Forty-eight hours ago,' he murmured, 'you assumed, quite rightly, that you were booked for five years' penal servitude. Instead of that, you're a free man. The triumphant sleuths of Vine Street found nothing on you, and had to release you with apologies. Doubtless they're swearing to make up for that bloomer, and make no mistakes about landing you with the goods next time, but that can't hurt you for the moment. And I expect you're still wondering what's going to be my price for having picked your pocket in the nick of time.'

'I've been wondering ever since.'

'I'm just going to tell you,' said the Saint. 'But first we'll get rid of this.'

He left the room with the packet, and through the open door came the sound of running water. In a few moments he was back, dusting his hands.

'That disposes of the evidence,' he said. 'Now I want you to tell me something. How did you get into this dope game?'

Stannard shrugged.

'You may as well know. There's no heroic or clever reason. It's just because I'm a waster. I was in the wrong set at Cambridge, and I knew most of the toughs in Town. Then my father died and left me without a bean. I tried to get a job, but I couldn't do anything useful. And all the time, naturally, I was mixing with the same bad bunch. Eventually they roped me in. I suppose I ought to have fought against it, but I just hadn't the guts. It was easy money, and I took it. That's all.'

There was a short silence, during which the Saint blew monotonously regular smoke rings towards the ceiling.

'Now I'll tell you something,' he said. 'I've made all the enquiries I need to make about you. I know your family history for two generations back, your early life, your school record – everything. I know enough to judge that you don't belong where you are now. For one thing, I know you're engaged to a rather nice girl, and she's worried about you. She doesn't know anything, but she suspects. And you're worried. You're not as quiet and comfortable in this crime racket as you'd like to make out. You weren't cut out for a bad man. Isn't that true?'

'True enough,' Stannard said flatly. 'I'd give anything to be out of it.'

'And you're straight about this girl – Gwen Chandler?'

'Straight as a die. Honest, Templar! But what can I do? If I drop Hayn's crowd, I shan't have a cent. Besides, I don't know that they'd let me drop out. I owe money. When I was at Cambridge, I lost a small fortune – for me – in Hayn's gambling rooms, and he's got IOU's of mine for close on a thousand. I've been extravagant – I've run up bills everywhere. You can't imagine how badly in the cart I am!'

'On the contrary, son,' said the Saint calmly, 'I've a very good guess about that. That's why you're here now. I wanted an agent inside Hayn's gang, and I ran through the whole deck before I chose you.'

He rose from his chair and took a turn up and down the room. Stannard waited; and presently the Saint stopped abruptly.

'You're all right,' he said.

Stannard frowned.

'Meaning?'

'Meaning I'm going to trust you. I'm going to take you in with me for this campaign. I'll get you enough out of it to square off your debts, and at the end of it I'll find you a job. You'll keep in with Hayn, but you'll be working for me. And you'll give me your word of honour that you'll go straight for the rest of your life. That's my offer. What about it?'

The Saint leant against the mantelpiece languidly enough, but there had been nothing languid about his crisp incisive sentences. Thinking it over afterwards, it seemed to Stannard that the whole thing had been done in a few minutes, and he was left to marvel at the extraordinary force of personality which in such a short time could override the prejudice of years and rekindle a spark of decency that had been as good as dead. But at the instant, Stannard could not analyse his feelings.

'I'm giving you a chance to get out and make good,' the Saint went on. 'I'm not doing it in the dark. I believe you when you say you'd be glad of a chance to make a fresh start. I believe there's the makings of a decent man in you. Anyway, I'll take a risk on it. I won't even threaten you, though I could, by telling you what I shall do to you if you double-cross me. I just ask you a fair question, and I want your answer now.'

Stannard got to his feet.

'There's only one answer,' he said, and held out his hand.

The Saint took it in a firm grip.

'Now I'll tell you exactly where you stand,' he said.

He did so, speaking in curt sentences as before. His earlier grimness had relaxed somewhat, for when the Saint did anything he never did it by halves, and now he spoke to Stannard as a friend and an ally. He had his reward in the eager attention with which the youngster followed his discourse. He told him everything that there was any need for him to know.

'You've got to think of everything, and then a heap, if you're going to come out of this with a whole skin,' Simon concluded, with some of his former sternness. 'The game I'm on isn't the kind they play in nurseries. I'm on it because I just can't live happily ever after. I've had enough adventures to fill a dozen books, but instead of satisfying me they've only left me with a bigger appetite. If I had to live the ordinary kind of safe, civilized life, I'd die of boredom. Risks are food and drink to me. You may be different. If you are, I'm sorry about it, but I can't help it. I need some help in this, and you're going to give it to me; but it wouldn't be fair to let you whale in without showing you what you are up against. Your bunch of bad hats aren't childish enemies. Before you're through, London's likely to be just about as healthy for you as the Cannibal Islands are for a nice plump missionary. Get me?'

Stannard intimated that he had got him.

'Then I'll give you your orders for the immediate future,' said the Saint.

He did so, in detail, and had everything repeated over to him twice before he was convinced that there would be no mistake and that nothing would be forgotten.

'From now on, I want you to keep away from me till I give you the all-clear,' he ended up. 'If the Snake's anywhere round, I shan't last long in Danny's, and it's essential to keep you out of suspicion for as long as possible. So this'll be our last open meeting for some time, but you can communicate by telephone – as long as you make sure nobody can hear you.'

'Right you are, Saint,' said Stannard.

Simon Templar flicked a cigarette into his mouth and reached for the matches.

The other had a queer transient feeling of unreality. It seemed fantastic that he should be associated with such a project as that into which the Saint had initiated him. It seemed equally fantastic that the Saint should have conceived it and brought it into being. That cool, casual young man, with his faultless clothes, his clipped and slangy speech, and his quick clear smile – he ought to have been lounging his amiable, easy-going way through a round of tennis and cricket and cocktail-parties and dances, instead of…

And yet it remained credible – it was even, with every passing second, becoming almost an article of the re-awakened Stannard's new faith. The Saint's spell was unique. There was a certain quiet assurance about his bearing, a certain steely quality that came sometimes into his blue eyes, a certain indefinable air of strength and recklessness and quixotic bravado, that made the whole fantastic notion acceptable. And Stannard had not even the advantage of knowing anything about the last eight years of the Saint's hell-for-leather career – eight years of gay buccaneering which, even allowing for exaggeration, made him out to be a man of no ordinary or drawing-room toughness…

The Saint lighted his cigarette and held out his hand to terminate the interview; and the corners of his mouth were twitching to his irresistible smile.

'So long, son,' he said. 'And good hunting!'

'Same to you,' said Stannard warmly.

The Saint clapped him on the shoulder.

'I know you won't let me down,' he said. 'There's lots of good in you, and I guess I've found some of it. You'll pull out all right.

I'm going to see that you do. Watch me!'

But before he left, Stannard got a query off his chest.

'Didn't you say there were five of you?'

His hands in his pockets, teetering gently on his heels, the Saint favoured Stannard with his most Saintly smile.

'I did,' he drawled. 'Four little Saints and Papa. I am the Holy Smoke. As for the other four, they are like the Great White Woolly Wugga-Wugga on the plains of Astrakhan.'

Stannard gaped at him.

'What does that mean?' he demanded.

'I ask you, sweet child,' answered the Saint, with that exasperating seraphic smile still on his lips, 'has anyone ever seen a Great White Woolly Wugga-Wugga on the plains of Astrakhan? Sleep on it, my cherub – it will keep your mind from impure thoughts.'

5

To all official intents and purposes, the proprietor and leading light of Mr Edgar Hayn's night club in Soho was the man after whom it was named – Danny Trask.

Danny was short and dumpy, a lazy little tub of a man, with a round red face, a sparse head of fair hair, and a thin sandy moustache. His pale eyes were deeply embedded in the creases of their fleshy lids; and when he smiled – which was often, and usually for no apparent reason – they vanished altogether in a corrugating mesh of wrinkles.

His intelligence was not very great. Nevertheless he had discovered quite early in life that there was a comfortable living to be made in the profession of 'dummy' – a job which calls for no startling intellectual gifts – and Danny had accordingly made that his vocation ever since. As a figurehead, he was all that could have been desired, for he was unobtrusive and easily satisfied. He had a type of mind common to his class of lawbreaker. As long as his salary – which was not small – was paid regularly, he never complained, showed no ambition to join his employer on a more equal basis of division of profits, and, if anything went wrong, kept his mouth shut and deputised for his principal in one of His Majesty's prisons without a murmur. Danny's fees for a term of imprisonment were a flat rate of ten pounds a week, with an extra charge of two pounds a week for 'hard'. The astuteness of the CID and the carelessness of one or two of his previous employers, had made this quite a profitable proposition for Danny.

He had visions of retiring one day, and

ending his life in comparative luxury, when his savings had reached a sufficiently large figure; but this hope had received several setbacks of late. He had been in Mr Hayn's service for four years, and Mr Hayn's uncanny skill at avoiding the attentions of the police were becoming a thorn in the side of Danny Trask. When Danny was not in 'stir', the most he could command was a paltry seven pounds a week, and living expenses had to be paid out of this instead of out of the pocket of the Government. Danny felt that he had a personal grievance against Mr Hayn on this account.

The club theoretically opened at 6 pm, but the food was not good, and most of its members preferred to dine elsewhere. The first arrivals usually began to drift in about 10 pm, but things never began to get exciting before 11 o'clock. Danny spent the hours between 6 o'clock and the commencement of the fun sitting in his shirtsleeves in his little cubicle by the entrance, sucking a foul old briar and tentatively selecting the next day's losers from an evening paper. He was incapable of feeling bored – his mind had never reached the stage of development where it could appreciate the idea of activity and inactivity. It had never been active, so it didn't see any difference.

He was engaged in this pleasant pursuit

towards 8 o'clock on a certain evening when Jerry Stannard arrived.

'Has Mr Hayn come in yet, Danny?'

Danny made a pencil note of the number of pounds which he had laboriously calculated that Wilco would have in hand over Man of Kent in the Lingfield Plate, folded his paper, and looked up.

'He don't usually come in till late, Mr Stannard,' he said. 'No, he ain't here now.'

Danny's utterances always contrived to put the cart before the horse. If he wanted to give you a vivid description of a deathbed scene, he would have inevitably started with the funeral.

'Oh, it's all right – he's expecting me,' said Stannard. 'When he arrives you can tell him I'm at the bar.'

He was plainly agitated. While he was talking, he never stopped fiddling with his signet ring; and Danny, whose shrewd glances missed very little, noticed that his tie was limp and crooked, as if it had been subjected to the clumsy wrestling of shaky fingers.

'Right you are, sir.'

It was none of Danny's business, anyway.

'Oh – and before I forget…'

'Sir?'

'A Mr Templar will be here later. He's O.K. Send down for me when he arrives, and I'll sign him in.'

'Very good, sir.'

Danny returned to his study of equine form, and Stannard passed on.

He went through the lounge which occupied the ground floor, and turned down the stairs at the end. Facing these stairs, behind a convenient curtain, was a secret door in the panelling, electrically operated, which was controlled by a button on the desk in Hayn's private office. This door, when opened, disclosed a flight of stairs running upwards. These stairs communicated with the upstairs rooms which were one of the most profitable features of the club, for in those rooms *chemin-de-fer,* poker, and *trente-et-quarante* were played every night with the sky for a limit.

Hayn's office was at the foot of the downward flight. He had personally supervised the installation of an ingenious system of mirrors, by means of which, with the aid of a large sound-proof window let into the wall at one end of the office, without leaving his seat, he was able to inspect everyone who passed through the lounge above. Moreover, when the secret doors swung open in response to the pressure of his finger on the control button, a further system of mirrors panelled up the upper flight of stairs gave him a view right up the stairway itself and round the landing into the gaming rooms. Mr Hayn was a man with a cunning turn of mind, and he was pre-eminently cautious.

Outside the office, in the basement, was the dance floor, surrounded with tables, but only two couples were dining there. At the far end was the dais on which the orchestra played, and at the other end, under the stairs, was the tiny bar.

Stannard turned in there, and roused the white-coated barman from his perusal of *La Vie Parisienne.*

'I don't know what would meet the case,' he said, 'but I want something steep in corpse-revivers.'

The man looked him over for a moment with an expert eye, then busied himself with the filling of a prescription. The result certainly had a kick in it. Stannard was downing it when Hayn came in.

The big man was looking pale and tired, and there were shadows under his eyes. He nodded curtly to Jerry.

'I'll be with you in a minute,' he said. 'Just going to get a wash.'

It was not like Mr Hayn, who ordinarily specialized in the boisterous hail-fellow-well-met method of address, and Stannard watched him go thoughtfully.

Braddon, who had remained outside, followed Hayn into the office.

'Who's the boy friend?' he asked, taking a chair.

'Stannard?' Hayn was skimming through

the letters that waited on his desk. 'An ordinary young fool. He lost eight hundred upstairs in his first couple of months. Heaven knows how much he owes outside – he'd lost a packet before I started lending him money.'

Braddon searched through his pockets for a cigar, and found one. He bit off the end, and spat.

'Got expectations? Rich papa who'll come across?'

'No. But he's got the clothes, and he'd pass anywhere. I was using him.'

'*Was?*'

Hayn was frowningly examining the postmark on one of his letters.

'I suppose I shall still,' he said. 'Don't bother me – this artistic hijacker's got me all ends up. But he's got a fiancée – I've only recently seen her. I like her.'

'Any good?'

'I shall arrange something about her.'

Hayn had slit open the letter with his thumbnail, but he only took one glance at what it contained. He tossed it over to Braddon, and it was the manager of Laserre who drew out the now familiar sketch.

'One of those came to my house by the first post this morning,' Hayn said. 'It's as old as the hills, that game. So he thinks he's going to rattle me!'

'Isn't he?' asked Braddon, in his heavily

cynical way.

'He damned well isn't!' Hayn came back savagely. 'I've got the Snake and the men who were with him prowling round the West End just keeping their eyes peeled for the man who beat them up in the Brighton train. If he's in London, he can't stay hid for ever. And when Ganning's found him, we'll soon put paid to his joke!'

Then he pulled himself together.

'I'm giving Stannard dinner,' he said. 'What are you doing now?'

'I'll loaf out and get some food, and be back later,' said Braddon. 'I thought I'd take a look in upstairs.'

Hayn nodded. He ushered Braddon out of the office, and locked the door behind him, for even Braddon was not allowed to remain in that sanctum alone. Braddon departed, and Hayn rejoined Stannard at the bar.

'Sorry to have kept you waiting, old man,' he apologized, with an attempt to resume his pose of bluff geniality.

'I've been amusing myself,' said Stannard, and indicated a row of empty glasses. 'Have a spot?'

Hayn accepted, and Stannard looked at his watch.

'By the way,' he said, 'there's a man due here in about an hour. I met him the other day, and he seemed all right. He said he was a South African, and he's sailing back the day after tomorrow. He was complaining that he couldn't get any real fun in England, so I dropped a hint about a private gambling club I might be able to get him into and he jumped at it. I thought he might be some use – leaving England so soon he could hardly make a kick – so I told him to join us over coffee. Is that all right?'

'Quite all right, old man.' A thought struck Mr Hayn. 'You're quite sure he wasn't one of these clever dicks?'

'Not on your life!' scoffed Stannard. 'I think I know a busy when I see one by now. I've seen enough of 'em dancing here. And this man seems to have money to burn.'

Hayn nodded.

'I meant to come to some arrangement with you over dinner,' he said. 'This bird can go down as your first job, on commission. If you're ready, we'll start.'

Stannard assented, and they walked over to the table which had been prepared.

Hayn was preoccupied. If his mind had not been simmering with other problems, he might have noticed Stannard's ill-concealed nervousness, and wondered what might have been the cause of it. But he observed nothing unusual about the young man's manner.

While they were waiting for the grapefruit, he asked a question quite perfunctorily.

'What's this South African's name?'

'Templar – Simon Templar,' answered Jerry.

The name meant nothing at all to Mr Hayn.

6

Over the dinner, Hayn made his offer – a twenty per cent commission on business introduced. Stannard hardly hesitated before accepting.

'You don't want to be squeamish about it,' Hayn argued. 'I know it's against the law, but that's splitting hairs. Horse-racing is just as much a gamble. There'll always be fools who want to get rich without working, and there's no reason why we shouldn't take their money. You won't have to do anything that would make you liable to be sent to prison, though some of my staff would be jailed if the police caught them. You're quite safe. And the games are perfectly straight. We only win because the law of probabilities favours the bank.'

This was not strictly true, for there were other factors to influence the runs of bad luck which attended the players upstairs; but this sordid fact Mr Hayn did not feel called upon to emphasize.

'Yes – I'll join you,' Stannard said. 'I've known it was coming. I didn't think you went on giving and lending me money for looking decorative and doing an odd job or two for you now and again.'

'My dear fellow–'

'Dear-fellowing doesn't alter it. I know you want more of me than my services in decoying boobs upstairs. Are you going to tell me you didn't know I was caught the other day?'

Hayn stroked his chin.

'I was going to compliment you. How you got rid of that parcel of snow–'

'The point that matters is that I did get rid of it,' cut in Stannard briefly. 'And if I hadn't been able to, I should have been on remand in Brixton Prison now. I'm not complaining. I suppose I had to earn my keep. But it wasn't square of you to keep me in the dark.'

'You knew–'

'I guessed. It's all right – I've stopped kicking. But I want you to let me right in from now on, if you're letting me in at all. I'm joining you, all in, and you needn't bother to humbug me any longer. How's that?'

'That's all right,' said Mr Hayn. 'If you must put things so crudely. But you don't even have to be squeamish about the dope side of it. If people choose to make fools of themselves like that, it's their own lookout. Our share is simply to refuse to quibble about whether it's legal or not. After all, alcohol is sold legally in this country, and nobody blames the publican if his customers get drunk every night and eventually die of DT's.'

Stannard shrugged.

'I can't afford to argue, anyhow,' he said. 'How much do I draw?'

'Twenty per cent – as I told you.'

'What's that likely to make?'

'A lot,' said Hayn. 'We play higher here than anywhere else in London, and there isn't a great deal of competition in the snow market. You might easily draw upwards of seventy pounds a week.'

'Then will you do something for me, Mr Hayn? I owe a lot of money outside. I'll take three thousand flat for the first year, to pay off everybody and fit myself up with a packet in hand.'

'Three thousand pounds is a lot of money,' said Hayn judicially. 'You owe me nearly a thousand as it is.'

'If you don't think I'm going to be worth it–'

Mr Hayn mediated, but not for long. The making of quick decisions was the whole reason for his success, and he didn't mind how much a thing cost if he knew it was worth it. He had no fear that Stannard would attempt to double-cross him. Among the other purposes which it served, Danny's formed a working headquarters for the Snake's Boys; Stannard could not help knowing the reputation of the gang, and he must also know that they had worked Hayn's vengeance on traitors before. No – there was no chance that Stannard would dare to try a double cross…

'I'll give you a cheque tonight,' said Hayn.

Stannard was effusively grateful.

'You won't lose by it,' he promised. 'Templar's a speculation, granted, but I've met him only once. But there are other people with mints of money, people I've known for years, that I can vouch for absolutely…'

He went on talking, but Hayn only listened with half an ear, for he was anxious to turn the conversation on to another topic, and he did so at the first opportunity.

Under pretence of taking a fatherly interest in his new agent's affairs, he plied him with questions about his private life and interests. Most of the information which he elicited was stale news to him, for he had long since taken the precaution of finding out everything of importance that there was to know about his man; but in these new inquiries Mr Hayn contrived to make Stannard's fiancée the centre of interrogation. It was very cleverly and surreptitiously done, but the fact remains that at the end of half an hour, by this process of indirect questioning, Hayn had discovered all that he wanted to know about the life and habits of Gwen Chandler.

'Do you think you could get her along here to supper on Thursday?' he suggested. 'The only time I've met her, if you remember, I think you rather prejudiced her against me. It's up to you to put that right.'

'I'll see what I can do,' said Stannard.

After that, his point won, Hayn had no further interest in directing the conversation, and they were chatting desultorily when Simon Templar arrived.

The Saint, after weighing the relative merits of full evening dress or an ordinary lounge suit for the auspicious occasion, had decided upon a compromise, and was sporting a dinner jacket; but he wore it, as might have been expected, as if he had been an ambassador paying a state visit in full regalia.

'Hullo, Jerry, dear angel!' he hailed Stannard cheerfully.

Then he noticed Mr Hayn, and turned with outstretched hand.

'Then you must be Uncle Ambrose,' he greeted that gentleman cordially. 'Pleased to meet you... That's right, isn't it, Jerry? This is the uncle who died and left all his money to the Cats' Home?... Sorry to see you looking so well, Uncle Ambrose, old mongoose!'

Mr Hayn seemed somewhat taken aback. This man did not wear his clothes in the manner traditionally associated with raw colonials with money to burn; and if his speech was typical of that of strong silent men from the great open spaces of that vintage, Mr Hayn decided that the culture of Piccadilly must have spread farther abroad into the British Empire than Cecil Rhodes had ever hoped in his wildest dreams. Mr Hayn had never heard of Rhodes – to him, Rhodes was an island where they bred red hens – but if he had heard of Rhodes he might reasonably have expressed his surprise like that.

He looked round to Jerry Stannard with raised eyebrows, and Stannard tapped his forehead and lifted his glass significantly.

'So we're going to see a real live gambling hell!' said the Saint, drawing up a chair. 'Isn't this fun? Let's all have a lot of drinks on the strength of it!'

He called for liqueurs, and paid for them from a huge wad of banknotes which he tugged from his pocket. Mr Hayn's eyes lit up at the sight, and he decided that there were excuses for Templar's eccentricity. He leant forward and set himself out to be charming.

The Saint, however, had other views on

the subject of the way in which the conversation should go, and at the first convenient pause, he came out with a remark that showed he had been paying little attention to what had gone before.

'I've bought a book about card tricks,' he said. 'I thought it might help me to spot sharpers. But the best part of it was the chapter on fortune-telling by cards. Take a card, and I'll tell you all your sins.'

He produced a new pack from his pocket and pushed it across the table towards Hayn.

'You first, Uncle,' he invited. 'And see that your thoughts are pure when you draw, otherwise you'll give the cards a wrong impression. Hum a verse of your favourite hymn, for instance.'

Mr Hayn knew nothing about hymns, but he complied tolerantly. If this freak had all that money, and perhaps some more, by all means let him be humoured.

'Now, isn't that sweet!' exclaimed the Saint, taking up the card Hayn had chosen. 'Jerry, my pet, your Uncle Ambrose had drawn the ace of hearts. That stands for princely generosity. We'll have another brandy with you, Uncle, just to show how we appreciate it. Waiter!... Three more brandies, please. Face Ache – I mean Uncle Ambrose – is paying... Uncle, you must try your luck again!'

Simon Templar pored over Hayn's second card until the drinks arrived. It was noticeable that his shoulders shook silently at one time. Mr Hayn attributed this to represent hiccups, and was gravely in error. Presently the Saint looked up.

'Has an aunt on your mother's side,' he asked solemnly, 'ever suffered from a bilious attack following a meal of sausages made by a German pork butcher with a hammer-toe and three epileptic children?'

Mr Hayn shook his head, staring.

'I haven't any aunts,' he said.

'I'm so sorry,' said the Saint, as if he were deeply distressed to hear of Mr Hayn's plight of pathetic auntlessness. 'But it means the beastly book's all wrong. Never mind. Don't lets bother about it.'

He pushed the pack away. Undoubtedly he was quite mad.

'Aren't you going to tell us any more?' asked Stannard, with a wink to Hayn.

'Uncle Ambrose would blush if I went on,' said Templar. 'Look at the brick I've dropped already. But if you insist, I'll try one more card.'

Hayn obliged again, smiling politely. He was starting to get acclimatized. Clearly the secret of being on good terms with Mr Templar was to let him have his own irrepressible way.

'I only hope it isn't the five of diamonds,'

said the Saint earnestly, 'Whenever I do this fortune-telling stuff, I'm terrified of somebody drawing the five of diamonds. You see, I'm bound to tell the truth, and the truth in that case is frightfully hard to tell to a comparative stranger. Because, according to my book, a man who draws the five of diamonds is liable at any moment to send an anonymous donation of ten thousand pounds to the London Hospital. Also, cards are unlucky for him, he is an abominable blackguard, and he has a repulsively ugly face.'

Hayn kept his smile nailed in position, and faced his card.

'The five of diamonds, Mr Templar,' he remarked gently.

'No – is it really?' said Simon, in most Saintly astonishment. 'Well, well, *well!*... There you are, Jerry – I warned you your uncle would be embarrassed if I went on. Now I've dropped another brick. Let's talk of something else, quickly, before he notices. Uncle Ambrose, tell me, have you ever seen a hot dog fighting a cat-o'-nine-tails?... No?... Well, shuffle the pack, and I'll show you a conjuring trick.'

Mr Hayn shuffled and cut, and the Saint rapidly dealt off five cards, which he passed face downwards across the table.

It was about the first chance Mr Hayn had had to sidle a word in, and he felt compelled to protest about one thing.

'You seem to be suffering from a delusion, Mr Templar,' he said. 'I'm not Jerry's uncle – I'm just a friend of his. My name's Hayn – Edgar Hayn.'

'Why?' asked the Saint innocently.

'It happens to be the name I was christened with, Mr Templar,' Hayn replied with some asperity.

'Is – that – so!' drawled the Saint mildly. 'Sorry again!'

Hayn frowned. There was something peculiarly infuriating about the Saint in that particular vein – something that, while it rasped the already raw fringe of his temper, was also beginning to send a queer, indefinable creeping up his back.

'And I'm sorry if it annoys you,' he snapped.

Simon Templar regarded him steadily.

'It annoys me,' he said, 'because, as I told you, it's my business never to make mistakes, and I just hate being wrong. The records of Somerset House told me that your name was once something quite different – that you weren't christened Edgar Hayn at all. And I believed it.'

Hayn said nothing. He sat quite still, with that tingling thrill of apprehension crawling round the base of his scalp. And the Saint's clear blue gaze never left Hayn's face.

'If I was wrong about that,' the Saint went

on softly, 'I may quite easily have been wrong about other things. And that would annoy me more than ever, because I don't like wasting my time. I've spent several days figuring out a way of meeting you for just this little chat – I thought it was about time our relationship became a bit more personal – and it'd break my heart to think it had all been for nothing. Don't tell me that, Edgar, beloved – don't tell me it wasn't any use my finding out that dear little Jerry was a friend of yours – don't tell me that I might have saved myself the trouble I took scraping an acquaintance with the said Jerry just to bring about this informal meeting. Don't tell me that, dear heart!'

Hayn moistened his lips. He was fighting down an insane, unreasoning feeling of panic; and it was the Saint's quiet, level voice and mocking eyes, as much as anything, that held Edgar Hayn rooted in his chair.

'Don't tell me, in fact, that you won't appreciate the little conjuring trick I came here especially to show you,' said the Saint, more mildly than ever.

He reached out suddenly and took the cards he had dealt from Hayn's nerveless fingers. Hayn had guessed what they would prove to be, long before Simon, with a flourish, had spread the cards out face upwards on the table.

'Don't tell me you aren't pleased to see our visiting cards, personally presented!' said Simon, in his very Saintliest voice.

His white teeth flashed in a smile, and there was a light of adventurous recklessness dancing in his eyes as he looked at Edgar Hayn across five neat specimens of the sign of the Saint.

7

'And if it's pure prune juice and boloney,' went on the Saint, in that curiously velvety tone which still contrived somehow to prickle all over with little warning spikes – 'if all that is sheer banana oil and soft roe, I shan't even raise a smile with the story I was going to tell you. It's my very latest one, and it's about a loose-living land-shark called Hayn, who was born in a barn in the rain. What he'd struggled to hide was found out when he died – there was mildew all over his brain. Now, that one's been getting a big hand everywhere I've told it since I made it up and it'll be one of the bitterest disappointments of my life if it doesn't fetch you, sweetheart!'

Hayn's chair went over with a crash as he kicked to his feet. Strangely enough, now that the murder was out and the first shock absorbed, the weight on his mind seemed lightened, and he felt better able to cope with the menace.

'So you're the young cub we've been looking for!' he rasped.

Simon raised his hand.

'I'm called the Saint,' he murmured. 'But don't let us get melodramatic about it, son. The last man who got melodramatic with me was hanged at Exeter six months back. It don't seem to be healthy!'

Hayn looked round. The diners had left, and as yet no one had arrived to take their places; but the clatter of his chair upsetting had roused three startled waiters, who were staring uncertainly in his direction. But a review of these odds did not seem to disturb the Saint, who was lounging languidly back in his seat with his hands in his pockets and a benign expression on his face.

'I suppose you know that the police are after you,' grated Hayn.

'I didn't,' said the Saint. 'That's interesting. Why?'

'You met some men in the Brighton train and played poker with them. You swindled them right and left, and when they accused you you attacked them and pinched the money. I think that's good enough to put you away for some time.'

'And who's going to identify me?'

'The four men.'

'You surprise me,' drawled Simon. 'I seem to remember that on that very day, just outside Brighton racecourse, those same four bums were concerned in beating up a poor little coot of a lame bookie named Tommy Mitre and pinching *his* money. There didn't happen to be any policemen about – they arranged it quite cleverly – and the crowd that saw it would most likely be all too scared of the Snake to give evidence. But yours truly and a couple of souls also saw the fun. We were a long way off, and the Snake and his Boys were over the horizon by the time we got to the scene, but we could identify them all, and a few more who were not there – and we shouldn't be afraid to step into the witness-box and say our peace. No, sonnikins – I don't think the police will be brought into that. That must go down to history as a little private wrangle between Snake and me. Send one of your beauty chorus out for a Robert and give me in charge, if you like, but don't blame me if Ganning and the Boys come back at you for it. Knowing their reputations, I should say they'd get the "cat" as well as their six months' hard, and that won't make them love you a lot. Have it your own way, though.'

The argument was watertight, and Hayn realized it. He was beginning to cool down.

He hadn't a kick – for the moment, the Saint had got him right down in the mud with a foot on his face. But he didn't see what good that was doing the Saint. It was a big bluff, Hayn was starting to think, and he had sense enough to realize that it wasn't helping him one bit to get all hot under the collar about it. In fact – such was the exhilarating effect of having at last found an enemy that he could see and hit back at – Hayn was rapidly reckoning that the Saint might lose a lot by that display of bravado.

Clearly the Saint didn't want the police horning in at all. It didn't even matter that the Saint knew things about Hayn and his activities that would have interested the police. The Saint was on some lay of his own, and the police weren't being invited to interfere. Very well. So be it. The cue for Hayn was to bide his time and refuse to be rattled. But he wished the Saint hadn't got that mocking, self-possessed air of having a lot more high cards up his sleeve, just waiting to be produced. It spoilt Hayn's happiness altogether. The Saint was behaving like a fool; and yet, in some disconcertingly subtle way, he managed to do it with the condescending air of putting off a naturally tremendous gravity in order to amuse the children.

Hayn righted his chair and sat down again slowly; the alert waiters relaxed – they were a tough crowd, and selected more for their qualities of toughness than for their clean fingernails and skill at juggling with plates and dishes. But as Hayn sat down his right hand went behind his chair – his back was towards the group of waiters – and with his fingers he made certain signs. One of the waiters faded away inconspicuously.

'So what do you propose to do?' Hayn said.

'Leave you,' answered the Saint benevolently. 'I know your ugly dial isn't your fault, but I've seen about as much of it as I can stand for one evening. I've done what I came to do, and now I think you can safely be left to wonder what I'm going to do next. See you later, I expect, my Beautiful Ones…'

The Saint rose and walked unhurriedly to the stairs. By that time, there were five men ranged in a row at the foot of the stairs, and they showed no signs of making way for anyone.

'We should hate to lose you so soon, Mr Templar,' said Hayn.

The Saint's lounging steps slowed up, and stopped. His hands slid into his pockets, and he stood for a moment surveying the quintet of waiters with a beatific smile. Then he turned.

'What are these?' he inquired pleasantly. 'The guard of honour, or the cabaret beauty chorus?'

'I think you might sit down again, Mr Templar,' suggested Hayn.

'And I think not,' said the Saint.

He walked swiftly back to the table – so swiftly that Hayn instinctively half rose from his seat, and the five men started forward. But the Saint did not attack at that moment. He stopped in front of Hayn, his hands in his pockets; and although that maddening little smile still lurked on his lips, there was something rather stern about his poise.

'I said I was going to leave you, and I am,' he murmured, with a gentleness that was in amazing contrast to the intent tautness of his bearing. 'That's what I came here for, ducky – to leave you. This is just meant for a demonstration of all-round superiority; you think you can stop me – but you watch! I'm going to prove that nothing on earth can stop me when I get going. Understand, loveliness?'

'We shall see,' said Hayn.

The Saint's smile became, if possible, even more Saintly. Somehow that smile, and the air of hair-trigger alertness which accompanied it, was bothering Edgar Hayn a heap. He knew it was all bravado – he knew the Saint had bitten off more than he could chew for once – he knew that the odds were all against a repetition of the discomfiture of the Ganning combine. And yet he couldn't feel happy about it. There was a kind of quivering strength about the Saint's lazy bearing – something that reminded Edgar Hayn of wire and whipcord and indiarubber and compressed steel springs and high explosives.

'In the space of a few minutes,' said the Saint, 'you're going to see a sample of rough-housing that'll make your bunch of third-rate hoodlums look like two cents' worth of oxtail. But before I proceed to beat them up, I want to tell you this – which you can pass on to your friends. Ready?'

Hayn spread out his hands.

'Then I'll shoot,' said the Saint. 'It's just this. We Saints are normally souls of peace and goodwill towards men. But we don't like crooks, blood-suckers, traders in vice and damnation, and other verminous excrescences of that type – such as yourself. We're going to beat you up and do you down, skin you and smash you, and scare you off the face of Europe. We are not bothered about the letter of the Law, we act exactly as we please, we inflict what punishments we think suitable, and no one is going to escape us. Ganning got hurt, but still you don't believe me. You're the next on the list, and by the time I've finished with you, you'll be an example to convince others. And it will go on. That's all I've got to say now, and when I've left you you can go forth and spread the glad news. I'm leaving now!'

He stooped suddenly, and grasped the leg of Hayn's chair and tipped it backwards with one jerking heave. As Hayn tried to scramble to his feet, the Saint put an ungentle foot in his face and upset the table on top of him.

The five tough waiters were pelting across the floor in a pack. Simon reached out for the nearest chair and sent it skating over the room at the height of six inches from the ground, with a vimful swing of his arms that give it the impetus of a charging buffalo. It smashed across the leader's knees and skins with bone-shattering force, and the man went down with a yell.

That left four.

The Saint had another chair in his hands by the time the next man was upon him. The waiter flung up his arms to guard his head, and tried to rush into a grapple; but the Saint stepped back and reversed the swing of his chair abruptly. It swerved under the man's guard and crashed murderously into his short ribs.

Three...

The next man ran slap into a sledge-hammer left that hurled him a dozen feet away. The other two hesitated, but the Saint was giving no breathing space. He leapt in at the nearest man with a pile-driving, left-right-left tattoo to the solar plexus.

As the tough crumpled up with a choking

groan under that battering-ram assault, some sixth sense flashed the Saint a warning.

He leapt to one side, and the chair Hayn had swung to his head swished harmlessly past him, the vigour of the blow toppling Hayn off his balance. The Saint assisted his downfall with an outflung foot which sent the man hurtling headlong.

The last man was still coming on, but warily. He ducked the Saint's lead, and replied with a right swing to the side of the head which gingered the Saint up a peach. Simon Templar decided that his reputation was involved, and executed a beautiful feint with his left which gave him an opening to lash in a volcanic right squarely upon the gangster's nose.

As the man dropped, the Saint whipped round and caught Stannard.

'Fight, you fool!' the Saint hissed in his ear. 'This is for local colour!'

Stannard clinched, and then the Saint broke away and firmly but regretfully clipped him on the ear.

It was not one of the Saint's heftiest punches, but it was hard enough to knock the youngster down convincingly; and then the Saint looked round hopefully for something else to wallop, and found nothing. Hayn was rising again, shakily, and so were those of the five roughs who were in a fit state to do so, but there was no notable enthusiasm to renew the battle.

'Any time any of you bad cheeses want any more lessons in rough-housing,' drawled the Saint, a little breathlessly, 'you've only got to drop me a postcard and I'll be right along.'

This time, there was no attempt to bar his way.

He collected hat, gloves and stick from the cloakroom, and went through the upstairs lounge. As he reached the door, he met Braddon returning.

'Hullo, Sweetness,' said the Saint genially. 'Pass right down the car and hear the new joke the Boys of the Burg downstairs are laughing at.'

Braddon was still trying to guess the cause for and meaning of this extraordinary salutation by a perfect stranger, when the Saint, without any haste or heat, but so swiftly and deftly that the thing was done before Braddon realized what was happening, had reached out and seized the brim of Braddon's hat and forced it well down over his eyes. Then, with a playful tweak of Braddon's nose, and a cheery wave of his hand to the dumbfounded Danny, he departed.

Danny was not a quick mover, and the street outside was Saintless by the time Braddon had struggled out of his hat and reached the door.

When his vocabulary was exhausted, Braddon went downstairs in search of Hayn, and stopped open-mouthed at the wreckage he saw.

Mr Hayn, turning from watching the Saint's triumphant vanishment, had swung sharply on Stannard. The Saint's unscathed exit had left Hayn in the foulest of tempers. All around him, it seemed, an army of tough waiters in various stages of disrepair were gathering themselves to their feet with a muttered obbligato of lurid oaths. Well, if there wasn't an army of them, there were five – five bone-hard heavyweights – and that ought to have been enough to settle any ordinary man, even on the most liberal computation of odds. But the Saint had simply waded right through them, hazed and manhandled and roasted them, and walked out without a scratch. Hayn would have taken a bet that the Saint's tie wasn't even a millimetre out of centre at the end of it. The Saint had made fools of them without turning a hair.

Hayn vented his exasperation on Jerry, and even the fact that he had seen the boy help to tackle the Saint and get the worst of it in the company did not mitigate his wrath.

'You damned fool!' he blazed. 'Couldn't you see he was up to something? Are you taken in by everyone who tells you the tale?'

'I told you I couldn't guarantee him,'

Stannard protested. 'But when I met him he wasn't a bit like he was tonight. Honestly, Mr Hayn – how could I have known? I don't even know what he was after yet. Those cards...'

'South African grandmothers,' snarled Hayn.

Braddon intervened.

'Who was this gentleman, anyway?' he demanded.

'Gentleman' was not the word he used.

'Use your eyes, you lunatic!' Hayn flared, pointing to the table, and Braddon's jaw dropped as he saw the cards.

'You've had that guy in here?'

'What the hell d'you think? You probably passed him coming in. And from what the Snake said, and what I've seen myself, he's probably right at the top – he might even be the Saint himself.'

'So that was the gentleman!' said Braddon, only once again he described Simon Templar with a more decorative word.

Hayn snorted.

'And that fool Stannard brought him here,' he said.

'I've told you, I didn't know much about him, Mr Hayn,' Stannard expostulated. 'I warned you I couldn't answer for him.'

'The kid's right,' said Braddon. 'If he put it over on the Snake, he might put it over on anybody.'

There was logic in the argument, but it was some time before Hayn could be made to see it. But presently he quietened down.

'We'll talk about this, Braddon,' he said. 'I've got an idea for stopping his funny stuff. He didn't get clean away – I put Keld on to follow him. By tonight we'll know where he lives, and then I don't think he'll last long.'

He turned to Jerry. The boy was fidgeting nervously, and Hayn became diplomatic. It wasn't any use rubbing a valuable man up the wrong way.

'I'm sorry I lost my temper, old man,' he said. 'I can see it wasn't your fault. You just want to be more careful. I ought to have warned you about the Saint – he's dangerous! Have a cigar.'

It was Mr Hayn's peace-offering. Stannard accepted it.

'No offence,' he said. 'I'm sorry I let you down.'

'We won't say anything more about it, old man,' said Hayn heartily. 'You won't mind if I leave you? Mr Braddon and I have some business to talk over. I expect you'll amuse yourself upstairs. But you mustn't play any more, you know.'

'I shan't want to,' said Stannard. 'But, Mr Hayn–'

Hayn stopped.

'Yes, old man?'

'Would you mind if I asked you for that

cheque? I'll give you an IOU now...'

'I'll see that you get it before you leave.'

'It's awfully good of you, Mr Hayn,' said Stannard apologetically. 'Three thousand pounds it was.'

'I hadn't forgotten,' said Hayn shortly.

He moved off, cursing the damaged waiters out of his path; and Stannard watched him go, thoughtfully. So far, it had all been too easy, but how long was it going to last?

He was watching the early dancers assembling when a waiter, whose face was obscured by a large piece of sticking-plaster, came through with a sealed envelope. Stannard ripped it open, inspected the cheque it contained, and scribbled his signature to the promissory note that came with it. He sent this back to Hayn by the same waiter.

Although he had disposed of several cocktails before dinner, and during the meal had partaken freely of wine, and afterwards had done his full share in the consumption of liqueurs, his subsequent abstemiousness was remarkable. He sat with an untasted brandy-and-soda in front of him while the coloured orchestra broke into its first frenzies of syncopation, and watched the gyrating couples with a jaundiced eye for an hour. Then he drained his glass, rose, and made his way to the stairs.

Through the window of the office he saw

Hayn and Braddon still engaged in earnest conversation. He tapped on the pane, and Hayn looked up and nodded. The hidden door swung open as Stannard reached it, and closed after him as he passed through.

He strolled through the gaming rooms, greeted a few acquaintances, and watched the play for a while without enthusiasm. He left the club early, as soon as he conveniently could.

The next morning, he hired a car and drove rapidly out of London. He met the Saint on the Newmarket road at a prearranged milestone.

'There was a man following me,' said the Saint happily. 'When I got on my bus, he took a taxi. I wonder if he gave up, or if he's still toiling optimistically along, bursting the meter somewhere in the wilds of Edmonton.'

He gave Stannard a cigarette, and received a cheque in return.

'A thousand pounds,' said Stannard. 'As I promised.'

The Saint put it carefully away in his wallet.

'And why I should give it to you, I don't know,' said Stannard.

'It is the beginning of wisdom,' said the Saint. 'The two thousand that's left will pay off your debts and give you a fresh start, and I'll get your IOU's back for you in a day or two. A thousand pounds isn't much to pay for that.'

'Except that I might have kept the money and gone on working for Hayn.'

'But you have reformed,' said the Saint gently. 'And I'm sure the demonstration you saw last night will help to keep you on the straight and narrow path. If you kept in with Hayn, you'd have me to deal with.'

He climbed back into his car and pressed the self-starter, but Stannard was still curious.

'What are you going to do with the money?' he asked. 'I thought you were against crooks.'

'I am,' said the Saint virtuously. 'It goes to charity. Less my ten per cent commission charged for collecting. You'll hear from me again when I want you. *Au revoir* – or, in the Spanish, *hasta la vista* – or, if you prefer it in the German, *auf Wiedersehen!*'

8

About a week after the Saint's mercurial irruption into Danny's, Gwen Chandler met Mr Edgar Hayn in Regent Street one morning by accident. At exactly the same time, Mr Edgar Hayn met Gwen Chandler on purpose, for he had been at some pains to bring about that accidental meeting.

'We see far too little of you these days, my dear,' he said, taking her hand.

She was looking cool and demure in a summer frock on printed chiffon, and her fair hair peeped out under the brim of her picture hat to set off the cornflower blue of her eyes.

'Why, it seems no time since Jerry and I were having supper with you,' she said.

'No time is far too long for me,' said Mr Hayn cleverly. 'One could hardly have too much of anyone as charming as yourself, my dear lady.'

At the supper party which she had unwillingly been induced to join, he had set himself out to be an irreproachable host, and his suave geniality had gone a long way towards undoing the first instinctive dislike which she had felt for him, but she did not know how to take him in this reversion to his earlier pose of exaggerated heartiness. It reminded her of the playful romping advances of an elephant, but she did not find it funny.

Mr Hayn, however, was for the moment as pachydermatous as the animal on whose pleasantries he appeared to have modelled his own, and her slightly chilling embarrassment was lost on him. He waved his umbrella towards the window of the shop outside which they were standing.

'Do you know that name, Miss Chandler?' he asked.

She looked in the direction indicated.

'Laserre? Yes, of course I've heard of it.'

'I am Laserre,' said Hayn largely. 'This is the opportunity I've been waiting for to introduce you to our humble premises – and how convenient that we should meet on the very doorstep!'

She was not eager to agree, but before she could frame a suitable reply he had propelled her into the glittering red-carpeted room where the preparations of the firm were purveyed in a hushed and reverent atmosphere reminiscent of a cathedral.

A girl assistant came forward, but in a moment she was displaced by Braddon himself – frock-coated, smooth, oleaginous, hands at washing position.

'This is my manager,' said Hayn, and the frock-coated man bowed. 'Mr Braddon, be so good as to show Miss Chandler some samples of the best of our products – the very best.'

Thereupon, to the girl's bewilderment, were displayed velvet-lined mahogany trays, serried ranks of them, brought from the shelves that surrounded the room, and set out with loving care on a counter, one after another, till she felt completely dazed. There were rows upon rows of flashing crystal bottles of scent, golden cohorts of lipsticks, platoons of little alabaster pots of rouge, orderly regiments of enamelled boxes of powder. Her brain reeled before the contemplation of such a massed quantity of luxurious panderings to vanity.

'I want you to choose anything you like,' said Hayn. 'Absolutely anything that takes your fancy, my dear Miss Chandler.'

'But – I – I couldn't possibly,' she stammered.

Hayn waved her objection aside.

'I insist,' he said. 'What is the use of being master of a place like this if you cannot let your friends enjoy it? Surely I can make you such a small present without any fear of being misunderstood? Accept the trifling gift graciously, my dear lady. I shall feel most hurt if you refuse.'

In spite of the grotesqueness of his approach, the circumstances made it impossible to snub him. But she was unable to fathom his purpose in making her the object of such an outbreak. It was a hot day, and he was perspiring freely, as a man of his build is unhappily liable to do, and she wondered hysterically if perhaps the heat had temporarily unhinged his brain. There was something subtly disquieting about his exuberance.

She modestly chose a small vanity-case

and a little flask of perfume, and he seemed disappointed by her reluctance. He pressed other things upon her, and she found herself forced to accept two large boxes of powder.

'Make a nice parcel of those things for Miss Chandler, Mr Braddon,' said Hayn, and the manager carried the goods away to the back of the shop.

'It's really absurdly kind of you, Mr Hayn,' said the girl confusedly. 'I don't know what I've done to deserve it.'

'Your face is your fortune, my dear young lady,' answered Hayn, who was obviously in a brilliant mood.

She had a terrifying suspicion that in a moment he would utter an invitation to lunch, and she hastily begged to be excused on the grounds of an entirely fictitious engagement.

'Please don't think me rude, hurrying away like this,' she pleaded. 'As a matter of fact, I'm already shockingly late.'

He was plainly crestfallen.

'No one can help forgiving you anything,' he said sententiously. 'But the loss to myself is irreparable.'

She never knew afterwards how she managed to keep her end up in the exchange of platitudes that followed, until the return of Braddon with a neat package enabled her to make her escape.

Hayn accompanied her out into the street,

hat in hand.

'At least,' he said, 'promise me that the invitation will not be unwelcome, if I ring you up soon and ask you to suggest a day. I could not bear to think that my company was distasteful to you.'

'Of course not – I should love to – and thank you ever so much for the powder and things,' she said desperately. 'But I must fly now.'

She fled as best she might.

Hayn watched her out of sight, standing stock-still in the middle of the pavement where she had left him, with a queer gleam in his pale eyes. Then he put his hat on, and marched off without re-entering the shop.

He made his way to the club in Soho, where he was informed that Snake Ganning and some of the Boys were waiting to see him. Hayn let them wait while he wrote a letter, which was addressed to M. Henri Chastel, Poste Restante, Athens; and he was about to ring for the Snake to be admitted when there was a tap on the door and Danny entered.

'There are five of them,' said Danny helpfully.

'Five of whom?' said Hayn patiently.

'Five,' said Danny, 'including the man who pulled Mr Braddon's hat down over his eyes. They said they must see you at once.'

Mr Hayn felt in the pit of his stomach the

dull sinking qualm which had come to be inseparable from the memory of the Saint's electric personality. Every morning without fail since the first warning he had received, there had been the now familiar envelope beside his plate at breakfast, containing the inevitable card; and every afternoon, when he reached Danny's, he found a similar reminder among the letters on his desk.

He had not had a chance to forget Simon Templar, even if he had wished to do so – as a matter of fact, the Snake and his Boys were at that moment waiting to receive their instructions in connection with a plot which Hayn had formed for disposing of the menace.

But the Saint's policy was rapidly wearing out Hayn's nerves. Knowing what he did, the Saint could only be refraining from passing his knowledge along to Scotland Yard because he hoped to gain more by silence, yet there had been no attempt to blackmail – only those daily melodramatic reminders of his continued interest.

Hayn was starting to feel like a mouse that has been tormented to the verge of madness by an exceptionally sportive cat. He had not a doubt that the Saint was scheming and working against him still, but his most frenzied efforts of concentration had failed to deduce the most emaciated shred of an idea of the direction from which the next assault would be launched, and seven days and nights of baffled inaction had brought Edgar Hayn to the borders of a breakdown.

Now the Saint – and the rest of his gang also, from all appearances – was paying a second visit. The next round was about to begin, and Hayn was fighting in a profounder obscurity than ever.

'Show them in,' he said in a voice that he hardly recognized as his own.

He bent over some writing, struggling to control his nerves for the bluff that was all he had to rely on, and with an effort of will he succeeded in not looking up when he heard the door opening and the soft footsteps of men filing into the room.

'Walk right in, souls,' said the Saint's unmistakably cheery accents. 'That's right... Park yourselves along that wall in single rank and stand easy.'

Then Hayn raised his eyes, and saw the Saint standing over the desk regarding him affectionately.

'Good morning, Edgar,' said the Saint affably. 'How's Swan?'

'Good morning, Mr Templar,' said Hayn.

He shifted his gaze to the four men ranged beside the door. They were a nondescript quartet, in his opinion – not at all the sort of men he had pictured in his hazy attempts to visualize Templar's partners. Only one of them could have been under thirty, and the clothes of all of them had seen better days.

'These are the rest of the gang,' said the Saint. 'I noticed that I was followed home from here last time I called, so I thought it'd save you a lot of sleuthing if I brought the other lads right along and introduced them.'

He turned.

'Squad – shun! – Souls, this is dear Edgar, whom you've heard so much about. As I call your names reading from left to right, you will each take one pace smartly to your front, bow snappily from the hips, keeping the eyebrows level and the thumb in line with the seam of the trousers, and fall in again... First, Edgar, meet Saint Winston Churchill. Raise your hat, Winny... On his left, Saint George Robey. Eyebrows level, George... Next, Saint Herbert Hoover, President of the United States, and no relation to the vacuum cleaner. Wave your handkerchief to the pretty gentleman, Herb! Last, but not least, Saint Hannen Swaffer. Keep smiling, Hannen – I won't let anyone slap your face here... That's the lot, Edgar, except for myself. Meet me!'

Hayn nodded.

'That's very considerate of you, Mr Templar,' he said, and his voice was a little shaky, for an idea was being born inside him. 'Is that all you came to do?'

'Not quite, Precious,' said the Saint, settling down on the edge of the deck. 'I came to talk business.'

'Then you won't want to be hurried,' said Hayn. 'There are some other people waiting to see me. Will you excuse me while I go and tell them to call again later?'

The Saint smiled.

'By all manner of means, sonny,' said he. 'But I warn you it won't be any use telling the Snake and his Boys to be ready to beat us up when we leave here, because a friend of ours is waiting a block away with a letter to our friend Inspector Teal – and that letter will be delivered if we don't report safe and sound in ten minutes from now!'

'You needn't worry,' said Hayn. 'I haven't underrated your intelligence!'

He went out. It was a mistake he was to regret later – never before had he left even his allies alone in that office, much less a confessed enemy. But the urgency of his inspiration had, for the moment, driven every other thought out of his head. The cleverest criminal must make a slip sooner or later, and it usually proves to be such a childish one that the onlooker is amazed that it should have been made at all. Hayn made his slip then, but it must be remembered that he was a very rattled man.

He found Snake Ganning sitting at the bar with three picked Boys, and beckoned them out of earshot of the bartender.

'The Saint and the rest of his band are in

the office,' he said, and Ganning let out a virulent exclamation. 'No – there won't be any rough business now. I want to have a chance to find out what his game is. But when the other four go, I want you to tail them and find out all you can about them. Report here at midnight, and I'll give you your instructions about Templar himself.'

'When I get hold of that swine,' Ganning ground out vitriolically, 'he's going to–'

Hayn cut him short with an impatient sweep of his hand.

'You'll wait till I've finished with him,' he said. 'You don't want to charge in like a bull at a gate, before you know what's on the other side of the gate. I'll tell you when to start – you can bet your life on that!'

And in that short space of time the Saint, having shamelessly seized the opportunity provided by Hayn's absence, had comprehensively ransacked the desk. There were four or five IOU's with Stannard's signature in an unlocked drawer, and these he pocketed. Hayn had been incredibly careless. And then the Saint's eye was caught by an envelope on which the ink was still damp. The name 'Chastel' stood out as if it had been spelt in letters of fire, so that Simon stiffened like a pointer…

His immobility lasted only an instant. Then, in a flash, he scribbled something on a blank sheet of notepaper and folded it into a blank envelope. With the original before him for a guide, he copied the address in a staggeringly lifelike imitation of Hayn's handwriting…

'I shall now be able to give you an hour, if you want it,' said Hayn, returning, and the Saint turned with a bland smile.

'I shan't take nearly as long as that, my cabbage,' he replied. 'But I don't think the proceedings will interest the others, and they've got work to do. Now you've met them, do you mind if I dismiss the parade?'

'Not at all, Mr Templar.'

There was a glitter of satisfaction in Hayn's eyes; but if the Saint noticed it, he gave no sign.

'Move to the right in column o' route – etcetera,' he ordered briskly. 'In English, hop it!'

The parade, after a second's hesitation, shuffled out with expressionless faces. They had not spoken a word from the time of their entrance to the time of their exit.

It may conveniently be recorded at this juncture that Snake Ganning and the Boys spent eleven laboriously profitless hours following a kerbstone vendor of bootlaces, a pavement artist, and a barrel-organ team of two ex-Service men, whom the Saint had hired for ten shillings apiece for the occasion; and it may also be mentioned that the quartet, assembling at a nearby dairy to celebrate the windfall, were no less mystified than were the four painstaking bloodhounds who dogged their footsteps for the rest of the day.

It was the Saint's idea of a joke – but then, the Saint's sense of humour was remarkably broad.

9

'And now let's get down to business – as the bishop said to the actress,' murmured Simon, fishing out his cigarette-case and tapping a gasper on his thumbnail. 'I want to ask you a very important question.'

Hayn sat down.

'Well, Mr Templar?'

'What would you say,' said the Saint tentatively, 'if I told you I wanted ten thousand pounds?'

Hayn smiled.

'I should sympathize with you,' he answered. 'You're not the only man who'd like to make ten thousand pounds as easily as that.'

'But just suppose,' said Simon persuasively – 'just suppose I told you that if I didn't get ten thousand pounds at once, a little dossier about you would travel right along to Inspector Teal to tell him the story of the upstairs rooms here and the inner secrets of the Maison Laserre? I could tell him enough to send you to penal servitude for five years.'

Hayn's eyes fell on the calendar hung on the wall, with a sliding red ring round the date. His brain was working very rapidly then. Suddenly, he felt unwontedly confident. He looked down from the calendar to his watch, and smiled.

'I should write you a cheque at once,' he said.

'And your current account would stand it?'

'All my money is in a current account,' said Hayn. 'As you will understand, it is essential for a man in my position to be able to realize his estate without notice.'

'Then please write,' murmured the Saint.

Without a word, Hayn opened a drawer, took out his chequebook, and wrote. He passed the cheque to Templar, and the Saint's eyes danced as he read it.

'You're a good little boy, son,' said the Saint. 'I'm so glad we haven't had any sordid argument and haggling about this. It makes the whole thing so crude, I always think.'

Hayn shrugged.

'You have your methods,' he said. 'I have mine. I ask you to observe the time.' He showed his watch, tapping the dial with a stubby forefinger. 'Half past twelve of a Saturday afternoon. You cannot cash that cheque until nine o'clock on Monday morning. Who knows what may have happened by then? I say you will never pay that cheque into your bank. I'm not afraid to tell you that. I know you won't set the police on to me until Monday morning, because you think you're going to win – because you think that at nine o'clock on Monday morning you'll be sitting on the bank's doorstep waiting for it to open. I know you won't. Do you honestly believe I would let you blackmail me for a sum like that – nearly as much money as I have saved in five years?'

The crisis that he had been expecting for so long had come. The cards were on the table, and the only thing left for Edgar Hayn to wonder was why the Saint had waited so many days before making his demand. Now the storm which had seemed to be hanging fire interminably had broken, and it found Edgar Hayn curiously unmoved.

Templar looked at Hayn sidelong, and the Saint also knew that the gloves were off.

'You're an old cove,' he said. 'Your trouble is that you're too serious. You'll lose this fight because you've no sense of humour – like all second-rate crooks. You can't laugh.'

'I may enjoy the last laugh, Templar,' said Hayn.

The Saint turned away with a smile, and picked up his hat.

'You kid yourself,' he said gently. 'You won't, dear one.' He took up his stick and swung it delicately in his fingers. The light of battle glinted in his blue eyes. 'I presume I may send your kind donation to the London Hospital anonymously, son?'

'We will decide that on Monday,' said Hayn.

The Saint nodded.

'I wonder if you know what my game is?' he said soberly. 'Perhaps you think I'm a kind of hijacker – a crook picking crooks' pockets? Bad guess, dearie. I'm losing money over this. But I'm just a born-an'-bred fighting machine, and a quiet life on the moss-gathering lay is plain hell for this child. I'm not a dick, because I can't be bothered with red tape, but I'm on the same side. I'm out to see that unpleasant insects like you are stamped on, which I grant you the dicks could do; but to justify my existence I'm going to see that the said insects contribute a large share of their ill-gotten gains to charity, which you've got to grant me the dicks can't do. It's always seemed a bit tough to me that microbes of your breed should be able to make a pile swindling, and then be free to enjoy it after they've done a month or two in stir – and I'm here to put that right. Out of the money

I lifted off the Snake I paid Tommy Mitre back his rightful property, plus a bonus for damages; but the Snake's a small bug, anyway. You're big, and I'm going to see that your contribution is in proportion.'

'We shall see,' said Hayn.

The Saint looked at him steadily.

'On Monday night you will sleep at Marlborough Street Police Station,' he said dispassionately.

The next moment he was gone. Simon Templar had a knack of making his abrupt exits so smoothly that it was generally some minutes before the other party fully realized that he was no longer with them.

Hayn sat looking at the closed door without moving. Then he glanced down, and saw the envelope that lay on the blotter before him, addressed in his own hand to M. Henri Chastel. And Hayn sat fascinated, staring, for although the imitation of his hand might have deceived a dozen people who knew it, he had looked at it for just long enough to see that it was not the envelope he had addressed.

It was some time before he came out of his trance, and forced himself to slit open the envelope with fingers that trembled. He spread out the sheet of paper on the desk in front of him, and his brain went numb. As a man might have grasped a concrete fact through a murky haze of dope, Hayn realized that his back was to the last wall. Underneath the superficial veneer of flippancy, the Saint had shown for a few seconds the seriousness of his real quality and the intentness of his purpose, and Hayn had been allowed to appreciate the true mettle of the man who was fighting him.

He could remember the Saint's last words. 'On Monday night you will sleep at Marlborough Street Police Station.' He could hear the Saint saying it. The voice had been the voice of a judge pronouncing sentence, and the memory of it made Edgar Hayn's face go grey with fear.

10

The Saint read Edgar Hayn's letter in the cocktail bar of the Piccadilly, over a timely Martini, but his glass stood for a long time untasted before him, for he had not to read far before he learned that Edgar Hayn was bigger game than he had ever dreamed.

Then he smoked two cigarettes, very thoughtfully, and made certain plans with a meticulous attention to detail. In half an hour he had formulated his strategy, but he spent another quarter of an hour and another cigarette going over it again and again in search of anything that he might have overlooked.

He did not touch his drink until he had decided that his plans were as foolproof as he could make them at such short notice.

The first move took him to Piccadilly Post Office, where he wrote out and despatched a lengthy telegram in code to one Norman Kent, who was at that time in Athens on the Saint's business; and the Saint thanked his little gods of chance for the happy coincidence that had given him an agent on the spot. It augured well for the future.

Next he shifted across from the counter to a telephone-box, and called a number. For ten minutes he spoke earnestly to a certain Roger Conway, and gave minute directions. He had these orders repeated over to him to make sure that they were perfectly memorized and understood, and presently he was satisfied.

'Hayn will have found out by now that I know about his connection with Chastel,' he concluded, 'that is, unless he's posted that letter without looking at it. We've got to act on the assumption that he *has* found out, and therefore the rule about having nothing to do with me except through the safest of safe channels is doubly in force. I estimate that within the next forty-four hours a number of very strenuous efforts will be made to bump me off, and it won't be any good shutting your eyes to it. It won't be dear Edgar's fault if I haven't qualified for Kensal Green by Monday morning.'

Conway protested, and the Saint dealt shortly with that.

'You're a heap more useful to me working unknown,' he said. 'I can't help it if your natural vanity makes you kick at having to hide your light under a bushel. There's only need for one of us to prance about in the line of fire; and since they know me all round and upside down as it is, I've bagged the job. You don't have to worry, I've never played the corpse yet, and I don't feel like starting now!'

He was in the highest of spirits. The imminent prospect of violent and decisive action always got him that way. It made his blood tingle thrillingly through his veins, and set his eyes dancing recklessly, and made him bless the perfect training in which he had always kept his nerves and sinews. The fact that his life would be charged a five hundred per cent premium by any cautious insurance company failed to disturb his cheerfulness one iota. The Saint was made that way.

The 'needle' was a sensation that had never troubled his young life. For the next few hours there was nothing that he could do for the cause that he had made his own, and he therefore proposed to enjoy those hours on his own to the best of his ability. He was completely unperturbed by the thought of the hectic and perilous hours which were to follow the interlude of enjoyment – rather, the interlude gathered an added zest from the approach of zero hour.

He could not, of course, be sure that Hayn had discovered the abstraction of the letter; but that remained a distant probability in spite of the Saint's excellent experiment in forgery. And even without the discovery, the cheque he had obtained, and Hayn's confidence in giving it, argued that there were going to be some very tense moments before the Monday morning. Simon Templar's guiding principle, which had brought him miraculously unscathed through innumerable desperate adventures in the past, was to assume the worst and take no chances; and in this instance subsequent events were to prove that pessimistic principle the greatest and most triumphant motto that had ever been invented.

The Saint lunched at his leisure, and then relaxed amusingly in a convenient cinema until half past six. Then he returned home to dress, and was somewhat disappointed to find no reply to his cable waiting for him at his flat.

He dined and spent the night dancing at the Kit-Cat with the lovely and utterly delightful Patricia Holm, for the Saint was as human as the next man, if not more so, and Patricia Holm was his weakness then.

It was a warm evening, and they walked up Regent Street together, enjoying the fresh air. They were in Hanover Square, just by the corner of Brook Street, when the Saint saw the first thunder cloud, and unceremoniously caught Patricia Holm by the shoulders and jerked her back round the corner and out of sight. An opportune taxi came prowling by at that moment, and the Saint had hailed it and bundled the girl in before she could say a word.

'I'm telling him to take you to the Savoy,' he said. 'You'll book a room there, and you'll stay there without putting even the tip of your pretty nose outside the door until I come and fetch you. You can assume that any message or messenger you receive is a fake. I don't think they saw you, but I'm not risking anything. Refuse to pay any attention to anything or anybody but myself in person. I'll be round Monday lunchtime, and if I'm not you can get hold of Inspector Teal and the lads and start raising Cain – but not before.'

The girl frowned suspiciously.

'Saint,' she said, in the dangerous tone that he knew and loved, 'you're trying to elbow me out again.'

'Old darling,' said the Saint quietly, 'I've

stopped trying to elbow you out and make you live a safe and respectable life. I know it can't be done. You can come in on any game I take up, and I don't care if we have to fight the massed gangs of bad hats in New York, Chicago, Berlin and London. But there's just one kind of dirty work I'm not going to have you mixed up in, and this is it. Get me, old Pat?... Then s'long!'

He closed the door of the taxi, directed the driver, and watched it drive away. The Saint felt particularly anxious to keep on living at that moment... And then the taxi's tail-light vanished round the corner, and Patricia Holm went with it; and the Saint turned with a sigh and an involuntary squaring of the shoulders, and swung into Brook Street.

He had observed the speedy-looking closed car that stood by the kerb directly outside the entrance to his flat, and he had seen the four men who stood in a little group on the pavement beside it conversing with all apparent innocence, and he had guessed the worst. The sum total of those deceptively innocuous fixtures and fittings seemed to him to bear the unmistakable hall-mark of the Hayn confederacy; for the Saint had what he called a nasty suspicious mind.

He strolled on at a leisurely pace. His left hand in his trouser pocket, was sorting out the key of his front door; in his right hand he twirled the stick that in those days he never travelled without. His black felt hat was tilted over to the back of his head. In everything outward and visible he wore the mildest and most Saintly air of fashionable and elegant harmlessness, for the Saint was never so cool as when everything about him was flaming with red danger-signals. And as he drew near the little group he noticed that they fell suddenly silent, all turning in his direction.

'Excuse me,' said the tallest of the four, taking a step forward to meet him.

'I'm afraid I can't excuse you, Snake,' said the Saint regretfully, and swayed back from his toes as Ganning struck at him with a loaded cane.

The Saint felt the wind of the blow caress his face, and then a lightening left uppercut came rocketing up from his knees to impact on the point of Snake's jaw, and Ganning was catapulted back into the arms of his attendant Boys.

Before any of them could recover from their surprise, Templar had leapt lightly up the steps to the portico, and had slipped the key into the lock. But as he turned and withdrew it, the other three came after him, leaving their chief to roll away into the gutter, and the Saint wheeled round to face them with the door swinging open behind him.

He held his stick in both hands, gave it a half-turn, and pulled. Part of the stick stripped away, and in the Saint's right hand a long slim blade of steel glinted in the dim light. His first thrust took the leading Boy through the shoulder, and the other two checked.

The Saint's white teeth flashed in an unpleasant smile.

'You're three very naughty children,' said the Saint, 'and I'm afraid I shall have to report you to your Sunday School teacher. Go a long way away, and don't come near me again for years and years!'

The rapier in his hand gleamed and whistled, and the two Boys recoiled with gasps of agony as the supple blade lashed across their faces. And then, as they sprang blindly to attack, the Saint streaked through the door and slammed it on them.

He turned the sword back into a stick, and went unhurriedly up the stairs to his flat, which was the first floor.

Looking down from the window, he saw four men gathered together engaged in furious deliberation. One of them was mopping about inside his coat with an insanitary handkerchief, and the Snake was sagging weakly back against the side of the car holding his jaw. There were frequent gesticulations in the direction of the Saint's windows. After a time, the four men climbed into the car and drove away.

The brief affray had left the Saint completely unruffled. If you had taken his pulse then, you would have found it ticking over at not one beat above or below its normal 75. He sauntered across the room, switched on the lights, and put away his hat and stick, still humming gently to himself.

Propped up on the table, in a prominent position, was a cable envelope. Without any hurry, the Saint poured himself out a modest whisky, lighted a cigarette, and then fetched a small black notebook from its hiding-place behind a picture. Provided with these essentials, the Saint settled down on the edge of the table, ripped up the envelope, and extracted the flimsy.

'Elephant revoke,' the message began. A little further on was the name Chandler. And near the end of the closely-written sheet were the words: 'Caterpillar diamonds ten spades four chicane hearts knave overcall'.

'Elephant' was the code word for Hayn; Chastel was 'Caterpillar'. 'Revoke' meant 'has changed his mind'. And the Saint could almost decode the sentence which included the words 'chicane' and 'overcall' at sight.

In his little black book, against the names of every card in the pack, and every bridge and poker term, were short sentences broadly applicable to almost any purpose about which his fellowship of freebooters might wish to communicate; and with the aid of this book, and a pencil, the Saint translated the message and wrote the interpretation between the lines. The information thus gleaned was in confirmation of what he had already deduced since purloining and reading Hayn's letter to Chastel, and the Saint was satisfied.

He opened his portable typewriter, and wrote a letter. It was the Saint's first official communiqué.

To Chief Inspector Teal
Criminal Investigation Department
New Scotland Yard
SW1
Sir,

I recommend to your notice Edgar Hayn, formerly Heine, of 27, Portugal Mansions, Hampstead. He is the man behind Danny's Club in Soho, and a well-timed raid on that establishment, with particular attention to a secret door in the panelling of the ground floor lounge (which is opened by an electric control in Hayn's office in the basement) will give you an interesting insight into the methods of card-sharping de luxe.

More important than this, Hayn is also the man behind Laserre, the Regent Street perfumiers, the difference being that George Edward Braddon, the manager, is not a figurehead, but an active partner. A careful watch kept on future consignments received from the Continent by Laserre will provide adequate proof that the main reason for the existence of Laserre is cocaine. The drug is smuggled into England in cases of beauty preparations shipped by Hayn's foreign agents and quite openly declared – as dutiable products, that is. In every case, there will be found a number of boxes purporting to contain face powder, but actually containing cocaine.

Hayn's European agent is a French national of Levantine extraction named Henri Chastel. The enclosed letter, in Hayn's own handwriting, will be sufficient to prove that Hayn and Chastel were up to their necks in the whole European dope traffic.

Chastel, who is at present in Athens, will be dealt with by my agent there. I regret that I cannot hand him over to the regular processes of justice; but the complications of nationality and extradition treaties would, I fear, defeat this purpose.

By the time you receive this, I shall have obtained from Hayn the donation to charity which it is my intention to exact before passing him on to you for punishment, and you may at once take steps to secure his arrest. He has a private Moth aeroplane at Stag Lane Aerodrome, Edgware, which has for some time been kept in readiness against the necessity for either himself or one of his valued agents to make a hasty getaway. A watch kept on the aerodrome, therefore, should ensure the frustration of this scheme.

In the future, you may expect to hear from me at frequent intervals.

Assuring you of my best services at all times,

I remain, etc,

THE SAINT.

With this epistle, besides Hayn's letter, Templar enclosed his artistic trademark. So that there should be no possibility of tracing him, he had had the paper on which it was drawn, specially obtained by Stannard from the gaming rooms at Danny's for the purpose.

He addressed the letter, and after a preliminary survey of the street to make sure that the Snake had not returned or sent deputies, he walked to a nearby pillarbox and posted it. It would not be delivered until Monday morning, and the Saint reckoned that that would give him all the time he needed.

Back in his flat, the Saint called up the third of his lieutenants, who was one Dicky Tremayne, and gave him instructions concerning the protection of Gwen Chandler.

Finally he telephoned another number and called Jerry Stannard out of bed to receive orders.

At last he was satisfied that everything had been done that he had to do.

He went to the window, drew the curtains aside a cautious half-inch, and looked down again. A little further up Brook Street, on the other side of the road, a blue Furillac sports saloon had drawn up by the kerb. The Saint smiled approvingly.

He turned out the lights in the sitting-room, went through to his bedroom, and began to undress. When he rolled up his left sleeve, there was visible a little leather sheath strapped to his forearm, and in this sheath he carried a beautifully-balanced knife – a mere six inches of razor-keen, leaf-shaped blade and three inches of carved ivory hilt. This was Anna, the Saint's favourite throwing-knife. The Saint could impale a flying champagne cork with Anna at twenty paces. He considered her present place of concealment a shade too risky, and transferred the sheath to the calf of his right leg. Finally, he made sure that his cigarette-case contained a supply of a peculiar kind of cigarette.

Outside, in the street, an ordinary bulb motor-horn hooted with a peculiar rhythm. It was a pre-arranged signal, and the Saint did not have to look out again to know that

Ganning had returned. And then, almost immediately, a bell rang, and the indicator in the kitchen showed him that it was the bell of the front door.

'They must think I'm a mug!' murmured the Saint.

But he was wrong – he had forgotten the fire-escape across the landing outside the door of his flat.

A moment later he heard, down the tiny hall, a dull crash and a sound of splintering wood. It connected up in his mind with the ringing of the front door bell, and he realized that he had no monopoly of pre-arranged signals. That ringing had been to tell the men who had entered at the back that their companions were ready at the front of the building. The Saint acknowledged that he had been trapped into underrating the organizing ability of Edgar Hayn.

Unthinkingly, he had left his automatic in his bedroom. He went quickly out of the kitchen into the hall, and at the sound of his coming the men who had entered with the aid of a jemmy swung round. Hayn was one of them, and his pistol carried a silencer.

'Well, well, *well!'* drawled the Saint, whose mildness in times of crisis was phenomenal, and prudently raised his hands high above his head.

'You are going on a journey with me,

Templar,' said Hayn. 'We are leaving at once, and I can give no date for your return. Kindly turn round and put your hands behind you.'

Templar obeyed. His wrists were bound, and the knots tightened by ungentle hands.

'Are you still so optimistic, Saint?' Hayn taunted him, testing the bonds.

'More than ever,' answered the Saint cheerfully. 'This is my idea of a night out – as the bishop said to the actress.'

Then they turned him round again.

'Take him downstairs,' said Hayn.

They went down in a silent procession, the Saint walking without resistance between two men. The front door was opened and a husky voice outside muttered: 'All clear. The flattie passed ten minutes ago, and his beat takes him half an hour.'

The Saint was passed on to the men outside and hustled across the pavement into the waiting car. Hayn and two other men followed him in; a third climbed up beside the driver. They moved off at once, heading west.

At the same time, a man rose from his cramped position on the floor of the Furillac that waited twenty yards away. He had been crouched down there for three-quarters of an hour, without a word of complaint for his discomfort, to make it appear that the car was empty, and the owner inside the house opposite which the car stood. The self-starter whirred under his foot as he sidled round behind the wheel, and the powerful engine woke to a throaty whisper.

The car in which the Saint rode with Hayn flashed up the street, gathering speed rapidly; and as it went by, the blue sports Furillac pulled out from the kerb and purred westwards at a discreet distance in its wake.

Roger Conway drove. The fit of his coat was spoiled by the solid bulge of the automatic in one pocket, and there was a stern set to his face which would have amazed those who only knew that amiable young man in his more flippant moods.

From his place in the leading car Simon Templar caught in the driving mirror a glimpse of the following Furillac, and smiled deep within himself.

11

Gwen Chandler lived in a microscopic flat in Bayswater, the rent of which was paid by the money left her by her father. She did the housekeeping herself, and, with this saving on a servant, there was enough left over from her income to feed her and give her a reasonably good time. None of the few relations she had ever paid much attention to her.

She would have been happy with her friends, and she had been, but all that had stopped abruptly when she had met and fallen in love, head over heels, with Jerry Stannard.

He was about twenty-three. She knew that, for the past two years, he had been leading a reckless life, spending most of his time and money in night clubs and usually going to bed at dawn. She also knew that his extravagant tastes had plunged him into debt, and that since the death of his father he had been accumulating bigger and bigger creditors; and she attributed these excesses to his friends, for the few people of his acquaintance she had met were of a type she detested. But her advice and inquiries had been answered with such a surliness, that at last she had given up the contest and nursed her anxiety alone.

But a few days ago her fiancé's grumpiness had strangely vanished. Though he still seemed to keep the same Bohemian hours, he had been smiling and cheerful whenever she met him; and once, in a burst of good spirits, he had told her that his debts were paid off and he was making a fresh start. She could get no more out of him than this, however – her eager questions had made him abruptly taciturn, though his refusal to be cross-examined had been kindly enough. He would be able to tell her all about it one day, he said, and that day would not be long coming.

She knew that it was his practice to lie in bed late on Sunday mornings – but then, it was his practice to lie in bed late on all the other six days of the week. On this particular Sunday morning, therefore, when a ring on the front door bell had disturbed her from the task of preparing breakfast, she was surprised to find that he was her visitor.

He was trying to hide agitation, but she discerned that the agitation was not of the harassed kind.

'Got any breakfast for me?' he asked. 'I had to come along at this unearthly hour, because I don't know that I'll have another chance to see you all day. Make it snappy, because I've got an important appointment.'

'It'll be ready in a minute,' she told him.

He loafed about the kitchen, whistling, while she fried eggs and bacon, and sniffed the fragrant aroma appreciatively.

'It smells good,' he said, 'and I've got the appetite of a lifetime!'

She would have expected him to breakfast in a somewhat headachy silence; but he talked cheerfully.

'It must be years since you had a decent holiday,' he said. 'I think you deserve one, Gwen. What do you say if we get married by special licence and run over to Deauville next week?'

He laughed at her bewildered protests.

'I can afford it,' he assured her. 'I've paid off everyone I owe money to, and in a fortnight I'm getting a terribly sober job, starting at five pounds a week.'

'How did you get it?'

'A man called Simon Templar found it for me. Have you ever met him, by any chance?'

She shook her head, trying to find her voice.

'I'd do anything in the world for that man,' said Jerry.

'Tell me about it,' she stammered.

He told her – of his miraculous rescue by the Saint and the interview that followed it, of the Saint's persuasiveness, of the compact they had made. He also told her about Hayn; but although the recital was fairly inclusive, it did not include the machinations of the Maison Laserre. The Saint never believed in telling anybody everything, and even Hayn had secrets of his own.

The girl was amazed and shocked by the revelation of what Stannard's life had been and might still have been. But all other emotions were rapidly submerged in the great wave of relief which swept over her when she learned that Stannard had given his word to break away, and was even then working on the side of the man who had brought him back to a sense of honour – even if that honour worked in an illegal method.

'I suppose it's crooked, in one way,' Stannard admitted. 'They're out to get Hayn and his crowd into prison, but first they're swindling them on behalf of charity. I don't know how they propose to do it. On the other hand, though, the money they've got back for me from Hayn is no more than I lost in cash at his beastly club.'

'But why did Hayn let you keep on when he knew you'd got no money left?'

Stannard made a wry grimace.

'He wanted to be able to force me into his gang. I came in, too – but that was because Templar told me to agree to anything that would make Hayn pay me that three thousand pound cheque.'

She digested the information in a daze. The revelation of the enterprise in which Jerry Stannard was accompliced to the Saint did not shock her. Womanlike, she could see only the guilt of Hayn and the undoubted justice of his punishment. Only one thing made her afraid.

'If you were caught–'

'There'll be no fuss,' said Jerry. 'Templar's

promised me that, and he's the kind of man you'd trust with anything. I haven't had to do anything criminal. And it'll all be over in a day or two. Templar rang me up last night.'

'What was it about?'

'That's what he wouldn't tell me. He told me to go to the Splendide at eleven and wait there for a man called Tremayne, who may arrive any time up to one o'clock, and he'll tell me the rest. Tremayne's one of Templar's gang.'

Then she remembered Hayn's peculiar behaviour of the previous morning. The parcel she had brought away from Laserre still lay unopened on her dressing-table.

Jerry was interested in the account. Hayn's association with Laserre, as has been mentioned, was news to him. But he could make nothing of the story.

'I expect he's got some foolish crush on you,' he suggested. 'It's only the way you'd expect a man like that to behave. I'll speak to Templar about it when I see him.'

He left the dining-room as soon as he had finished breakfast, and was back in a moment with his hat.

'I must be going now,' he said, and took her in his arms. 'Gwen, dear, with any luck it'll all be over very soon, and we'll be able to forget it. I'll be back as soon as ever I can.'

She kissed him.

'God bless you. And be careful, my darling!'

He kissed her again, and went out singing blithely. The world was very bright for Jerry Stannard that morning.

But the girl listened to the cheerful slamming of the door with a little frown, for she was troubled with misgivings. It had all seemed so easy at the time, in the optimistic way in which he had told her the story, but reviewed in cold blood it presented dangers and difficulties in legion.

She wished, for both their sakes, that he had been able to stay with her that day, and her fears were soon to be justified.

Half an hour after he had gone, when the breakfast things had been cleared away, and she was tidying herself to go out for a walk, there was a ring on the front door bell.

She answered it; and when she saw that it was Edgar Hayn, after what Jerry had been able to tell her, she would have closed the door in his face. But he had pushed through before she could collect her wits.

He led the way into the sitting-room, and she followed in mingled fear and anger. Then she saw that there were dark rings round his eyes, and his face was haggard.

'What is it?' she asked coldly.

'The police,' he said. 'They're after me – and they're after you, too. I came to warn you.'

'But why should they be after me?' she demanded blankly.

He was in a terrible state of nerves. His hands fidgeted with his umbrella all the time he was talking, and he did not meet her eyes.

'Drugs!' he said gruffly. 'Illicit drugs. Cocaine. You know what I mean! There's no harm in your knowing now – we're both in the same boat. They've been watching me, and they saw me with you yesterday and followed you.'

'But how do you know?'

'I've got friends at Scotland Yard,' he snapped. 'It's necessary. Policemen aren't incorruptible. But my man let me down – he never gave me the tip till the last moment. They're going to raid this flat and search it this morning.'

Her brain was like a maelstrom, but there was one solid fact to hold on to.

'There's nothing for them to find.'

'That's where you're wrong! Those things I gave you – one of our other boxes got mixed up in them. I've just found that out. That's why I'm here. There's six ounces of cocaine in this flat!'

She recoiled, wide-eyed. Her heart was thumping madly. It all seemed too impossible, too fantastic… And yet it only bore out and amplified what Jerry had been able to tell her. She wondered frantically if the excuse of innocence would convince a jury. Hayn saw the thought cross her mind, and shattered it.

'You know how Jerry's lived,' he said. 'No one would believe that you weren't both in it!'

He looked out of the window. She was impelled to follow his example, and she was in time to see two broad-shouldered men in bowler hats entering the house.

'They're here!' said Hayn breathlessly. 'But there may be a chance. I recognized one of the men – he's a friend of minc. I may be able to square him.'

Outside, a bell rang.

Hayn was scribbling something on a card.

'Take this,' he muttered. 'My car's outside. If I can get them away from you for a moment, slip out and show the card to the chauffeur. I've got a house at Hurley. He'll take you there, and I'll come down later and discuss how we're going to get you and Jerry out of the country.'

The bell rang again, more urgently. Hayn thrust the pasteboard into the girl's hand.

'What're you hesitating for?' he snarled. 'Do you want to stand in the dock at the Old Bailey beside your brother?'

Hardly knowing what she did, she put the card in her bag.

'Go and open the door,' Hayn commanded. 'They'll break in if you don't.'

As he spoke, there came yet a more insistent ringing, and the flat echoed with the thunder of a knocker impatiently plied.

The girl obeyed, and at the same time she was thinking furiously. Jerry – or his chief, this man Templar – would know how to deal with the crisis; but for the moment there was no doubt that Hayn's plan was the only practical one. Her one idea was to stay out of the hands of the police long enough to make sure that Jerry was safe, and to give them time to think out an escape from the trap in which Hayn had involved them.

The two broad-shouldered men entered without ceremony as she opened the door.

'I am Inspector Baker, of Scotland Yard,' said one of them formally, 'and I have a warrant to search your flat. You are suspected of being in illegal possession of a quantity of cocaine.'

The other man took her arm and led her into the sitting-room. Hayn came forward, frowning.

'I must protest about this,' he said. 'Miss Chandler is a friend of mine.'

'That's unlucky for you,' was the curt reply.

'I'll speak to Baker about this,' threatened Hayn hotly, and at that moment Baker came in.

He was carrying a small cardboard box with the label of Laserre. 'Poudre Laserre', the label said; but the powder was white and crystalline.

'I think this is all we need,' said Baker; and stepped up to Gwen. 'I shall take you into custody on a charge–'

Hayn came between them.

'I should like a word with you first,' he said quietly.

Baker shrugged.

'If you must waste your time–'

'I'll take the risk,' said Hayn. 'In private, please.'

Baker jerked his thumb.

'Take Chandler into another room, Jones.'

'Jones had better stay,' interrupted Hayn. 'What I have to say concerns him also. If you will let Miss Chandler leave us for a minute, I will guarantee that she will not attempt to escape.'

There was some argument, but eventually Baker agreed. Hayn opened the door for the girl, and as she went out gave her an almost imperceptible nod. She went into her bedroom and picked up the telephone. It seemed an eternity before the paging system of the Splendide found Jerry. When he answered, he told him what had happened.

'I'm going to Hayn's house at Hurley,' she said. 'It's the only way to get out at the moment. But tell Tremayne when he comes, and get hold of Templar, and do something quickly!'

He was beginning to object, to ask questions, but there was no time for that, and she hung up the receiver. She had no means of knowing what Hayn's methods of 'squaring' were, or how long the negotiations might be expected to keep the detectives occupied.

She tiptoed down the hall, and opened the door.

From the window, Hayn, Baker and Jones watched her cross the pavement and enter the car.

'She's a peach, boss,' said Baker enviously.

'You've said all I wanted you to say,' Hayn returned shortly. 'But it's worked perfectly. If I'd simply tried to kidnap her, she'd have been twice as much nuisance. As it is, she'll be only too glad to do everything I say.'

Dicky Tremayne arrived two minutes after Hayn's car had driven off. He should have been there over an hour ago, but the cussedness of Fate had intervened to baulk one of the Saint's best-laid plans. A bus had skidded into Tremayne's car in Park Lane, the consequent policeman had delayed him interminably, the arrangements for the removal of his wrecked car had delayed him longer, and when at last he had got away in a taxi a series of traffic blocks had held him up at every crossing.

Now he had to act on his own initiative.

After a second's indecision, Tremayne

realized that there was only one thing to do. If Hayn and his men were already in the flat, he must just blind in and hope for the best; if they had not yet arrived, no harm would be done.

He went straight into the building, and on the way up the stairs he met Hayn and two other men coming down. There was no time for deliberation or planning a move in advance.

'You're the birds I'm looking for,' Tremayne rapped, barring the way. 'I'm Inspector Hancock, of Scotland Yard, and I shall arrest you–'

So far he got before Hayn lashed out at him. Tremayne ducked, and the next instant there was an automatic in his hand.

'Back up those stairs to the flat you've just left,' he ordered, and the three men retreated before the menace of his gun.

They stopped at the door of the flat, and he told Hayn to ring. They waited.

'There seems to be no reply,' said Hayn sardonically.

'Ring again,' Tremayne directed grimly.

Another minute passed.

'There can't really be anyone at home,' Hayn remarked.

Tremayne's eyes narrowed. It was something about the tone of Hayn's sneering voice…

'You swine!' said Tremayne though his

teeth. 'What have you done with her?'

'With whom?' inquired Hayn blandly.

'With Gwen Chandler!'

Tremayne could have bitten his tongue off as soon as the words were out of his mouth. That fatal, thoughtless impetuosity which was always letting him down! He saw Hayn suddenly go tense, and knew that it was useless to try to bluff further.

'So you're a Saint!' said Hayn softly.

'Yes, I am!' Tremayne let out recklessly. 'And if you scabs don't want me to plug you full of holes–'

He had been concentrating on Hayn, the leader, and so he had not noticed the other men edging nearer. A hand snatched at his gun, and wrenched… As Dicky Tremayne swung his fist to the man's jaw, Hayn dodged behind him and struck at the back of his head with a little rubber truncheon…

12

Jerry Stannard never understood how he managed to contain himself until one o'clock. Much less did he understand how he waited the further half hour which he gave Dicky Tremayne for grace. Perhaps no other man in the world but Simon Templar could have inspired such a blind loyalty. The Saint was working some secret stratagem of his own, Stannard argued, and he had to meet Tremayne for reasons appertaining to the Saint's tactics. In any case, if Gwen had left when she telephoned, he could not have reached the flat before she had gone – and then he might only have blundered into the police trap that she had tried to save him from.

But it all connected up now – Gwen's Laserre story, and what Stannard himself knew of Hayn, and more that he suspected – and the visions that it took only a little imagination to conjure up were dreadful.

When half past one came, and there was still no sign of Tremayne, the suspense became intolerable. Stannard went to the telephone, and fruitlessly searched London over the wires for Simon Templar. He could learn nothing from any of the clubs or hotels or restaurants which he might have frequented, nor was he any more successful with his flat. As for Dicky Tremayne, Stannard did not even know him by sight – he had simply been told to leave his card with a page, and Tremayne would ask for him.

It was after two o'clock by that time, and Tremayne had not arrived. He tried to ring up Gwen Chandler's flat, but after an interminable period of ringing, the exchange reported 'No reply.'

Jerry Stannard took a grip on himself. Perhaps that emergency was the making of him, the final consolidation of the process that had been started by the Saint, for Stannard had never been a fighting man. He had spoken the truth when he told Templar that his weakness was lack of 'guts'. But now he'd got to act. He didn't know nearly everything about Hayn, but he knew enough not to want to leave Gwen Chandler with that versatile gentleman for a moment longer than was absolutely necessary. But if anything was going to be done, Stannard had got to do it himself.

With a savage resolution, he telephoned to a garage where he was known. While he waited, he scribbled a note for Tremayne in which he described the whole series of events and stated his intentions. It was time wasted, but he was not to know that.

When the car arrived, he dismissed the mechanic who had brought it round, and drove to Hurley.

He knew how to handle cars – it was one of his few really useful accomplishments. And he sent the Buick blazing west with his foot flat down on the accelerator for practically every yard of the way.

Even so, it was nearly five o'clock when he arrived there, and then he realized a difficulty. There were a lot of houses at

Hurley, and he had no idea where Hayn's house might be. Nor had the post office, nor the nearest police.

Stannard, in the circumstances, dared not press his inquiries too closely. The only hope left to him was that he might be able to glean some information from a villager, for he was forced to conclude that Hayn tenanted his country seat under another name. With this forlorn hope in view, he made his way to the Bell, and it was there that he met a surprising piece of good fortune.

As he pulled up outside, a man came out, and the man hailed him.

'Thank the Lord you're here,' said Roger Conway without preface. 'Come inside and have a drink.'

'Who are you?' asked a mystified Jerry Stannard.

'You don't know me, but I know you,' answered the man. 'I'm one of the Saint's haloes.'

He listened with a grave face to Stannard's story.

'There's been a hitch somewhere,' he said, when Jerry had finished. 'The Saint kept you in the dark because he was afraid your natural indignation might run away with you. Hayn had designs on your girl friend – you might have guessed that. The Saint pinched a letter of Hayn's to Chastel –

Hayn's man abroad – in which, among other things, Edgar described his plot for getting hold of Gwen. I suppose he wanted to be congratulated on his ingenuity. The rough idea was to plant some cocaine on Gwen in a present of powder and things from Laserre, fake a police raid, and pretend to square the police for her. Then, if she believed the police were after you and her – Hayn was banking on making her afraid that you were also involved – he thought it would be easy to get her away with him.'

'And the Saint wasn't doing anything to stop that?' demanded Jerry, white-lipped.

'Half a minute! The Saint couldn't attend to it himself, having other things to deal with, but he put Tremayne, the man you were supposed to have met at the Splendide, on the job. Tremayne was to get hold of Gwen before Hayn arrived, and tell her the story – we were assuming that you hadn't told her anything – and then bring her along to the Splendide and join up with you. The two of you were then to take Gwen down by car to the Saint's bungalow at Maidenhead and stay down there till the trouble had blown over.'

The boy was gnawing his fingernails. He had had more time to think over the situation on the drive down, and Conway's story had only confirmed his own deductions. The vista of consequences that it opened up was appalling.

'What's the Saint been doing all this time?'

'That's another longish story,' Conway answered. 'He'd got Hayn's cheque for five figures, and that made the risk bigger. There was only one way to settle it.'

Roger Conway briefly described the Saint's employing of the four spoof Cherubs. 'After that was found out, Simon reckoned Hayn would think the gang business was all bluff, and he'd calculate there was only the Saint against himself. Therefore he wouldn't be afraid to try on his scheme about Gwen, even though he knew the Saint knew it, because the Saint was going to be out of the way. Anyhow, Hayn's choice was between getting rid of the Saint and going to prison, and we could guess which he'd try first. The Saint had figured out that Hayn wouldn't simply try a quick assassination, because it wouldn't help him to be wanted for murder. There had got to be a murder, of course, but it would have to be well planned. So the Saint guessed he'd be kidnapped first and taken away to some quiet spot to be done in, and he decided to play stalking-horse. He did that because if Hayn were arrested, his cheques would be stopped automatically, so Hayn had got to be kept busy till tomorrow morning. I was watching outside the Saint's flat in a fast car last night, as I'd been detailed to do, in case of accidents. The Saint was going to make a fight of it. But they got him somehow – I saw him taken out to a car they had waiting – and I followed down here. Tremayne was to be waiting at the Splendide for a 'phone call from me at two o'clock. I've been trying to get him ever since, and you as well, touring London over the toll line, and it's cost a small fortune. And I didn't dare to go back to London, because of leaving the Saint here. That's why I'm damned glad you've turned up.'

'But why haven't you told the police?'

'Simon'd never forgive me. He's out to make the Saint the terror of the Underworld, and he won't do that by simply giving information to Scotland Yard. The idea of the gang is to punish people suitably before handing them over to the law, and our success over Hayn depends on sending five figures of his money to charity. I know it's a terrible risk. The Saint may have been killed already. But he knew what he was doing. We were ordered not to interfere and the Saint's the head man in this show.'

Stannard sprung up.

'But Hayn's got Gwen!' he half sobbed. 'Roger, we can't hang about, not for anything, while Gwen's–'

'We aren't hanging about any longer,' said Roger quietly.

His hand fell with a firm grip on Jerry Stannard's arm, and the youngster steadied up. Conway led him to the window of the smokeroom, and pointed.

'You can just see the roof of the house, over there,' he said. 'Since last night, Hayn's gone back to London, and his car came by again about two hours ago. I couldn't see who was in it, but it must have been Gwen. Now–'

He broke off suddenly. In the silence, the drone of a powerful car could be heard approaching. Then the car itself whirled by at speed, but it did not pass too quickly for Roger Conway to glimpse the men who rode in it.

'Hayn and Braddon in the back with Dicky Tremayne between them!' he said tensely.

He was in time to catch Stannard by the arm as the boy broke away wildly.

'What the blazes are you stampeding for?' he snapped. 'Do you want to go charging madly in and let Hayn rope you in, too?'

'We can't wait!' Stannard panted, struggling.

Conway thrust him roughly into a chair and stood over him. The boy was as helpless as a child in Conway's hands.

'You keep your head and listen to me!' Roger commanded sharply. 'We'll have another drink and tackle this sensibly. And

I'm going to see that you wolf a couple of sandwiches before you do anything. You've been in a panic for hours, with no lunch, and you look about all in. I want you to be useful.'

'If we 'phone the police–'

'Nothing doing!'

Roger Conway's contradiction ripped out almost automatically, for he was not the Saint's right-hand man for nothing. He had learnt the secret of the perfect lieutenant, which is the secret of, in any emergency, divining at once what your superior officer would want you to do. It was no use simply skinning out any old how – the emergency had got to be dealt with in a way that would dovetail in with the Saint's general plan of campaign.

'The police are our last resort,' he said. 'We'll see if the two of us can't fix this alone. Leave this to me.'

He ordered a brace of stiff whiskies and a pile of sandwiches, and while these were being brought he wrote a letter which he sealed. Then he went in search of the proprietor, whom he knew of old, and gave him the letter.

'If I'm not here to claim that in two hours,' he said, 'I want you to open it and telephone what's inside to Scotland Yard. Will you do that for me, as a great favour, and ask no questions?'

The landlord agreed, somewhat perplexedly.

'Is it a joke?' he asked good humouredly.

'It may grow into one,' Roger Conway replied. 'But I give you my word of honour that if I'm not back at eight o'clock, and that message isn't opened and 'phoned punctually, the consequences may include some of the most un-funny things that ever happened!'

13

The Saint hadn't slept. As soon as they had arrived at the house at Hurley (he knew it was Hurley, for he had travelled that road many times over the course of several summers) he had been pushed into a bare-furnished bedroom and left to his own devices. These were not numerous, for the ropes had not been taken off his wrists.

A short tour of inspection of the room had shown that, in the circumstances, it formed an effective prison. The window, besides being shuttered, was closely barred; the door was of three-inch oak, and the key had been taken away after it had been locked. For weapons with which to attack either window or door there was the choice of a light table, a wooden chair, or a bedpost. The Saint might have employed any of these, after cutting himself free – for they had quite overlooked, in the search to which he had been subjected, the little knife strapped to his calf under his sock – but he judged that the time was not yet ripe for any such drastic action. Besides, he was tired; he saw strenuous times ahead of him, and he believed in husbanding his energies. Therefore, he had settled down on the bed for a good night's rest, making himself as comfortable as a man can when his hands are tied behind his back, and it had not been long before he had fallen into an untroubled sleep. It had struck him, drowsily, as being the most natural thing to do.

Glints of sunlight were stabbing through the interstices of the shutters when he was awakened by the sound of his door opening. He rolled over, opening one eye, and saw two men enter. One carried a tray of food, and the other carried a club. This concession to the respect in which the gang held him, even when bound and helpless, afforded the Saint infinite amusement.

'This is sweet of you,' he said; and indeed he thought it was, for he had not expected such a consideration, and he was feeling hungry. 'But, my angels of mercy,' he said, 'I can't eat like this.'

They sat him down in a chair and tied his

ankles to the legs of it, and then the cords were taken off his wrists and he was able to stretch his cramped arms. They watched him eat, standing by the door, and the cheerful comments with which he sought to enliven the meal went unanswered. But a request for the time evoked the surly information that it was past one o'clock.

When he had finished, one of the men fastened his hands again, while the other stood by with his bludgeon at the ready. Then they untied his ankles and left him, taking the tray with them.

The searchers had also left him his cigarette-case and matches, and with some agility and a system of extraordinary contortions the Saint managed to get a cigarette into his mouth and light it. This feat of double-jointed juggling kept him entertained for about twenty minutes; but as the afternoon wore on he developed, in practice, a positively brilliant dexterity. He had nothing else to do.

His chief feeling was one of boredom, and he soon ceased to find any enjoyment in wondering how Dick Tremayne had fared in Bayswater. By five o'clock he was yawning almost continuously, having thought out seventeen original and foolproof methods of swindling swindlers without coming within reach of the law, and this and similar exercises of ingenuity were giving him no more kick at all.

He would have been a lot more comfortable if his hands had not been bound, but he decided not to release himself until there was good cause for it. The Saint knew the tactical advantage of keeping a card up his sleeve.

The room, without any noticeable means of ventilation, was growing hotter and stuffier, and the cigarettes he was smoking were not improving matters. Regretfully, the Saint resigned himself to giving up that pleasure, and composed himself on the bed again. Some time before, he had heard a car humming up the short drive, and he was hazily looking forward to Hayn's return and the renewed interest that it would bring. But the heaviness of the atmosphere did not conduce to mental alertness. The Saint found himself dozing…

For the second time, it was the sound of his door opening that roused him, and he blinked his eyes open with a sigh.

It was Edgar Hayn who came in. Physically he was in much worse case than the Saint, for he had had no sleep at all since the Friday night, and his mind had been much less carefree. His tiredness showed in the pallor of his face and the bruise-like puffiness of his eyes, but he had the air of one who feels himself the master of a situation.

'Evening,' murmured Simon politely.

Hayn came over to the beside, his lips drawn back in an unlovely smile.

'Still feeling bumptious, Templar?' he asked.

'Ain't misbehavin',' answered the Saint winningly, 'I'm savin' my love for you.'

The man who had held the bludgeon at lunch stood in the doorway. Hayn stood aside and beckoned him in.

'There are some friends of yours downstairs,' said Hayn. 'I should like to have you all together.'

'I should be charmed to oblige you – as the actress said to the bishop,' replied the Saint.

And he wondered whom Hayn could be referring to, but he showed nothing of the chill of uneasiness that had leaped at him for an instant like an Arctic wind.

He was not left long in doubt.

The bludgeon merchant jerked him to his feet and marched him down the corridor and down the stairs, Hayn bringing up the rear. The door of a room opening off the hall stood ajar, and from within came a murmur of voices which faded into stillness as their footsteps were heard approaching. Then the door was kicked wide, and the Saint was thrust into the room.

Gwen Chandler was there – he saw her at once. There were also three men whom he knew, and one of them was a dishevelled

Dicky Tremayne.

Hayn closed the door and came into the centre of the room.

'Now, what about it, Templar?' he said.

'What, indeed?' echoed the Saint.

His lazy eyes shifted over the assembled company.

'Greeting, Herr Braddon,' he murmured. 'Hullo, Snake … Great heavens, Snake! – what's the matter with your face?'

'What's the matter with my face?' Ganning snarled.

'Everything, honeybunch,' drawled the Saint. 'I was forgetting. You were born like that.'

Ganning came close, his eyes puckered with fury.

'I owe you something,' he grunted, and let fly with both fists.

The Saint slipped the blows, and landed a shattering kick to the Snake's shins. Then Braddon interposed a foot between the Saint's legs, and as Simon went down Ganning loosed off with both feet…

'That'll do for the present,' Hayn cut in at last.

He took Templar by the collar and yanked him into a sitting position on a chair.

'You filthy blots!' Tremayne was raving, with the veins standing out purply on his forehead. 'You warts – you flaming, verminous…'

It was Braddon who silenced him, with a couple of vicious, backhand blows across the mouth. And Dick Tremayne, bound hand and foot, wrestled impotently with ropes that he could not shift.

'We'll hear the Haynski speech,' Simon interrupted. 'Shut up, Dicky! We don't mind, but it isn't nice for Gwen to have to watch!'

He looked across at the girl, fighting sobbingly in Hayn's hold.

'It's all right, Gwen, old thing,' he said. 'Keep smiling, for Jerry's sake. We don't worry about anything that these dregs can do. Don't let them see they can hurt you!'

Hayn passed the girl over to Braddon and Ganning, and went over to the Saint's chair.

'I'm going to ask you one or two questions, Templar,' he said. 'If you don't want to let the Snake have another go at you, you'll answer them truthfully.'

'Pleasure,' said the Saint briefly. 'George Washington was the idol of my childhood.'

Everything he had planned had suffered a sudden reversal. Gwen Chandler had been caught, and so had Dicky. Their only hope was in Roger Conway – and how long would it be before he discovered the disaster and got busy?... The Saint made up his mind.

'How many of you are there?'

'Seventy-six,' said the Saint. 'Two from five – just like when you were at Borstal.'

There was no one behind him. He had got his legs well back under the chair. His arms were also reaching back, and he was edging his little knife out of its sheath.

'You can save the rest of your questions,' he said. 'I'll tell you something. You'll never get away with this. You think you're going to find out all about my organization, the plans I've made, whether I've arranged for a squeal to the police. Then you'll counter-move accordingly. Hold the line while I laugh!'

'I don't think so,' said Hayn.

'Then you don't think as much as a weevil, with sleeping sickness,' said the Saint equably. 'You must think I was born yesterday! Listen, sweetheart! Last night I posted a little story to Inspector Teal, which he'll get Monday morning. That letter's in the post now – and nothing will stop it – and the letter to friend Henri I enclosed with it will make sure the dicks pay a lot of attention to the rest of the things I had to say. You haven't an earthly, Edgarvitch!'

Hayn stepped back as if he had received a blow, and his face was horribly ashen. The Saint had never imagined that he would cause such a sensation.

'I told you he'd squeak!' Braddon was raging. 'You fool – I told you!'

'I told him, too,' said the Saint. 'Oh, Edgar – why didn't you believe your Uncle Simon?'

Hayn came erect, his eyes blazing. He swung round on Braddon.

'Be quiet, you puppy!' he commanded harshly. 'We've all come to this – that's why we've got those aeroplanes. We leave tonight, and Teal can look for us tomorrow as long as he likes.'

He turned on the Saint.

'You'll come with us – you and your friend. You will not be strapped in. Somewhere in mid-Channel we shall loop the loop. You understand ... Templar, you've undone years of work, and I'm going to make you pay for it! I shall escape, and after a time, I shall be able to come back and start again. But you–'

'I shall be flitting through Paradise, with a halo round my hat,' murmured the Saint. 'What a pleasant thought!'

And as he spoke he felt his little knife biting into the cords on his wrists.

'We lose everything we've got,' Braddon babbled.

'Including your liberty,' said the Saint softly, and the knife was going through his ropes like a wire through cheese.

They all looked at him. Something in the way he had spoken those three words, something in the taut purposefulness of his body, some strange power of personality, held them spellbound. Bound and at their mercy, for all they knew, an unarmed man, he was yet able to dominate them. There was hatred and murder flaring in their eyes, and yet for a space he was able to hold them on a curb and compel them to listen.

'I will tell you why you have lost, Hayn,' said the Saint, speaking in the same, gentle, leisured tones that nevertheless quelled them as definitely as if he had backed them up with a gun. 'You made the mistake of kidding yourself that when I told you I was going to put you in prison, I was bluffing. You were sure that I'd never throw away such an opening for unlimited blackmail. Your miserable warped temperament couldn't conceive the idea of a man doing and risking all that I did and risked for nothing but an ideal. You judged me by your own crooked standards. That's where you crashed, because I'm not a crook. But I'm going to make crooks go in fear of me. You and your kind aren't scared of the police. You've got used to them – you call them by their first names and swap cigarettes with them when they arrest you – it's become a game to you, with prison as a forfeit for a mistake, and bull-baiting's just the same as tiddlywinks, in your lives. But I'm going to give you something new to fear – the Unknown. You'll rave about us in the dock, and all the world will hear. And when we have finished with you, you will go to prison, and you will be an example to make others afraid. But you will tell the police that you cannot describe us, because there are still three left whom you do not know; and if we two came to any harm through you, the other three would deal with you, and they would not deal gently. You understand? You will never dare to speak…'

'And do you think you will ever be able to speak, Templar?' asked Hayn in a quivering voice, and his right hand was leaping to his hip pocket.

And the Saint chuckled, a low triumphant murmur of a laugh.

'I'm sure of it!' he said, and stood up with the cords falling from his wrists.

The little throwing-knife flashed across the room like a chip of flying quicksilver, and Hayn, with his automatic half out of his pocket, felt a pain like the searing of a hot iron across his knuckles, and all the strength went out of his fingers.

Braddon was drawing at that moment, but the Saint was swift. He had Edgar Hayn in a grip of steel, and Hayn's body was between the Saint and Braddon.

'Get behind him, Snake!' Braddon shrilled; but as Ganning moved to obey, the Saint reached a corner.

'Aim at the girl, you fool!' Hayn gasped, with the Saint's hand tightening on his throat.

The Saint held Hayn with one hand only,

but the strength of that hold was incredible. With the other hand, he was fumbling with his cigarette-case.

Braddon had turned his gun into Gwen Chandler's face, while Ganning pinioned her arms. And the Saint had a cigarette in his mouth and was striking a match with one hand.

'Now do you surrender?' Braddon menaced.

'Like hell I do!' cried the Saint.

His match touched the end of his cigarette, and in the same movement he threw the cigarette far from him. It made an explosive hiss like a launched rocket, and in a second everything was blotted out in a swirl of impenetrable fog.

Templar pushed Hayn away into the opacity. He knew to a fraction of a square inch where his knife had fallen after it had severed the tendons of Hayn's hand, and he dived for it. He bumped against Tremayne's chair, and cut him free in four quick slashes.

Came, from the direction of the window, the sound of smashing glass. A shadow showed momentarily through the mist.

'Gwen!'

It was Jerry Stannard's agonized voice. The girl answered him. They sought each other in the obscurity.

A sudden draught parted the wreathing clouds of the Saint's rapid-action smokescreen. Stannard, with the girl in his arms, saw that the door was open. The Saint's unmistakable silhouette loomed in the oblong of light.

'Very, very efficient, my Roger,' said the Saint.

'You can always leave these little things to me,' said Mr Conway modestly, leaning against the front door, with Edgar Hayn, Braddon, and Snake Ganning herded into a corner of the hall at the unfriendly end of his automatic.

14

They took the three men into a room where there was no smoke.

'It was my fiancée,' pleaded Jerry Stannard.

'That's so,' said the Saint tolerantly. 'Dicky, you'll have to be content with Braddon. After all, he sloshed you when your hands were tied. But nobody's going to come between the Snake and this child!'

It lasted half an hour all told, and then they gathered up the three components of the mess and trussed them very securely into chairs.

'There were two other men,' said the Saint

hopefully, wrapping his handkerchief round a skinned set of knuckles.

'I stuck them up, and Jerry dotted them with a spanner,' said Conway. 'We locked them in a room upstairs.'

The Saint sighed.

'I suppose we'll have to leave them,' he said. 'Personally, I feel I've been done. These guys are rotten poor fighters when it comes to a showdown.'

Then Conway remembered the message he had left in the landlord's hands at the Bell, and they piled hurriedly into the car in which Conway and Stannard had driven up. They retrieved the message, tidied themselves, and dined.

'I think we can call it a day,' said the Saint comfortably, when the coffee was on the table. 'The cheque will be cashed on Monday morning, and the proceeds will be registered to the London Hospital, as arranged – less our ten per cent commission, which I don't mind saying I think we've earned. I think I shall enclose one of my celebrated self-portraits – a case like this ought to finish in a worthily dramatic manner, and that opportunity's too good to miss.'

He stretched himself luxuriously, and lighted a fresh cigarette which did not explode.

'Before I go to bed tonight,' he said, 'I'll

drop a line to old Teal and tell him where to look for our friends. I'm afraid they'll have a hungry and uncomfortable night, but I can't help that. And now, my infants, I suggest that we adjourn to London.'

They exchanged drinks and felicitations with the lord and master of the Bell, and it should stand to the eternal credit of that amiable gentleman that not by the twitch of an eyebrow did he signify any surprise at the somewhat battered appearance of two of the party. Then they went out to their cars.

'Who's coming back with me?' asked Tremayne.

'I'm going back without you, laddie,' said Jerry Stannard. 'Gwen's coming with me!'

They cheered the Buick out of sight; and then the Saint climbed into the back of the Furillac and settled himself at his ease.

'Mr Conway will drive,' he said. 'Deprived of my charming conversation, you will ponder over the fact that our friend is undoubtedly for it. You may also rehearse the song which I've just composed for us to sing at his funeral – I mean wedding. It's about a wicked young lover named Jerry, who had methods decidedly merry. When the party got rough, was he smart with his stuff? Oh, very! Oh, very!... Oh, very!... Take me to the Savoy, Roger. I have a date... Night-night, dear old bacteria!'

THE POLICEMAN WITH WINGS

1

By this time all the world has heard of the Saint. It has been estimated (by those industrious gentlemen who estimate these things) that if all the columns that the newspapers have devoted to the Saint were placed end to end, they would reach from the south-east corner of the Woolwich Building, New York, to a point seventeen inches west of the commissionaire outside the Berkeley Street entrance of the Mayfair Hotel, London – which, as was remarked at the time, only goes to prove that the bridging of the gulf between rich and poor can be materially helped by the vigorous efforts of a democratic Press.

It was not to be hoped, however, that the Saint could remain for ever under the shroud of anonymity in which he had made his *début.* Policemen, in spite of the libels of the mystery novelist, possess a certain amount of intelligence, and a large amount of plodding patience; and the Saint's campaign was a definite challenge. The actual episode in which Chief Inspector Teal began to suspect that Simon Templar might know more about the Saint than he told the world, is, as it happens, of no absorbing interest for the purposes of this chronicle; but it may be recorded that the Saint returned one day from one of his frequent trips aboard, and found reason to believe that unauthorized persons had entered his apartment while he was away.

The detectives who had discovered the flat in Brook Street had searched it thoroughly, as was their duty. They had found nothing, but the traces of their passage were everywhere visible.

'They might have tidied the place up after them,' remarked the Saint mildly, standing at gaze before the disorder.

Orace, the Saint's devoted servant, ran his thumb through the accumulated dust on the mantelpiece, and made strangled snuffling noises of disgust.

He was still struggling ferociously with the mess when they went to bed that night. The Saint, wandering towards his bath the next morning, caught through an open door a glimpse of a sitting-room become magically clean and shipshape, and was moved to investigate further. Eventually he came upon Orace frying eggs in the kitchen.

'I see you've been spring cleaning,' he said.

'Yus,' said Orace, savagely. 'Brekfuss narf a minnit.'

'Good scout,' drawled the Saint, and drifted on.

The Saint refused to behave like a hunted man. He went out and about his lawful occasions, and in consequence it was five days before the police noticed his return. There are times when barefaced effrontery is the most impenetrable disguise.

But it could not last. There are constables, and they patrol beats, and not the least of their duties is to embody in their reports an account of anything unusual they may notice. There was a night when the Saint, looking out from behind his curtains, saw two men in bowler hats staring up long and earnestly at the lighted windows, which should have been in deserted darkness; and then he knew that it would not be long before the Law reached out an inquiring hand towards him. But he said nothing at the time.

Roger Conway came in at lunchtime the following afternoon to find the Saint in his dressing-gown. Simon Templar was smoking a thin cigar, with his feet on the sill of the open window, and Roger knew at once, from the extraordinary saintliness of his expression, that something had happened.

'Teal's been here,' said Roger, after a hawkeyed glance round the room.

'Claud Eustace himself,' murmured the Saint, admiringly. 'How did you guess?'

'There's a discarded piece of chewing gum in that ashtray, and that scrap of pink paper in the fireplace must once have enclosed the piece he went out with. Giving my well-known impersonation of Sherlock Holmes–'

Simon nodded.

'You look dangerously like developing an intelligence, my Roger. Yes, Teal has called. I knew he was coming, because he told me so himself.'

'Liar!' said Mr Conway, pleasantly.

'He told me over the telephone,' said the Saint calmly. 'I rang up and asked him, and he told me.'

'He didn't!'

'He did. I said I was Barney Malone, of the *Clarion,* and I told him we'd heard a rumour that he was on the Saint's trail, and asked him if he could say anything about it. "Not yet," says Teal, who's pally with Barney, "but I'm going to see about it this morning. Come down after lunch and get the story." "Right," I said. And there we were.'

'You have a nerve, Simon.'

'Not so bad, sonny boy. I then proceeded to ring up my solicitors, and Uncle Elias whiffled round and held my hand while we waited for the Law, which arrived about eleven-thirty. There was some argument, and then Teal went home. I hope he doesn't wait too long for Barney,' added the Saint piously.

Roger Conway sat down and searched for cigarettes.

'He went like a lamb?'

'Like a lamb. In all our exploits, you see, his case depends on the evidence of the injured parties – and none of the said IP's seem anxious to prosecute. I simply told Teal to get on with it and try to prove something – the innocent-citizen-falsely-accused stunt. Of course, he bluffed for all he was worth, but Uncle Elias and I made him see that his chance wasn't too hopeful.'

'So you parted like brothers?'

The Saint shrugged.

'I should call it an armed truce. He asked me if I was going on, and I said I hadn't anything to go on with. I said we were so good that the light of virtue glowing within us made us faintly luminous in the dark.'

'And that was that?'

'He sailed out on a note of warning, very grim and stern and law-abiding. For, of course, he didn't believe me. And yet I won't swear that he winked. Uncle Elias didn't see it, anyway. But I'm afraid Uncle Elias was rather shocked by the whole palaver. However, if you reach out and ring the bell twice, Orace will understand...'

They solemnly toasted each other over the

tankards which came in answer to the summons; and then Roger Conway spoke.

'There's a problem which might interest us–'

'Professionally?'

'It's quite possible. It starts with a girl I met in Torquay last summer.'

Simon sighed.

'You insist on meeting girls in these outlandish places,' he complained. 'Now, if you'd only met her in Gotham, for instance, I should have had a song all ready for you. When you came in, I was just perfecting a little song about a wild woman of Gotham, who made love to young men and then shot 'em – till she started to shoot at a hard-hearted brute, who just grabbed her and walloped her for all he was worth. But don't let that cramp your style. You were saying?'

'This girl I met in Torquay–'

'Did she think that love ought to be free?'

'My dear Mr Templar–'

'I was recalling,' said the Saint impenitently, 'another girl you met in Torquay who thought that love ought to be free. She clung to this view till she chanced to meet you– Oh, send back my bonny to me! But you were telling me about someone else.'

'She has an uncle–'

'Impossible!'

'She has an uncle, and she lives with the uncle, and the uncle has a house at Newton.'

'They have an abbot there, haven't they?'

'Newton Abbot is the place. The uncle built this house nearly seven years ago. He intended to settle down and spend the rest of his life there – and now a man insists on buying the place.'

'Insists?'

'It comes to something like that. This man–'

'Let's have it clear, sonny boy. What's uncle's name?'

'Sebastian Aldo.'

'Then he must be rich.'

'He's happy.'

'And Whiskers – the bloke who wants to buy the house?'

'We don't know his name. He sent his secretary, an oily excrescence called Gilbert Neave.'

The Saint settled deeper in his armchair.

'And the story?' he prompted.

'There's very little of it – or there was until today. Uncle refused to sell. Neave bid more and more – he went up to twenty thousand pounds, I believe – and he was so insistent that finally Uncle lost his temper and kicked him out.'

'And?'

'Three days later, Uncle was pottering about the garden when his hat flew off. When he picked it up there was a bullet hole through it. A week later he was out in his car and the steering came unstuck. He'd have been killed if he'd been driving fast. A week after that everybody in the house was mysteriously taken ill, and the analysts found arsenic in the milk. A couple of days later, Neave 'phoned up and asked if Uncle had changed his mind about selling.'

'Uncle Sebastian still gave him the razz?'

'Betty says he fused the telephone wires for miles around.'

'Who's Betty?'

'His niece – the girl I met in Torquay.'

'I see. A lovely young lady named Betty, made such noises when eating spaghetti, it played absolute hell with the *maître d'hotel,* and made sensitive waiters quite – er – self-conscious. And when did they bury Uncle?'

Roger Conway was smoothing out the evening paper which he had bought at twelve-thirty.

'Betty told me all this in her letters while we were down at Maidenhead,' he said. 'Now you can read the sequel.'

Roger indicated the column, but that was hardly necessary. There was one heading that caught the eye – that could not have helped being the first thing to catch the eye of a man like the Saint. For by that simple title an inspired sub-editor had made a sensation out of a simple mystery.

'The Policeman With Wings,' said the heading; and the point of the story was that a policeman had called on a certain Mr Sebastian Aldo three days before, a perfectly ordinary and wingless policeman, according to the testimony of the housekeeper who admitted him, but a most unusual policeman according to the testimony of subsequent events. For, after a short interview, Mr Aldo had left his house with the policeman in his car, saying that he would be back to lunch; but neither the policeman nor Mr Aldo had been heard of since, and the police of all the surrounding districts, appealed to, declared that none of their policemen were missing, and certainly none had been sent to see Mr Aldo.

'I observe,' said the Saint thoughtfully, 'that Miss Aldo was in Ostend at the time, and has just returned upon hearing of her uncle's disappearance. So the paper says.'

'She told me she was going to Ostend for a week in August to stay with friends. Have you any ideas?'

'Millions,' said the Saint.

The door opened, and a head came in.

'Lunch narf a minnit,' said the head, and went out again.

The Saint rose.

'Millions of ideas, Roger, old dear,' he murmured. 'But none of them, at the moment, tells me why anyone should be so absorbingly interested in one particular house at Newton Abbot. On the other hand, if you like to sing softly to me while I dress, I may produce something brilliant over the cocktail you will be shaking up while you sing.'

He vanished, and was back again in an amazingly short space of time to collect the Martini which Conway was decanting from the shaker as Orace came in with the soup. The Saint's speed of dressing was an unending source of envious admiration to his friends.

'We are interested,' said the Saint, holding his glass up to the light, and inspecting it with an appreciative eye, 'and we have produced a brilliant idea.'

'What's that?'

'After lunch, we will go out into the wide world and buy a nice-looking car, and in the car we will travel down to Newton Abbot this very afternoon.'

'Arriving in time to have dinner with Betty.'

'If you insist.'

'Any objections?'

'Only that, knowing you, I feel that for her sake–'

'She's a nice girl,' said Roger, reminiscently.

'She hasn't known you long,' said the Saint.

'Cheer-ho!' said Conway.

'Honk, honk!' said the Saint.

They drank.

'Further to mine of even date,' said the Saint, 'when we've bought this car, we will continue on our way through the wide world, and seek a place where we can buy you a policeman's uniform. You can grow the wings yourself.'

Roger stared.

'Uniform!' he repeated feebly. 'Wings?'

'As a Policeman with Wings,' said the Saint comfortably, 'I think you'd be a distant hit. That's part of my brilliant idea.'

And the Saint grinned, hands on hips, tall and fresh and immaculate in grey. His dark hair was at its sleekest perfection, his clear blue eyes danced, his brown face was alight with an absurdly boyish and hell-for-leather enthusiasm.

The Saint in those days had moods in which he was unwontedly sober. He was then nearly twenty-eight, and in those twenty-eight years of his life he had seen more than most men would see in eighty years, and done more than they would have done in a hundred and eighty. And yet he had not fulfilled himself. He was then only upon the threshold of his destiny; but it seemed sometimes that he glimpsed wider visions through the opening door ahead. But this was not so much a dulling of his impetuous energy as the acquiring of a more solid foundation for it. He remained the

Saint – the flippant dandy with the heart of a crusader, a fighter who laughed as he fought, the reckless, smiling swashbuckler, the inspired and beloved leader of men, the man born with the sound of trumpets in his ears. And the others followed him.

He was impatient through the lunch, but he made the meal. And after it he lighted a cigarette and set it canting up between smiling lips, and leapt to his feet as if he could contain himself no longer.

'Let's go!' cried the Saint.

He clapped Roger Conway on the shoulder, and so they went out arm in arm. Roger Conway would have followed in the same spirit if the Saint had announced that their objective was the Senate House, Timbuctoo.

And so they went.

2

If Simon Templar had been a failure, he would have been spoken of pityingly as a man born out of his time. The truth was that in all the fields of modern endeavour – except the crazy driving of high-powered cars, the suicidal stunting of aeroplanes, and the slick handling of boxing gloves – the

Saint was cheerfully useless. Golf bored him. He played tennis with vigour and shameless inefficiency, erratically scrambling through weeks of rabbitry to occasional flashes of a positively Tildenesque *maestria*. He was always ready to make his duck or bowl his wides in any cricket game that happened to be going; and his prowess at baseball, on an expedition which he once made to America, brought tears to the eyes of all beholders.

But put a fencing foil in Simon Templar's hand; throw him into dangerous swimming water; invite him to slither up a tree or the side of a house; set him on the wildest horse that ever bucked; ask him to throw a knife into a visiting card or shoot the three leaves out of an ace of clubs at twenty paces; suggest that he couldn't put an arrow through a greengage held between your finger and thumb at the same range – and then you'd see something to tell your grandchildren.

Of course he was born out of his time. He ought to have lived in any age but the present – any age in which his uncanny flair for all such mediaeval accomplishments would have brought him to the front of his fellows.

And yet you didn't notice the anachronism, because he wasn't a failure. He made for himself a world fit for himself to live in.

It is truly said that adventures are to the adventurous. Simon had about him that indefinable atmosphere of romance and adventurousness which is given to some favoured men in every age, and it attracted adventure as inevitably as a magnet attracts iron filings.

But it will be left for future generations to decide how much of the adventure which he found was made by himself. For adventure can only be born of the conflict of two adventurous men; the greatest adventurer would be baffled if he came into conflict with a dullard, and a dullard would find no adventure in meeting the greatest adventurer that ever stepped. The Saint found the seeds of adventure were everywhere around him. It was the Saint himself who saw the budding of the seed before anyone else would have noticed it, and who brought the thing to a full flowering glory with the loving care of a fanatic.

With a typical genius the Saint had already touched the story of the Policeman with Wings.

'A mug,' said the Saint kindly, as he pushed the Desurio towards Devonshire with the speedometer needle off the map – 'a mug, such as yourself, for instance, my beautiful,' said the Saint kindly, 'wouldn't have thought of anything like that.'

'He wouldn't,' agreed Roger fervently, as

the Saint shot the Desurio between two cars with the width of a matchbox to spare on either side.

'A mug,' said the Saint kindly, 'would have thought that it was quite sufficient either (*a*) to remove Betty to the comparative safety of his maiden aunt's home at Stratford–'

'Upon the Avon.'

'Upon the Avon – or (*b*) to entrench ourselves in Uncle's house at Newton and prepare to hold the place against the enemy.'

'A mug such as myself would have thought that,' confessed Roger, humbly.

The Saint paused for a moment to slide contemptuously past a Packard that was crawling along at sixty.

'But the mug's scheme,' said the Saint, 'wouldn't get us any forrader. I grant you that if we watched vigilantly and shot straight we might very well frustrate the invading efforts of the enemy for as long as we stayed in residence – which, if Betty is all you say she is, might keep us busy for weeks. But we still shouldn't know who is the power behind Mr Neave – if it isn't Mr Neave himself.'

'Whereas you suggest–'

'That we carry the war into the enemy's camp. Consider the position of the power behind Mr Neave, whom we'll call Whiskers for short. Consider the position of Whiskers.

There he's been and gone and thought out the charming scheme of abducting people by means of a fake policeman – a notable idea. No one ever suspects a policeman. I'll bet that the fake policeman simply said they'd arrested a man whom they suspected of having something to do with the doping of the milk, and would Mr Aldo come over to the station and see if the accused looked like Neave. And Uncle was removed without any of the fuss and bother you have when you kidnap people by force.'

'You suggest that we run a policeman of our own?'

'Obviously. Think of the publicity. A few days after the abduction of Uncle, the niece also disappears with a mysterious policeman. I'm afraid that'll make Betty out to be rather a dim bulb, but we can't help that. The fact remains that Whiskers, in his secret lair, will read of the leaf that's been taken out of his book, will wonder who's got on to his game, and will promptly arm himself to the teeth and set out to find and strafe us.'

'And we help him by leaving a trail of clues leading straight into a trap.'

The Saint sighed.

'You're getting on – as the actress said to the bishop,' he murmured. 'This brain of yours is becoming absolutely phenomenal. Now go ahead and invent the details of this trap we're going to lead Whiskers into, because I've thought enough for one day, and I'm tired.'

And the Saint languidly settled down to concentrate on the business of annihilating space; what time Roger Conway, after a few prayers, closed his eyes and proceeded with the train of thought which the Saint had initiated.

They broke the journey at Shaftesbury for liquid nourishment, and when they came out Roger approached the car unhappily. But he was always tactful.

'Shall I take a turn at the wheel?' he ventured.

'I'm not tired,' said the Saint breezily.

'You said just now you were too tired to think.'

'I don't think when I'm driving,' said the Saint.

Roger would have liked to say that he could very well believe it, but he thought of the retort too late.

They covered the next eighty-five miles in a shade under two hours, and ran up the drive of the house to which Roger pointed the way as the clocks were striking seven-thirty.

'It occurs to me,' said Simon, as he applied the brakes, 'that we ought to have sent a wire to announce ourselves. Does the girl know you're in England at all?'

Roger shook his head.

'I hadn't told her we were back.'

The Saint climbed out and stretched himself, and they walked up to the house together.

A face watched them from a ground-floor window, and before they had reached the steps the window was flung up and a voice spoke sharply and suspiciously.

'I'm sorry – Miss Aldo is out.'

The Saint stopped.

'Where's she gone?'

'She was going to the police station.'

Simon groaned.

'Not with a policeman?' he protested.

'Yes, she went with a policeman,' said the woman. 'But this one was all right. Miss Aldo rang up the police station to make sure. They've found Mr Aldo.'

'Is he alive?' asked Roger.

'Yes, he's alive.'

The Saint was staring up intently into the sky, revolving slowly on his heels, as though following a trail in the clouds.

'Somehow,' he said gently, 'that's more than I can believe.'

Conway said: 'She telephoned to the station–'

'Yes,' said the Saint, 'she telephoned.'

By that time he had turned right round.

'Which,' he said, 'is exactly what any strategist would expect an intelligent girl to do, in the circumstances.'

'But–'

The Saint's arm went out suddenly like a signpost.

'The telephone wire goes over those fields. And the line's cut by that group of trees over there, unless I'm mistaken. A man sitting there with an instrument–'

'My – hat!' snapped Roger, with surprising restraint.

But Simon was already on his way back to the car.

'How long ago did she leave?' he flung at the now frightened housekeeper.

'Not five minutes ago, sir, when I was just starting to serve dinner. She took her car–'

'Which way?'

The woman pointed.

The Saint let in the clutch as Roger swung into the place beside him.

'What's the betting, Roger?' he crisped. 'If they'd gone towards Exeter we'd have seen them. Therefore–'

'They've gone towards Bovey Tracey – unless they turned off towards Ashburton–'

The Saint stopped the car again so abruptly that Roger was almost lifted out of his seat.

'You can drive this car. You know the district backwards, and I don't. Take any chance you like, and never mind the damage. I'll bet they've gone towards Ashburton and Two Bridges. You can disappear on Dartmoor as well as anywhere in England.'

Conway was behind the wheel by the time Simon had reached the other side of the car. He was moving off as the Saint leapt for the running-board.

And then the Saint was lighting two cigarettes with perfect calm – one for Roger and one for himself.

'Nice of Whiskers,' said the Saint, with that irresponsible optimism which nothing could ever damp. 'He's done all the work for us, provided the policeman and everything. When I think of the money I spent on that outfit of yours–'

'*If* we catch him,' said Conway, hunched intently over the steering wheel, 'you'll be able to talk.'

'We'll catch him,' said the Saint.

If Simon Templar was a reckless driver, Roger could match him when the occasion arose. And, more valuable even than mere speed, Roger knew every inch of the road blindfolded. He sent the Desurio literally leaping over the macadam, cornering on two wheels without losing control for an instant, and cleaving a path through the other traffic without regard for anyone's nerves; but nerves were things which the Saint only knew by name.

'It's extraordinary how things happen to us,' drawled the Saint coolly, as the Desurio grazed out of what looked to be the certainty of a head-on collision. 'Perpetual melodrama – that's what we live in. Why will nobody let me live the quiet life I yearn for?'

Roger said nothing. He knew exactly why *his* life wasn't quiet. It was because he happened to be a friend of Simon Templar's, and Simon Templar was a man who couldn't help spreading melodrama all around him like an infectious disease.

3

But the Saint did not feel at all guilty about the adventure. He could not have seen, if the suggestion had been made to him, how he could possibly be blamed for an incidental melodrama therein involved. The girl was Roger's, the story so far had been Roger's, and the romantic rewards, if any, would be Roger's – therefore the whole shout was Roger's.

Anyhow, the Saint was quite happy.

He leaned back with half-closed eyes, enjoying his cigarette. Simon Templar had the gift of being able to relax instantaneously, and thereby being able to benefit to the full from the intervals of relative quiet between moments of crisis; and then, when the next crisis cropped up, he could snap back to a quivering steel-spring alertness without the loss of a second. That, he said, was the way he stayed young – by refusing to take anything quite as seriously as he should have done.

As a matter of fact, he was elaborating a really brilliant idea for a new improper story about a giraffe when Roger Conway rapped out: 'There's a car in front…'

'No!' demurred the Saint, dreamily. 'Are we going to hit it?'

But his eyes were wide open, and he saw the car at once – on the crest of the next switchback.

'What kind of car?'

'A Morris – and Betty's is a Morris. A man was driving, with a girl beside him, but he was wearing an ordinary soft hat–'

'Dear old ass,' said the Saint; 'naturally he'd have an ordinary coat on under his tunic, and a soft hat in his pocket, ready to transform himself on the first quiet piece of road. Policemen driving cars in uniform are so darn conspicuous. He might easily be our man. Step on it, son!'

'Damn it!' said Roger, 'the accelerator won't go down any further – unless I push it through the floor.'

'Then push it through the floor,' instructed the Saint, hopefully, and lighted another cigarette.

The car in front was out of sight then, but Roger was slamming the Desurio at the immediate slope with all the force of its eighty developed horses. Half a minute later they topped the rise and went bucketing down the subsequent slant in a roar and whistle of wind. They hurtled through the dip and slashed into the opposite grade with a deep-throated snarl…

'In England,' remarked the Saint mildly, as a proposition of philosophical interest, 'there is a speed limit of twenty miles an hour.'

'Is that so?'

'Yes, that is so.'

'Then I hope it keeps fine for them.'

'Kind of you, drawled the Saint. 'Kind of you, Mr Conway!'

The Desurio ate up the hill, whipped round the bend at the top. There was a breath-taking second in which, by a miracle that no one will ever be able to explain, they escaped being sandwiched to death between two motor coaches moving in opposite directions; then they skimmed round the next corner into the temporary safety of a straight stretch of road, on which, for the moment, there was only the Desurio and the Morris in front – a quarter of a mile in front.

The Desurio devoured the intervening distance like a hungry beast.

'I can see the number!' came Roger's voice like the crack of a whip. 'It's Betty's car–'

'O.K., Big Boy!'

But it never occurred to the Saint to abandon his half-smoked cigarette.

Another corner, taken at death-defying pace, and then another straight stretch with the Morris only thirty yards in the lead.

The klaxon blared under Roger's hand, and the man in front signalled them to pass.

'Slacken up as you come level,' ordered the Saint. 'I'll board the galleon. Ready?'

'Yes.'

'Then we'll go!'

The Saint had the door on his side of the car open in a flash. He slipped out on to the running-board and rode there, closing the door carefully behind him as the nose of the Desurio slid past the rear wing of the Morris. And he was serenely finishing off his cigarette.

On these occasions, the Saint's *sang-froid* would have made an icebox look like an overheated gas oven.

Then the driver of the Morris saw him in the mirror, and crowded on speed. The Saint saw the man's hand leave the wheel and dive for his pocket.

'Drop behind as soon as I'm aboard,' rapped the Saint. '*Now!*'

The Desurio came abreast, slackened, hung there.

For a second the two cars raced side by side, with a bare foot of space between them, at fifty miles an hour; and the Saint stepped across to the running board of the Morris as one might step across a garden path.

The Desurio fell astern instantly, with a scream of overworked brakes. It was scarcely too soon, for the Morris swerved drunkenly across the road as the Saint grabbed the steering wheel with one hand and struck twice with the other…

The driver sagged sideways, and the gun slipped through his fingers and thumped to the floor.

Simon straightened the car with a steady hand. They were losing speed rapidly, for the driver's foot had come off the accelerator when he collapsed under the Saint's two crashing blows to the jaw – otherwise, they would never have been able to take the next corner.

Round the corner, twenty yards away, a lane opened off the main road. The Saint signalled the turn, and then, reaching over, used the handbrake and spun the wheel. They ran a little way down the lane, and stopped; and Roger brought the Desurio to rest behind them.

Through all that violent and hair-raising action, the girl had never stirred. Her eyes were closed as if in sleep. The Saint looked at her thoughtfully, and thoughtfully felt in the pockets of the unconscious driver.

Roger was shaking her and called her name helplessly. He looked up at the Saint.

'They've doped her–'

'Yes,' said the Saint, thoughtfully examining a little glass hypodermic syringe that was still half-filled with a pale, straw-coloured liquid, 'they've certainly doped her.'

In the same thoughtful way, he lifted the driver's right arm, turned back the sleeve, drove the needle into the exposed flesh, and pressed home the plunger. The empty syringe went into a convenient ditch.

'I think, Roger,' said the Saint, 'we will now move with some speed. Get your bag out of the car and unload the police effects. I want to see you in those glad rags.'

'But where are we going?'

'I'll think while you're changing. The one safe bet is that we've got to go at once. The housekeeper bird will be spreading the alarm already, and we've got to get away before the roads are stopped. Jump to it, my beautiful cherub!'

The Saint sometimes said that Roger was too good looking to be really intelligent; but there were times when Roger could get off the mark with commendable promptness, and this was one of them.

While Conway was rustling into his

uniform, the Saint picked the driver out of the Morris, carried him over, and dumped him into the back of the Desurio.

'We'll do some third degree on him later,' said the Saint. 'If he recovers,' he added carelessly.

'Which way can we go?' asked Conway. 'It wouldn't be safe to go back through Newton, and we can't head out into the blue towards Land's End–'

'Why not?' drawled the Saint, who was apt to become difficult on the slightest provocation. 'Land's End sounds a good romantic place to establish a piratical base, and we must have one somewhere. Besides, it has the great advantage that nobody's ever used it before. The only alternative is to make for Tavistock and Okehampton, and either take the north coast road through Barnstaple and Minehead or chance going through Exeter.'

'I thought you wanted to be seen.'

'I do – but some place where they can't stop us. They can see us go through any village, but they can hold us up in Exeter – it's a slow place to get through at the best of times.'

'You may be right. There's nowhere for us to go if we do head east. Unless we make back for Brook Street.'

'Teal knows about Brook Street,' said the Saint. 'He's liable to drop in there any time.

Your maiden aunt at Stratford upon Avon–'

'You don't know her,' snorted Roger, testing the fit of his helmet.

'I can imagine it,' said the Saint. 'No – we'll spare the feelings of Auntie, I can understand her getting rather excited when Whiskers tools up with his gang to re-capture the hostage.'

Roger picked up his discarded clothes and took them over to the Morris, and the Saint walked beside him. A barren waste of moorland stretched around them, and a hump of ground capped with gorse screened them from the main road.

'Then where can we go? Remember that anything that Whiskers gets to know through the papers will be known to the real police first. We've overlooked that.'

'Yes, we've overlooked that,' said the Saint thoughtfully; and he paused, with one foot propped up on the running-board of the Morris and his hands deep in his trouser pockets and his eyes fixed on the girl in a blank and distracted way. 'We've overlooked that,' he said.

'Well?'

Roger asked the question as if he had no hope of receiving a useful answer, yet it seemed quite natural to ask it. People naturally asked such impossible questions of the Saint.

Half an hour ago (Roger knew it was half

an hour because the Saint had smoked two cigarettes, and the Saint consumed four cigarettes an hour with the regularity of clockwork) they had calmly driven up to a house in Newton Abbot in the expectation of dinner, a short convivial evening, a bath, and a well-earned night's rest before proceeding with the problem in hand.

Now – it seemed only five minutes later – they had risked their necks a dozen times in a hectic motor chase, stopped the fugitive car, laid out the driver, doped him with his own medicine, and found themselves saddled with two bodies and the necessity of putting their plans forward by twenty-four hours.

And Simon Templar was quite unperturbed, and apparently unaware that there was, or had been, any excitement whatever.

'On the other hand,' said the Saint thoughtfully, still looking at the girl, 'we might revise our strategy slightly. There's one place in the whole of England where the police will never think of looking for anybody.'

'Where's that?'

'That,' said the Saint, 'is Uncle Sebastian's house.'

Roger was beyond being startled by anything the Saint suggested. Besides, he was swift on the uptake.

'You mean we should go there now?'

'No less.'

'But the housekeeper–'

'The housekeeper, with her heart full of the fear of winged policemen, and her boots full of feet, will have shut up the house and fled to the bosom of her family and Torquay – or wherever her family keeps its official bosom. We navigate first to a pub I wot of in St Marychurch, to demand liquor and provisions–'

'Not in these trousers,' said Roger, indicating his costume.

'In those trousers,' said the Saint, 'but not in that coat and hat. You'd better stick to as much of the outfit as you can, to save time, because you'll want it later in the evening. Speed, my angel, is the order of the night. The great brain is working...'

Roger, feeling somewhat dazed, but still on the spot, was starting to peel off his tunic. The Saint helped him on with his gent's jacket.

'I'll think out the further details on the way,' he said. 'I've got another colossal idea which won't work unless we get the dope bird to a quiet place before he comes to. I'll take the Desurio and the dope bird, and you take the Morris and the moll – and let's burn the road!'

He spoke the last words from his way back to the Desurio, and he was already reversing up the lane as Roger tipped his police lid into the dickey and climbed into the driving seat of the Morris.

As Conway backed round into the main road, the Desurio slid past him and the Saint leaned out.

'She's a nice girl, by appearance,' said the Saint. 'Mind you keep both hands on the steering wheel all the way home, sonny boy!'

Then he was gone, with a gay wave of his hand, and Roger pulled out the Morris after him.

It was still daylight, for the month was August. The rays of the sun slanted softly across the purple desert; overhead, a shadow on a pale blue sky, a curlew flew towards the sunset with a weird titter; the evening air went to Roger's head like wine.

Roger had got into his stride.

He should have been concentrating exclusively on the task of keeping on the tail of the Desurio; but he was not. With both hands clinging religiously to the steering wheel, he stole a sidelong glance at the girl. With one hand clinging religiously to the steering wheel, he reached out the other and tugged off her small hat – in order, he told himself, that the rush of cool air might help to revive her.

Black hair, straight and sleek, framing a face that was all wrong. Eccentric eyes, an absurd nose, a ridiculous mouth – all about as wrong as they could be. But a perfect skin. She must have been tall. 'No nonsense with tall girls,' thought Roger, as an expert.

'But,' thought Roger as an expert, 'there might be something doing. Adroitly handled...'

The pub at St Marychurch which both he and the Saint wotted of, where a friendly proprietor would not ask too many questions. The removal of the 'dope bird' to a quiet cellar where a ruthless interrogation could proceed without interruption. The development of the Saint's unrevealed stratagem. Then, perhaps–'

It was an utterly ridiculous mouth, but rather intriguing. And if a man couldn't yank a girl out of a maze of mysterious melodrama without claiming, and getting, something in return for romantic services rendered – by what right did he call himself a man?

Roger fumbled for a cigarette and drove on, characteristically grim, but quite contented.

4

Driving straight into the garage of the Golden Eagle Hotel, St Marychurch, Conway found the Saint's Desurio there before him. The Saint was not there, but the 'dope bird' remained in the back of the car in unprotesting tenancy. His mouth was open, and he appeared to snore with distressing violence.

Roger picked the girl out of the Morris and carried her through a back entrance to the hotel adjoining the garage. He was unobserved, for the population was at dinner. Finding an empty lounge, he put the girl down in an armchair and went on his way. There was no one to question his right to leave stray unconscious females lying about the place, for Roger himself happened to be the proprietor of the pub in his spare time.

He continued down the corridor to the hall, and there found Simon Templar interviewing the manageress.

'It has been,' the Saint was saying, staggering rhythmically, 'a b-beautiful b-binge. Champagne. An' brandy. An' beer. Barrels an' barrels of it.' He giggled inanely, and flung out his arms in a wide sweep to indicate the size of the barrels. 'Barrels,' he said. 'An' we won't go home till the morning, we won't go home till the morning, we won't go home till the mor-hor-*ning*–'

He caught sight of Roger, and pointed to him with one hand while he grasped the hand of the manageress passionately with the other.

'An' there's dear ole Roger!' he crowed. 'You ask dear ole Roger if it wasn't a b-beautiful b-binge. 'Cos we won't go home till the morning, we won't go home–'

'I'm afraid,' said Conway, advancing with solemn disapproval written all over his face, 'that my friend is rather drunk.'

The Saint wagged a wobbly forefinger at him.

'Drunk?' he expostulated, with portentous gravity. 'Roger, ole darling, that's unkind. Frightfully unkind. Now, if you'd said that about Desmond... Poor ole Dismal Desmond, he's passed right out ... I left him in the car. An' he won't go home till the morning, he won't–'

The shocked manageress drew Roger to one side.

'We can't let him in like that, Mr Conway,' she protested, twittering. 'There are guests staying in the hotel–'

'Are there any rooms vacant?' asked Roger.

'None at all. And people will be coming out from dinner in a minute–'

'But,' carolled the Saint unmelodiously, 'we won't go home till the mor-hor-*ning* – an' so say all of us. Gimme a drink.'

The manageress looked helplessly about her.

'Are there any more of them?'

'There's one in the car, but he's dead to the world.'

'Why don't you turn them out?'

'Drink,' warbled the Saint happily. 'Thousan's of drinks. Drink to me only wi-hith thine eye-heys an' I-hi will pledge with miiiiine…'

Roger glanced down the corridor. A red-faced man poked his head out of the smokeroom door and glared around to discover the source of the uproar. He discovered it, snuffled indignantly through a superb white moustache, and withdrew his head again, banging the door after it. The manageress seemed to be on the verge of hysterics.

'I,' chanted the Saint, pleasantly absorbed in his own serenade, 'sent thee late a ro-hosy wre-he-heath, not so much hon-hon'ring theeee, as giving it–'

'Can't you do something, Mr Conway?' pleaded the unfortunate manageress, almost wringing her hands.

'You can't sing without drink,' insisted the

Saint throatily, as a man propounding one of the eternal verities.

Conway shrugged.

'I can't very well turn him out,' he said. 'I've known him a long time, and he was coming to stay here. Besides, he isn't often like this.'

'But where can we put him?'

'How about the cellar?'

'What? Among all the bottles?'

Roger had to think fast.

'There's the porter's room. I'll shove him in there to cool off. And the other man can go in with him.'

'You can't sing without drink,' insisted the Saint pathetically. 'You can't, really, ole sweetheart.'

Conway took him insinuatingly by the arm.

'Then you'd better come and have another drink, old boy.'

'Good idea,' nodded the Saint, draping himself affectionately on Roger's neck. 'Less go on drinking. All night. All the silly ole night. That,' said the Saint, 'sha good idea.' He turned to blow the manageress an unsteady kiss. 'See you tomorrow, ole fruit, 'cos we're not going home till the morning, we're not-*hic!* ... Roger, old water-melon, why *does* this floor wave about so much? You ought to have it s-seen to...'

They reached the porter's room with

realistic unsteadiness, and lurched in; and then the Saint straightened up.

'Hustle Dismal Desmond along kiddo,' he said. 'Where did you put the girl?'

'In one of the lounges. Do you *have* to act like this?'

'Obviously, my pet – to account for Dismal Desmond. Get Betty out of the way, up to one of the rooms. Pretend you're just playing the fool. I leave it to you, partner!'

He literally pushed Conway out of the room, and the muffled sounds of his discordant singing followed Roger down the corridor. Conway felt like a wolf in sheep's clothing.

He hoisted the man out of the Saint's car and carried him in, and only the simmering manageress saw him plugged into the porter's cubicle.

Through the open door came the Saint's voice:

'Why, there's dear ole Desmond! How are you, Desmond, ole pineapple? I was juss sayin'–'

Roger closed the door, and assumed an air of official efficiency.

'Did you say all the rooms were taken, Miss Cocker?'

'Number Seven's empty at the moment, sir, but there's some people due in tonight–'

'Then I'm afraid they'll be unlucky. A girl friend of mine arrived at the same time as we did, and I must give her a room. Tell these people you're awfully sorry, but you've booked the same room twice by mistake – and pass them on to some other place.'

He turned on his heel and went back up the corridor. The manageress, standing petrified, heard a short conversation in which Roger's voice was the only one audible; and then Mr Conway reappeared from the lounge with the girl in his arms.

'Cavemen,' said Mr Conway strongly, 'are all the vogue; and there'll be no nonsense from you, Betty darling – see?' He swept rapidly past the scandalized Miss Cocker, and continued towards the stairs. 'Do you like being carried about the place? Does it make you love me any more? What's that? Right. I'll teach you to sham dead. You wait till I drop you in the bath…'

A bend in the staircase hid him from sight, but the conversation went on. Miss Cocker, rooted in her tracks, listened, appalled…

She was standing at the foot of the stairs when Roger came down, a few minutes later, feeling as if he had blasted his reputation for ever as far as his executive staff was concerned. And he was quite right.

'Will you be taking dinner, Mr Conway?' asked the manageress frostily, and Roger knew that he might as well be jugged for a julep as a jujube.

He grinned.

'Get sandwiches cut for twenty people,' he said, 'and tell the porter to get a couple of dozen Bass. I think we're all going for a moonlight picnic on the moors – and we won't be home till the morning.'

He passed on, comforted by the moral victory; and found the Saint sitting on the porter's bed, smoking a cigarette and surveying the man sprawled out on the floor. In much the same way an introspectively-minded cat might have surveyed a sleeping mouse.

He looked up, as Roger came in, with a lift of one questioning eyebrow; and Roger shook his head.

'I left her down at the other end of the corridor. And I should like to tell you that after this, either I shall have to fire her, or I shall have to fire myself.'

'Why worry?' demanded the Saint. 'Pub-keeping is no trade for an honest criminal. Where's Betty now?'

'I got her up to Number Seven.'

'Unsuspected?'

'I think so.'

'Good boy. Now let's look at you.'

He stood up. Suddenly his hands went out and stroked down each side of Roger's chin. Conway started back.

'What the blazes–'

'Hush,' said the Saint. 'Not so much excitement.'

He showed Roger his hands. The palms were black with dust.

'You ought to make your bell-hop sweep under his bed more carefully,' he said. 'However, in this case we'll forgive him. It helps to make you look really villainous. Now – off with that collar and tie. A choker'll suit you much better. That handkerchief–'

He jerked the square of fancy silk out of Roger's pocket.

'Knot this round your neck, and you'll start to look more like yourself. And unbutton the coat and turn up the collar at the back – it'll make you look tougher… And a rakish cap effect, as worn by college chums, would make it perfect. There ought to be a cap here somewhere – every self-respecting bell-hop has one for his night out…'

He opened the wardrobe unceremoniously, rummaged, and found what he sought.

'Put that on. Over one ear, and well down over the eyes. That's the stuff!'

Roger obeyed blindly. The Saint's staccato urgency would have overwhelmed anyone.

'But what's the idea?'

'Easy,' said the Saint. 'A real bull-dozing would make too much noise, and we haven't the place to do it. So we take Desmond on the bend, so to speak. I'd be the stoolpigeon myself, only he'd recognize me, so you have the honour. Meanwhile, I'll park myself in Betty's room and put her wise when she wakes up.'

'Yes, but–'

'I've got to leave it to your imagination what tale you tell Desmond when he comes to. The main point is that you're one of the gang, and you've been captured, too. You're the prisoners of the Saint, and you don't know where you are. This room won't tell anything.'

He pointed to the tiny window, set high up in the wall and looking out upon nothing more informative than another blank wall.

'Old-fashioned and unhygenic,' said the Saint, 'but useful on this occasion. It's much too small to get out through. And I'll lock the door and take the key with me. In half an hour's time I'll lock myself in the service room upstairs and start watching. When you're through, flutter your handkerchief out of this window, and I'll see it and be right down.'

'But why the rush?' asked Conway, with what breath had not been taken away by the Saint's machine-gun fire of directions.

'For the plan,' answered Simon. 'You have the advantage of getting on to Desmond while he's still hazy with dope. As a friend in the same boat as himself, you worm all you can out of him, put two and two together, and worm again. The great thing is to find out under what name Whiskers is known to the police, and where Desmond was supposed to meet him to hand over Betty.'

Roger took the Saint's place on the bed.

'And you want to know that tonight?'

'Of course. This is the night when Whiskers is expecting Betty to join her uncle and complete the family party. And that's what she'll do, if you pull your stuff. I'll take her there myself, roughly disguised as Dismal Desmond. And as soon as Whiskers has rumbled that joke, you, old haricot, having followed closely behind in your fancy dress will beetle in, and arrest the lot of us – thereby hoisting Whiskers with his own whatnot. How's that for a funny story?'

Roger looked up with enthusiasm kindling in his face.

'It gets a laugh,' he said.

'My funny stories,' said Simon Templar modestly, 'frequently do.'

'And once we've got Whiskers–'

'Exactly. The mystery of Uncle Sebastian's house will no longer be a mystery.'

The Saint took a quick glance round him, picked up a piece of printed hotel paper off the table and stuffed it into his pocket, and then reached up and removed the single bulb from its socket.

'It's getting dark,' he explained, 'and a bad

light might help you. All set?'

'You may always,' said Mr Conway tranquilly, 'leave these little things to me.'

It was one of Roger's pet expressions; and the Saint hailed it with a grin. Roger was not the star of the gang in the matter of purely abstract brains; but there could have been no greater lieutenant, when it came to the point, in the whole solar system.

The Saint opened the door cautiously, and peered out. The passage was deserted. He turned back.

'You're playing the hand,' he said. 'Don't miss any of the important tricks. And when Dismal Desmond's conversation gets boring, or if he starts to smell rats, just blip him over the head with the slop-pail and wave the flag.'

'Right you are, Saint.'

'So long, Beautiful.'

'So long, Ugly-Wugs.'

Roger heard the turning of the lock and the withdrawing of the key, but he never heard the Saint pad away down the corridor. He lighted a cigarette and stretched himself out on the bed, with one eye on the man on the floor, considering the memory of a most intriguing mouth.

5

Conway finished his cigarette, and lay for a time gazing at the ceiling. Then he tried to watch the minute-hand of his watch crawling round the dial. Time passed. The room was shrouded in a grey dusk. Roger yawned.

He wondered uneasily if the Saint had underestimated the potency of the drug in the hypodermic syringe. True, it had been only half full when Simon found it, and Simon had promptly injected the half on the assumption that what had been sauce for the goose might very justly be made sauce for the gander – but there was nothing to show that the syringe had ever been full. Perhaps Betty had only been given a few drops, the rest being kept for a repeat dose in case of need.

Roger speculated for a moment on his chance in a murder trial. He had never been able to acquire that dispassionate valuation of human life, nor that careless contempt for the law that forbids you to bounce off your neighbour simply because you have decided that his habits are objectionable and his face an outrage, which were among the charming simplicities of Simon Templar.

But the persistent snoring of Dismal Desmond, distasteful as it might be to a sensitive man, was reassuring. Roger lighted another cigarette…

Nevertheless, it was another ten minutes before the man on the floor gave any sign of returning consciousness. Then a snore was strangled into a grunt, and the grunt became a low moan.

Roger twisted over on to one shoulder to observe the recovery. The man twitched and moved one leg heavily; but after that, for some time, there seemed to be a relapse. Then another groan, and another movement more vigorous than the first.

'My head,' muttered the man foggily. 'He hit me…'

Silence.

Roger shifted up on to his elbow.

'Hullo, mate,' he said.

Another silence. Then, painfully–

'Who's that?'

'They seem to have got you all right, mate,' said Roger.

'There were two men in a car. One of 'em got out an' hit me. Must have smashed us up… Blast this head… Why's it so dark?'

'It's night. You've been out a long time.'

Silence for a long time. Roger could sense the man's struggle to pierce the drug-fumes that still murked his brain. He would have given much for a light, even while he realized that the darkness was helping his deception. But presently the voice came again.

'Who're you, anyway?'

'They got me, too.'

'Is that Carris?'

'Yes.'

The man strained to penetrate the gloom. Roger could see his eyes.

'That's not Bill Carris's voice.'

'This is George Carris,' said Roger. 'Bill's brother.'

He swung his legs off the bed and crossed the floor. The man had writhed up into a sitting position, and Conway put an arm round his shoulders.

'Come and lie down on the bed,' he suggested. 'You'll feel better in a minute.'

The man peered closely into his face.

'You don't look like Bill.'

'I'm not Bill – I'm George.'

'You ought to look like Bill. How do you come here?'

'I was with Bill.'

'On the telephone?'

'Yes.'

'Bill said he was going alone.'

'He changed his mind and took me. D'you think you could get over to that bed if I helped you?'

'I'll try. My head's going round and round...'

Roger helped the man up and more or less carried him to the bed, where he collapsed again limply. Roger sat down on the edge. He glanced at his watch; it was over half an hour since the Saint had left him.

'Who are you?' he asked.

'Why, don't you know?'

'I'm new, I don't know any of the gang except Bill.'

'You're a liar!' snarled the man. 'You're not in the gang at all. You're–'

'You fool!' retorted Roger, with an oath. 'What the – d'you think I'd be doing here if they hadn't caught me, too?'

The man appeared to cogitate this argument painfully for a time. Presently he said, as though satisfied:

'Where are we?'

'I don't know. I was laid out when they brought me here. What did you say your name was, mate?'

'My name's Dyson. "Slinky" Dyson. Who're these guys you keep talking about? Who're *they*?'

'The Saint's gang, of course.'

'The Saint–'

Dyson's voice choked on a note of fear.

'You're a liar!' he croaked.

'I tell you, it was the Saint. I saw him–'

'No one's ever seen the Saint an' got away with it.'

'But I've seen him. An' he said he was

going to torture us. I'm scared. Slinky, we've got to get out of this!'

Conway felt the bed shaking.

'He can't do anything to me,' said Dyson hoarsely. 'He's got nothing on me. He can't–'

'That's all you know. He wants you most – for doing that girl. Flog the hide off your back, that's what he said he was going to do.'

'They can't–'

Roger Conway, well as he knew the superstitious terror which the name of the Saint inspired, and the legends of ruthlessness which had grown up around him, had no need to act his contempt for the whining wretch on the bed. He caught the man's shoulder and shook him roughly.

'For heaven's sake, stop blubbering!' he snapped. 'D'you think that'll get us anywhere?'

'The Boss'll do something when he finds out.'

'He's too far away to be any use,' ventured Roger.

'I was nearly there when they got me.'

Nearly there! And they had been about five miles from Two Bridges. Somewhere on the moor, then ... Roger's heart leapt with a thrill of triumph, and he drove in upon the opening like lightning.

'You don't know how far away we are

now,' he said. 'We've both been out for over an hour. And if the Boss does find out, and knows the Saint, he'll most likely be too busy making his own getaway to bother about us.'

'That's all *you* know. You ever heard of "Spider" Sleat letting his bunch down?'

'Spider' Sleat! Point two ... Roger made his next remark almost with apprehension. It was a tremendous strain to keep up what he considered to be the right tone of voice, when his whole system was tingling with half-incredulous delight.

'They'll be bringing us some food soon. They said they would. I'm fitter than you are – I might make a bolt for it, if you keep them busy. And I'd fetch the Boss and the rest of the bunch along... Only I can never find the way alone, out on that moor. And it'd be dark...'

'How often you been there?'

'Only twice. And Bill took me each time.'

'It's easy. Where did you come from?'

'Exeter.'

'Through Okehampton?'

Something in the way the question was put – a faint, almost imperceptible hesitation, stabbed a sharp warning through Roger's flush of exultation. But he had no time to think. With his muscles tensed, he flashed back his gamble.

'No – you know that's not the way. We

came through Moreton Hampstead.'

Slinky Dyson's breath came again, audibly, through his teeth.

'Sorry, chum. I had to make sure you were straight. Well, you went about ten miles past Moreton Hampstead–'

'I suppose so.'

'That put you about two miles from Two Bridges. Don't you remember the knoll with three humps, on the right of the road near where you stopped?'

'That's about all I do remember.'

'Then you can't go wrong. You make two hundred yards due north of the knoll into the dip, and follow the low ground north-west till you come to a patch of gorse in the shape of an "S". Then you strike off north-east – and you're there.'

'But it'll be dark.'

'There'll be a moon.'

Roger appeared to meditate.

'It sounds easy, the way you put it,' he said. 'But–'

'It *is* easy!' Dyson snarled. 'But I don't believe you'll do it. You're yellow! You'd just cut and run, and no one'll ever see you again for dust. You miserable little dirty quitter!'

'What the blazes are you talking about?'

'What I say. I don't believe you. You're just trying to save your own skin an' get me to help you. You might make a bolt for it, you say, while *I* keep 'em busy. Thanks for nothing! You listen here – either we both make a bolt, or we both stay. I know your sort. Bill was always a yaller dog, an' you take after him. You–'

It struck Roger that Mr Dyson's conversation was certainly becoming monotonous. And his brain was humming with other things. 'Spider' Sleat – whoever he might be – and a knoll with three humps two miles from the Two Bridges on the Moreton Hampstead. Due north – a dip – north-west to a patch of gorse in the shape of an 'S' – turn north-east…

A fight, in that dark room, might have been troublesome. Dyson was no light weight – Roger had noticed that when helping him to the bed. And his strength must be returning rapidly.

The Saint, in parting, had suggested the slop-pail. But Roger had discovered something better than that – a hefty broken chair-leg, apparently used to switch off the electric light without getting out of bed. His fingers closed upon it lovingly.

6

'Sorry to have kept you waiting,' drawled the Saint, ten minutes later, 'but your manageress is wandering about in the line of retreat looking like a flat tyre, and I didn't dare let her see me. Roger, you've blighted her young life. I know she'll never smile again.'

Conway pointed his chair-leg at the bed.

'He sleeps.'

'After laying his egg?'

'He spilled a certain amount of beans. It ought to be enough to work on.'

'Let's see what you've got – as the actress said to the bishop,' murmured Simon. 'Half a sec – we'll have some light on the subject.'

He felt for the socket, extracted the bulb from his pocket, and adjusted it. Roger switched it on.

The Saint inspected Mr Dyson with interest.

'Do you think he'll die?' he asked.

'I don't think so.'

'A pity,' said the Saint. 'It means we'll have the trouble of roping him up. Make yourself look decent, and go out and find some string. You can talk while I tie.'

Roger removed the choker and replaced his collar while the Saint employed spit-and-polish methods, with a handkerchief, to his face. Then Roger snooped off on his errand.

He met Miss Cocker in the corridor.

'I've been looking for you, Mr Conway,' said the lady ominously. 'Where have you been all this time?'

'If I told you,' said Roger truthfully, 'you'd be shocked. What's the trouble?'

'A gentleman's been complaining about the noise.'

'Let him complain.'

'He's wanting to leave at once.'

'Don't stop him. Are the sandwiches and beer ready?'

'They've been waiting half an hour. But Mr Conway–'

'Tell the little fellows to be patient. I shan't be long now.'

He stalked away before the manageress could find her voice. But the woman was waiting for him when he came back, after a few minutes, with a couple of fathoms of stout cord in his pocket.

'Mr Conway–'

'Miss Cocker.'

'I'm not used to being treated like this, I'm not really. I think you must be drunk yourself. I'm used to respectable hotels, I am, and I never heard of such goings on, I didn't–'

'Miss Cocker,' said Roger kindly, 'take my advice and go and look for a nice respectable hotel. Because I'm turning this one into a high-class roadside gin palace, from which people will be removed, roaring drunk, in the small hours of every morning. Bye-bye, ole geranium.'

He entered the porter's room and closed the door in her face.

The Saint looked up with his quick smile.

'Domestic strife?' he queried.

'I'm used to respectable hotels, I am, and I never heard of such goings on, I didn't.'

'And you always such a nice quiet gentleman, Mr Conway!'

'It's the only way to carry it off – to pretend I'm canned. Tomorrow I shall have to see her and apologize profusely. Here's your string.'

The Saint took the cord and bent to his task with practised efficiency, while Roger described the interview with Mr Dyson. Simon listened intently, but his memory was baulked by the name of Sleat. It had a vague familiar ring about it, but nothing more.

'Spider Sleat,' he repeated. 'Can't place it. How many men are there supposed to be on the moor?'

'I didn't find that out.'

'There's only the two of us. Dicky Tremayne took his car for a golfing tour in Scotland, and I don't know where to find him. I sent Pat and Norman off to join Terry's yachting party at Cowes.'

'You wouldn't drag her into it, anyway.'

'There wouldn't be time if I wanted to. No, my seraph – you and I must tackle this alone, and damn the odds. There's one idea…'

'What's that?'

The Saint completed his last knot, tested it, and stepped back. He faced Roger.

'I hate to do it,' he said, 'but it's the most practical scheme. I know Teal's private 'phone number, and he'll probably be at home now. I'll ask if the name of Sleat means anything to him. Teal's got the longest memory of any man at the Yard. That means I'll have to tell him I'm on the tail of the Policeman with Wings.'

'Then he'll get on the 'phone to the police round here–'

'He won't. You don't know the CID like I do. They're as jealous as a mother at a baby show, and they think rather less of the country police than a Rolls chauffeur thinks of a Ford. I'll tell Teal to come down himself by the first train in the morning to collect the specimens, and he won't say a word to a soul. Now, filter out again and remove your manageress. Take her away to a quiet place and talk to her. Apologize now, if you like, instead of tomorrow morning. But give me a clear quarter of an hour to get that trunk call through.'

Roger nodded.

'I'll see to it. But that only gives us tonight and half tomorrow.'

'It'll be enough – to get Whiskers, find out the secret of this house, and act accordingly. We've got to make this a hurry order. Off you go, son.'

'Right. Where shall I meet you?'

'Betty's room – in about half an hour. Now skate!'

Roger skated.

He found the manageress spluttering about the hall, steered her into the office, and spent a desperate twenty minutes with her. He got out at last, minus his dignity, but still blessed with a manageress; and made his way up the stairs.

Of all the Saint's little band, Roger Conway had always been Simon's especial friend. There were many men scattered over the world who held Simon Templar in reverence bordering on idolatry; there were as many, if not more, in whose aid the Saint would not have stopped at any of the crimes in the calendar; but between Roger and the Saint was a greater bond than any of these. And Roger considered...

The Saint gave his ultimate affection to two people only – one man and one girl. The man was Roger Conway. The girl was Patricia Holm. She was the cream in his coffee. And those three, like the Three Musketeers had come together out of infinitely diverse worlds – and stuck.

And Roger considered, soberly for him, because he realized that the girl he had seen, in sleep only, that afternoon, and she almost a stranger, had moved him far more than it is safe for a man to be moved. Suppose she came to make a fourth inseparable, would the bonds that held the rest of them together hold as firmly. It was a fantastic castle to build in the air, but he had been moved, and he knew it.

Therefore he considered, in that brief breathing-space, and came to the girl's room in a subdued mood.

She was powdering her nose.

'Hullo, Roger darling,' she said. 'How are you?'

'I'm very fit,' said Roger. 'How are you?'

Commonplace. But comforting. He lighted a cigarette, and sat down on the bed where he could see her face in the dressing-table mirror.

They talked. He described, for the second time, the Dyson episode – and other matters. She said she thought it was clever of him to think of carrying her up the stairs as if she were teasing and he ragging. Roger preened himself visibly. She looked nicer with her eyes open, he thought.

'Your friend's very nice,' she said.

'Who – the Saint?'

'Is that what you call him? He said his name was Simon.'

'Everyone calls him the Saint.'

'He's a sheik.'

Roger eased up on the preening.

She was plainly frightened by her adventure, but he thought she bore up remarkably well. Her nerves were palpably fluttered, but there was no hint of hysterics in her voice. She explained the doping.

'I was driving, and I felt something prick my leg. He showed me a pin sticking out of the upholstery, and said it must have been that. But a minute or so later I began to feel horribly dizzy, and I had to stop the car. My leg seemed to have swollen up and gone numb. That's all I remember until I woke up here and found Simon – or the Saint – sitting in the armchair. He made me put my head under the cold tap, and then he made me lie down again and told me all about it.

The minutes seemed to fly. She sat down beside him, and he took her hand absent-mindedly and went on talking. She didn't seem to mind – he recalled that afterwards. But he had hardly got started when he was interrupted by a gentle tap on the door, and Simon Templar came in.

Roger was acutely conscious of his eccentric garb, for he was still wearing his police trousers with his ordinary coat, and his face was still somewhat soiled from the Saint's improvised make-up. Roger felt depressingly unlike a sheik; and the Saint was as offensively sleek and Savile Row and patent-leather as a man can possibly be.

'Sorry to have to barge in like this, boys and girls,' he said breezily, 'but I thought you ought to know that I've had a heart-to-heart chat with Teal over the long-distance wire – and worked the trick. He'll be at Exeter tomorrow afternoon to stand us a drink and remove the exhibits. But there'll be no sleep for the just between now and then, Roger!'

'Did you find out about Sleat?'

'And how.' The Saint swung round to the girl. 'Tell me, old dear – when did Uncle Sebastian start building that house?'

'I can tell you exactly,' said Betty, 'because it was a week before my birthday. I was staying with him in Torquay, and he took me over to see the foundations being dug.'

'You, all legs and pigtails, on your holidays,' said the Saint. 'I know. And when is this birthday?'

'The third of August.'

'Five days ago – and to think you didn't invite us to the party! But a week before that would be the twenty-seventh of July, seven years ago, makes it nineteen twenty-two... Roger, my archangel, it's too good to be true!'

'Why?'

'Because on the fifth of July, nineteen twenty-two, Harry Sleat, known as Spider Sleat, was arrested at Southampton. On the first of August, nineteen twenty-two, he was convicted at the Old Bailey and sent down for seven years for busting the strongroom of the *Presidential* and getting away at Plymouth with fifty thousand pounds' worth of diamonds that were on their way over to America. All that from the marvellous memory of our one and only Claud Eustace Teal.'

Roger forgot his clothes in the absorption of this cataract of facts. But his mind seized instantly on one clear idea.

'They never found the diamonds?'

'Never in all these days. But Whiskers was on the loose with the sparklers *before* Uncle Sebastian started to build his house. And Whiskers was in this district before they nobbled him – he must have been. *And* Whiskers, being an insubordinate convict, had to serve almost his full term. He came out on the eighth of June. What's he do first?'

Roger leapt into the breach, momentarily oblivious of the bewildered girl.

'He tries to buy the house. Then, when Uncle won't sell, he tries to scare him out. Then, when Uncle won't be scared, he kidnaps Uncle and follows through with kidnapping Betty–'

'Because Betty is Uncle's heir, and if Uncle merely vanishes the house goes to Betty–'

'So that Whiskers has to pinch them both, force them to sign a deed of sale dated some weeks before their disappearance–'

'And kill them – or otherwise keep them out of the way – while he takes possession, disinters the loot, and slithers off in the general direction of the tall timber. Roger, my pet, we're next to the goods this time!'

The girl was staring blankly at them.

'I haven't the least idea what you're talking about,' she said.

The Saint slapped his thigh.

'But it's marvellous!' he cried. 'It's the maddest, merriest story that ever brought the roof down. Think of it! Whiskers, having got clean away with his fifty thousand quids' worth of crystallized carbon, with the dicks hard on his heels, comes upon a field in the dead of night, and buries the diamonds deep down.

Roger chipped in: 'Then they catch him–'

'And he goes to jail quite cheerfully, knowing where he can find his fortune when he comes out. And he comes out, all ready to make a splash and enjoy himself – and finds somebody's bought his field and built a house on top of the treasures. Oh *Baby!* Can you beat it?'

The girl gasped. It was a perfect story. As an explanation of the whole mystery, it was the only possible one that was convincing at the same time – and even then it read like the creation of some imaginative novelist's brain. It wanted some digesting.

But the two men before her seemed to find it sufficiently accredited. The Saint, hands on hips, was shaking with silent laughter. Roger, always less effervescent by nature than the Saint, was grinning delightedly.

'It sounds good,' he said.

'It's the caterpillar's spats! Now, this is where we take the springboard for the high dive. Is there provender ready for the troops?'

'Yes.'

'Load it up in the Desurio. We'll park most of it at Betty's for future reference, on the way over, and just take what we need for supper to drink in the car as we go along. We'll leave the Morris, because the police'll be looking for it. You and Betty can go out quite openly, and I'll sneak along to the best bathroom – that's the one looking out on to the garage drive, isn't it? – and drop out of the window and meet you there.'

'What about Dyson? We can't leave him in the porter's room.'

'Toddle along and give him another clip over the ear. Then he won't yelp or struggle, and you can carry him out to the car. We'll take him with us. I couldn't bear to be parted from Dismal Desmond, even for an hour.'

'I ought to be able to do that,' said Conway. 'There's a door leading into the garden right opposite the porter's room, and it's dark enough now for no one to notice, if I'm quick.'

'That's fine! Betty, old sweetheart–'

The Saint's rattling volley of instructions was cut short as if by the turning off of a tap. He turned to the dazed girl with his most winning smile.

'Betty, old sweetheart, will you do it?'

'What do you want me to do?' she asked dazedly. 'I've hardly understood a word of what you've been saying.'

The Saint seemed wilted by her denseness. Unused (as in his sober moments he was always ready to confess) to the less mercurial habits of ordinary folk, he was invariably taken aback by anyone showing the least surprise at anything he did or said. The limitations of the ordinary person's outlook on life were to him a never-ending source of hurt puzzlement.

'My dear old peach-blossom–'

Roger, who was of a commoner humanity, and who knew by his own experience what a shock a first meeting with Simon Templar in such a mood could be, intervened sympathetically.

'Leave this to me, old boy.'

In language less picturesquely volcanic than the Saint would have employed, but language nevertheless infinitely more intelligible to a lay audience, he summarized the main features of the situation and what he knew of the plot, while the Saint listened with undisguised admiration. Simon had never ceased to admire and envy, without being able to imitate, Roger's gift for meeting every known species of human life on its own ground. People had to adapt themselves to the Saint; Roger was able to adapt himself to people.

He explained, and the girl understood. Then he came to the Saint's question, and he could see an automatic refusal starting to her lips.

The Saint stepped in again – but in this he was sure of himself. He had his own particular brand of parlour tricks, had Simon Templar.

'Betty, darling–'

This time it was Roger who listened in envious admiration.

It would be useless to attempt to record what the Saint said. The bare words, bereft of the magical charm of voice which the Saint could assume on occasion with such deadly ease, would appear banal, if not ridiculous. But the Saint spoke. He was pleading; he was friendly; he was masterful; he was confidential; he was flippant; he was romantic; he was impudent. And change followed effortless change with a crazily kaleidoscopic speed that would have left any girl battered into submission – and probably mazily wondering why she submitted.

And it was all done in a few minutes, and the girl was looking at him with wide eyes and saying: 'Do you really think I ought to do it?'

'I really do,' said the Saint, as if the fate of worlds depended on it.

She hesitated, looked helplessly at Roger. Then–

'All right,' she said. 'I'll go. But I don't mind telling you I'm terrified. Honestly. After this evening–'

'That's a good girl,' said the Saint, and brazenly hugged her.

Roger felt morosely pleased that he was shortly going to be able to give Mr Dyson another clip over the ear. Anyone else would have done equally well, but if it had to be Mr Dyson…

7

'That,' said the Saint, 'should be the place.'

He lay full length in the long damp grass, peering over the crest of a convenient hummock at the house.

When you have as extensive a wardrobe as the Saint's, you can afford to maltreat a Savile Row poem in light grey fresco by stretching it out full length in long damp grass. Roger Conway, mindful of the dignity of his police uniform, contented himself with sinking to a squatting position. The girl was a little way behind them.

They could see the cottage, a stumpy black bulk in the moonlight, with two windows sharply cut out in yellow luminance. The sky was as clear as a bowl of dark glass; and in spite of Mr Dyson's confident assurance, the fragments of moon that rode low down in the sky had been less help to them in their journey than the stars. A mile out, just off the road, the Desurio was parked with all its lights out.

The Saint squirmed down a little so that the flame of his match would not be visible to any watchers outside the cottage, and lighted a cigarette in his cupped hands.

'We might as well start now,' he murmured. 'Where's the girl?'

They crept back together to rejoin her.

'On the mark, kid?'

A clammy breath of wind had been born on the moor. She shivered in her thin coat.

'The sooner you get it over, the better I'll be pleased.'

'You'll soon be happy,' said the Saint.

His teeth gleamed in a smile – it was all they could distinguish of his expression in the gloom. But the faint tremor of eagerness in his voice was perceptible without the aid of eyes.

'All got your pieces ready to say?' he asked.

She said, nervously: 'I don't know what I've got to do–'

'Nor would you if you'd really been kidnapped. That's your piece. Anyhow, you're supposed to be dead to the world, having assimilated the second instalment of that syringeful. Roger, you've got your gun?'

Conway slapped his pocket for answer.

'Haven't you got a gun, Saint?' asked the girl.

Simon was heard to chuckle softly.

'Ask Roger if I ever carry guns,' he said. 'No – I leave them to other people. Personally, I can't stand the noise. I have my own copyright armoury, which is much more silent – and just as useful. So we're ready?'

'Yes.'

'Fine! Roger, we expect you to make your dramatic entrance in ten minutes. S'long.'

'So long, Saint… So long, Betty!'

Roger felt for the girl's hand and give it a reassuring pressure. A moment later he was alone.

The Saint, with one arm round the girl's waist to steady her, picked their way over the uneven ground with the uncanny sure-footedness of a cat. It was dark enough for his clothes to be unnoticeable. He wore Mr Dyson's soft hat pulled well down over his eyes, and he had turned up the collar of his coat to assist the crude disguise. Even before they were near the cottage, he was walking with knees bent and shoulders stooped so as to approximate more to the height of Mr Dyson.

Mr Dyson himself slept peacefully in the Desurio, roped hand and foot and gagged with is own handkerchief.

The Saint was not bothering to take precautions. He felt a thread snap across his chin, and knew he had sprung a trip-alarm, but he went on unabashed. Only the lights in the two windows went out suddenly…

He had no idea where the door of the cottage would be, but his preternaturally keen ears heard it creak open when he was still twenty yards away. Instantly he stopped, and his grip on the girl tightened. She felt his lips brush her ear.

'Now go dead,' he whispered. 'And don't worry. We win this game!'

He stooped quickly, and lifted her into his arms like a child. It seemed as if there was a rustling in the grass around him that was not of the wind; and the Saint grinned invisibly. He moved forward again, with slower steps…

Then, directly in front of him, the darkness was split by a probing finger of light.

The Saint halted.

His coat collar shrouded his chin; the girl he carried helped to cover his body; he lowered his head so that the hat-brim obscured most of his face, and kept his eyes away from the blinding beam of the torch.

There was a second's pause, broken only by the rustling of the grass; and then, from behind the light, a harsh voice spoke – half startled, half relieved.

'Dyson!'

'Who did you think it was?' Simon snapped back hoarsely. 'Put out that light!'

The light winked, and went out. The voice spoke again.

'Why didn't you give the signal?'

'Why should I?'

In the shadowy mass of the cottage, an upright oblong of light was carved out abruptly. That was the door. Just inside, a man was kindling an oil lamp. His back was turned to the Saint.

Simon straightened up, and walked in. He set the girl down on her feet, and in three quick smooth movements he took off his borrowed hat, turned down his collar, and settled his coat. But the man was still busy with the lamp, and the shout came from behind the Saint – from outside the door.

'That's not Dyson!'

The man spun round with a smothered exclamation.

Simon, standing at his elegant ease, was lighting a second cigarette from the stump of his first.

'No, this isn't Dyson, dear heart,' he murmured. 'But, if you remember, I never said it was. I should like to maintain my reputation for truthfulness for a few minutes longer.'

He looked up blandly, waving his match gently in the air to extinguish it, and saw the men crowding in behind him. One – two – three – four … and two of them displaying automatics. Slightly bigger odds than the Saint had seriously expected. Simon Templar's face became extraordinarily mild.

'Well, well, *well!*' he drawled. 'Look at all the flies, Spider – I congratulate you on the collection.'

The man by the lamp took a pace forward. The movement was queerly lopsided – the shuffling forward of one twisted foot, and the dragging of another twisted foot after it. Simon understood at once the origin of the nickname. The man was almost a dwarf, though tremendously broad of shoulder, with short deformed legs and long ape-like arms. In a small wrinkled face, incredibly faded blue eyes blinked under shaggy eyebrows.

'One of these matinée idols we read about,' thought the Saint in his mild way, and felt the girl's shoulder against his.

The man took another slithering step towards them, peering at them crookedly. Then–

'Who are you?' he asked, in that harsh cracked voice.

'His Royal Highness, the Prince What's-it of I-forget-where,' said the Saint. 'And you're Mr Sleat. Pleased to have you meet me. The introductions having been effected, do you curtsy first or do I? I'm afraid I hocked my table of precedence two seasons ago…'

'And this – lady?'

'Miss Betty Aldo. I believe you wanted to see her, so I brought her along. The escort you provided was unfortunately – er – unable to continue the journey. I'm afraid he hit his head on a piece of wood, or something. Anyway, the poor fellow was quite incapacitated, so I thought I'd better take his place.'

The pale eyes stared back horribly.

'So you've met Dyson?'

'"Slinky" – I believe – is what his friends call him. But I call him Dismal Desmond. Yes, I think I can say that we – er – made contact.'

Sleat looked round.

'Close that door.'

Simon saw the door shut and barred.

'Do you know,' he said conversationally, 'when I didn't know you so intimately as this, I used to call you Whiskers. And now I find you've shaved, it's terribly disappointing. However, to talk of pleasanter things–'

'Take them in here.'

'To talk of pleasanter things,' continued the Saint affably, taking Betty's hand and following without protest into the room where the dwarf led the way with the lamp – 'don't you find the air up here very bracing? And we've been having such lovely weather lately. My Auntie Ethel always used to say–'

Sleat turned with a snarl that bared a row of yellow teeth.

'That'll do, for a minute–'

'But I'm not nearly satisfied yet – as the actress said in one of her famous conversations with the bishop,' remarked Simon. 'Like the actress, I want more and more. For instance, what are your favourite indoor sports? Halma, ludo, funny faces–'

Without the least warning, the dwarf reached up and struck him, flat-handed, across the mouth.

Once before in Simon's life a man had dared to do that. And this time, as before, for one blinding second, Simon saw red.

There were two men covering him with automatics, and two men standing by with heavy sticks; but not even a battery of artillery and a land mine would have stopped the Saint in such a mood. His fist had leapt like a cannon-ball from his shoulder before he had consciously aimed the blow.

And the next second he was again as cool as ice, and the dwarf was picking himself off the floor with a trickle of blood running down from his smashed lips. Nobody else had moved.

'A distinct loss of temper,' murmured the Saint regretfully, flicking the ash from his cigarette. 'All the same, I shouldn't do that again if I were you, Beautiful – you might get hurt more next time. A joke's a joke, as Auntie Ethel used to say.'

'You–'

'Hush!' said the Saint. 'Not before the Bible class. They might misunderstand you. And if you want to know why they didn't shoot me, the answer is that they never had the nerve… Isn't that so, honeybunch?'

He swung round on one of the armed men

– and, without the least haste or heat, flicked him under the nose. He saw the man's finger tighten on the trigger, and threw up his hands.

'One moment!' he rapped. 'Hear my speech before you decide to shoot – or you may be sorry later. You, too, my pretty one!'

He turned to crack the warning at Sleat, whose right hand was sneaking down to his hip. There was a blaze of fury in the dwarf's eyes, and for a moment Simon thought he would shoot – without waiting to listen. Simon stood quite still.

'Who are you?' rasped Sleat.

'I am Inspector Maxwell, of Scotland Yard, and I've come to get y–'

Sleat's hand came up, deliberately.

'...your views on the much-disputed question. Why was Bernard Shaw?... And – seriously – I'll advise you to be careful with that popgun, because my men are all round this house, and anyone who's going to get through that cordon will have to be thinner than a lath before breakfast. You can't laugh that off, Rudolph!'

'I've a good mind–'

'To shoot and chance the consequences. I know. But I shouldn't. I shouldn't, really. Because if you do, you'll quite certainly be hanged by the neck until you're so dead that it'll be practically impossible to distinguish you from a corpse. Not that a little more length in the neck would improve your beauty, but the way they do the stretching–'

One of the armed guard cut in savagely: 'Dyson's squealed–'

'It was a good squeak,' said the Saint meditatively, 'as squeaks go. But the sweet pea had no choice. When we started to singe his second ear–'

'You're clever!' grated Sleat.

'Very,' agreed the Saint modestly. 'My Auntie Ethel always said–'

The sentence merged into a thunderous pounding on the outer door, and the Saint broke off with a smile.

'My men are getting anxious about me. It's my fault, for getting so absorbed in this genial chit-chat. But tell me, Spider,' said the Saint persuasively, 'is this or is this not entitled to be called a cop?'

Sleat drew back a pace.

His eyes fled round the room, like the eyes of a hunted animal seeking an avenue of escape. And yet – there was something about the eyes that was not surrendering. Pale, expressionless eyes in a mask-like wrinkled face. Something about the eyes that told Simon, with a weird certainty, that it was not going to be called a cop…

The guard stood like statues. Or like three statues – for the fourth was staring at Simon with a wild intentness.

Sleat's eyes came back to the Saint, palely,

expressionlessly. It was an eerie effect, that sudden paling out of their blaze of fury into a blind cold emptiness. Simon gripped the girl's arm to steady her, and felt her trembling.

'Don't look at me like that!' she mouthed sharply, shakily. 'It's horrible...'

'Bear up, old dear,' encouraged the Saint. 'He can't help it. If you had a face like that–'

Again the thunder on the door.

And Sleat came to life. He motioned back the two armed men of the guard.

'Behind those curtains! You take the girl – you take the man. And if they try to give one word of warning – if you hear them say anything that might have a double meaning – you'll shoot! Understand?'

The men nodded dumbly, moving to obey. Sleat turned to the other two, indicating each in turn with a jerky pointing finger.

'You stay here. You go and open the door. And you–'

He swung round on the Saint.

'You – you heard the orders I gave. They'll be carried out. So you'll dismiss your men, on any excuse you can invent–'

'Shall I, dear angel?'

'You will – unless you want to die where you stand, and the girl with you. If you had been alone, I might have been afraid that your sense of duty might have outweighed your discretion. But you have a – responsibility. I think you will be discreet. Now–'

The Saint heard the unbarring of the outer door, and the measured step of heavy feet. The curtains three yards away from him reached to the floor. They had settled down, and there was nothing to betray the presence of the men behind them. The third man, standing in one corner, was still staring at him.

Sleat's hands, with the automatic, had gone behind him.

Then Roger Conway walked in and saluted, and Simon's face was terribly Saintly.

'Yes, constable?'

'Beg pardon, sir,' said Roger stiffly, 'but your time's up. Sergeant Jones sent me in to see if you were all right.'

'Quite all right, thanks,' said the Saint. 'As a matter of fact–'

And then, out of the tail of his eye, Simon saw a strange light dawn in the face of the third man, the man in the corner, the man who had been staring.

'Boss–'

Sleat craned round at the exclamation, with a malignant threat in his face that should have silenced the man. But the man was not silenced. He was pointing at the Saint with a shaking hand.

'Boss, dat ain't no bull! De foist time I see him was when he stuck up de Paradiso, back of Nassau Street, in Noo Yoik, four years back. Dat guy wid de goil's de Saint!'

Sleat spun back with his gun hand leaping into view, but the Saint's hands were high in the air.

'OK, buddy!' he drawled. 'You take the Memory Prize. Roger, take that hand away from your pocket. There's a whole firing squad got the drop on you at this moment, and they mightn't believe you were only going to produce your birth certificate... Boys and girls, you may take it from me. This is our night out!'

8

Conway saw the gun in Sleat's hand even as the Saint warned him, and his hands went up slowly as he moved over to join the Saint. Then the curtains moved, and the hidden men came out.

'So!' said Sleat harshly. 'I thought you were a fraud from the first words you spoke. I've known a good many busies–'

'And you'll know a lot more before you're finished,' said the Saint equably. 'You've heard of me?'

'I have.'

'Then you'll know I have – friends. Three

of them are outside this house now. Unless you leave as my prisoners, you'll never pass them. They'll stalk you over the moor, in the dark, and take you one by one. Not one of you will reach the road alive. Those were my orders. You can smile at that one, sonny boy!'

'Your men don't kill.'

'They killed Chastel – you've heard of him? And there are others who've never been heard of. And for me they would kill you with as little compunction as they'd kill any other poisonous spider. If you don't believe me, send one of your men outside and see if he comes back.'

It was bluff – blind, desperate bluff. But it was the only card Simon could find in his hand at that moment. At least it gave him a few seconds' respite to think...

Sleat looked at him, his head on one side, as though seeking the first flaw in voice or manner. But the Saint stood as coldly solid as an iceberg, and his voice was as smooth and hard as polished steel.

'You think they'll obey your orders?' said Sleat.

'In anything.'

The dwarf nodded.

'Then you'll give me a key to let myself out of your trap. It used to be said that the Saint was clever, but it seems that he also makes his mistakes. You will call them in here – please.'

Simon laughed shortly.

'You have a hope!'

'Otherwise... Fetch me a rope, Wells.'

One of the men left the room.

'He's bluffing,' said Roger tensely.

'Of course he is,' murmured the Saint. 'But don't spoil his fun, if it amuses him. A plain man of simple amusements, our Whiskers. He reminds me of–'

'In a moment we shall see who's bluffing,' said Sleat.

He turned as the man came back with a length of rope. Sleat took it and tied it in a short loop.

'Just now,' he said, as he worked, 'you spoke to me of a way of stretching necks. Personally, I prefer to compress them horizontally.'

He tightened his knot carefully. The loop was just big enough to pass over a man's head. He passed it back to the man who had brought it.

'That rope, Wells, and the poker. You understand the principle of the garotte?... You put the loop round the man's neck, put the poker through the loop, and twist so that the rope tightens slowly. Very slowly, you understand, Wells... No–'

He broke off, and a gleam of venomous ferocity came into his faded eyes.

'No,' said Sleat. 'I made a mistake. Not

round the man's neck. Round the girl's.'

Roger started forward, and instantly an armed man barred his way menacingly. Conway, helpless before the automatic that drove into his chest, raved like a maniac: 'You filthy scum–'

'My shout, Roger!'

The Saint's voice came very quietly. A stick of dynamite may also be quiet for a long time.

Simon was facing Sleat.

'I admit the argument. And the answer is – there's no one outside. That's the truth.'

'I see – another bluff!'

'We don't get you, Funny Face.'

'Was his face as funny as that before you hit him?' asked Roger insultingly.

'No,' said the Saint. 'Before that, it was a tragedy.'

Sleat stepped forward, his face contorted in a spasm of rage. The Saint thought for a second that Sleat was going to strike him again, and braced himself for the shock; but with a tremendous effort the man controlled himself.

'I could deal with your humour more comfortably, Templar,' he said malevolently, 'if you were tied up. Some more rope, Wells.'

'Another of these brave men,' snapped Roger.

The Saint smiled. There had never been a time when the Saint could not smile.

'He's got a weak heart,' said the Saint, 'and his grandmother told him never to leave off his woollen drawers and never to risk the shock of being hit back. He forgot it just now, and he might have been killed. Wouldn't that have been dreadful?'

Then the man came back, this time with a great coil of rope over his arm. Two of the others seized the Saint.

'Search him,' said Sleat, 'and tie him up.'

The Saint was searched, but he had no fear of that. He never carried such obvious things as firearms – only the two little knives which he could throw with such supernatural skill. And they were where only one who knew the secret would ever have dreamed of searching – Anna, his favourite, in a sheath strapped to his left forearm, and Belle, the second, in a similar sheath strapped to his right calf under his sock.

Then they brought up a chair, and he sat down willingly. To have struggled would have been simply a useless waste of energy. They bound his hands behind his back, and roped his ankles to the legs of the chair. Simon encouraged them.

'This is the twenty-seventh time I've been tied up like this,' he said pleasantly, 'and every time I've got away somehow. Just like the hero of numberless hectic adventures in a storybook. But don't let that depress you. Just try and do better than your predecessors ... I'm afraid, though, your technique rather reminds me of the technique of the twenty-second man who did this. I called him Halfred the Hideous, and Auntie Ethel never took very kindly to him, either. He died, unhappily. I had to push him off the top of the house a few hours later. He fell into the orchard, and next season all the trees grew blood oranges...'

The Saint's voice was as calm as if he had been discussing the following day's racecard, and as cheerfully optimistic as if he had been discussing it in the spirit of having collected a packet over a twenty-to-one winner that afternoon. He did it, as much as anything, to lighten the hearts of the others – and particularly the girl's. But he would probably have behaved in the same way, for his own entertainment, if he had been alone. The Saint never believed in getting all hot under the collar about anything. It was so bad for the smartness of the collar...

Sleat stood by the wall in silence, his automatic in his hand. His fury had settled down into something horribly soft and deadly, like gently simmering vitriol. To anyone less reckless than the Saint, that sudden restraint might have been more paralysing to the tongue than any show of violence. Even Simon felt a chilly tingle slide up his spine like the touch of a clammy hand, and smiled more seraphically than ever.

Sleat spoke.

'Now the other man.'

'Roger–'

The girl's control broke for an instant, in that involuntary cry. Conway, forced into a chair like the Saint, with the men rapidly pinioning his arms and legs, answered her urgently: 'Don't worry, darling. These blistered rats can't do anything I care about. And when I get near that misshapen blot on the landscape, over by that wall, I'll–'

'You shall have the job of killing him, Roger,' said the Saint dispassionately. 'I promise you that. And I should recommend a sharply-pointed barge-pole. You wouldn't want to touch the skunk with anything shorter.'

The girl stifled a sob. She was white and shaking.

'But what are they going to do?'

'Nothing,' said Roger brusquely.

Sleat put his automatic away in his pocket.

'Now the girl,' he said.

Roger strained at his bonds in agony.

'You're even afraid of her, are you?' he blazed. 'That's sensible of you! Newborn babies would be about your fighting mark, you white-livered–'

'Why get excited, son?' Simon's voice drawled in. 'You'll only scare the girl.

Whereas there's really nothing–'

'All right, boss.'

Wells spoke. The roping was finished.

Sleat moved twistedly off the wall. 'Pale blue eyes,' thought the Saint. 'Pale blue eyes. All ruthless men – murderers and great generals – have them. This is our evening!' And Sleat picked up his loop of rope from the floor where it had fallen, and shuffled forward again.

He halted in front of the Saint.

'You are the professional humorist of the party, I believe, Templar?' he said, and his cracked voice was high-pitched and uneven.

Simon looked him steadily in the eyes.

'Quite right,' he said. 'At least, that's my reputation. And you're the monstrosity from the touring menagerie, aren't you? Let me know when you're ready to start your turn.'

Then he saw what was going to happen, and his voice ripped out again in a desperate command.

'Don't look, Betty! Whiskers is going to make one of his funny faces, and you might die laughing!'

'I dislike your kind of humour,' said Sleat, in the same tone as before, and swung the loose end of the rope.

The girl screamed once, and closed her eyes.

Roger swore foully, impotently.

Sleat babbled: '...that ... and that ... and that ... and that ... and that!' He paused, panting. 'And if you've any more humorous remarks to make, Templar–'

'Only,' said the Saint, with nothing but the least tremor in his voice, 'that my Auntie Ethel had a very good joke about an incorrigible bimetallist of Salt Lake City whose hobby was collecting freaks. He was quite happy until one day he noticed that all pigs had short curly tails. He went quite mad, and wore himself to a shadow touring all the pig-farms in the States looking for a pig with a long straight tail. For all I know, he's searching still, and it occurred to me that perhaps your tail–'

Sleat, with the face of a fiend, lifted his rope's end again.

'Then you can add that ... and that...'

It was Roger who interrupted, with an unprintable profanity which, for some reason, found its mark.

The dwarf turned on him.

'Another humorist?' he sneered. 'Then–'

He struck once, twice...

'You fool!' sobbed the girl hysterically. 'That won't help you! There aren't any men outside, I tell you–'

Sleat paused with his hand raised again – and slowly lowered it. And as slowly as that slow movement, the flush of madness froze under the surface of his face, leaving it grey and twitching.

'There aren't any men outside,' he muttered. 'That's what I wanted to be sure about, in case he was trying to make me walk out into a trap. But there aren't any men outside...'

He dropped the rope.

'Oh, Roger – Saint–'

The girl was sobbing weakly in her chair.

Conway called to her, insistently: 'Don't cry, dear – don't cry, please! It'll only make that walking ulcer think he's won. I'm not hurt. Don't cry!'

'You beasts – you beasts!'

Sleat shambled over to her and tilted back her head brutally.

'How did they come here?' he demanded.

'In a car – it's by the road – and your man's in it–'

'You little fool!' broke in the Saint's bitter voice. 'You're smashing the game to glory! Why don't you go down on your knees and beg the scab to spare us? That'd finish it splendidly.'

Sleat turned.

'Unless you want some more rope, Templar–'

'Thanks,' said the Saint clearly, with his head held high and the blood running down to stain his collar – 'that hurts me a lot less than the thought of all the clean mud you must have soiled by crawling through it.'

The dwarf lifted his hand; and then he mastered himself.

'I know all I want to know,' he said. 'And I have things to attend to at once.'

'Disposing of the body of Sebastian Aldo, for instance?' suggested the Saint insolently.

'Yes – I shall do that at the same time as I dispose of yours.'

'So he's dead?' said Roger.

'He died of heart failure.'

'When he saw you, I suppose?'

The girl said: 'You cowards! You murdered him–'

'I said he died of heart failure,' snarled the dwarf. 'Why should I trouble to lie, when none of you will ever be able to use anything I tell you? The shock killed him.'

'That is sufficient for me,' said the Saint. 'For that alone I shall be justified in ordering your execution. And the sentence will be carried out.'

Sleat shook his head. His eyes shifted over to the Saint, and a slow malevolent leer came into his wrinkled face.

'You will order nothing,' he said.

Only the dim yellow light of the oil lamp on the table illuminated that macabre scene. The four guards stood motionless around the walls. Simon, Roger and Betty, in their chairs, were ranged in a rough crescent. In the centre of the room stood Sleat, with a queer light flickering in his pale eyes, and his face twisted and ghoulish.

There was a moment's silence.

Conway sat grimly still. His face was white, save for two thick red weals that ran across either cheek, and behind his eyes burned a dull fire. He looked at the Saint, and saw the Saint's head thrown back with its old unconquerable mocking arrogance, and the Saint's face bruised and bloody. He looked at the girl, and met her eyes. Her quick breathing was then the only sound in that moment's silence.

'I warn you,' said the Saint clearly, 'that whatever you do – whether you fly to the end of the world, or hide yourself at the bottom of the sea – my friends will follow you and find you. And you will die.'

Again Sleat shook his head. It was like the wagging of the head of a grotesque doll.

'You will order nothing,' he repeated. 'Because you – and these two friends of yours – will die – tonight.'

A window rattled in the wind, and the flame of the lamp flickered like a tired soul.

9

The Saint felt the atmosphere weighing down as if with a tense, dark evil heaviness. And he laughed the laugh of a boy, and shattered that evil cloud with a breath.

'Very dramatic!' he mocked, in a voice that slipped through that murky room like a shaft of sunlight. 'But a shade theatrical, my pet. Never mind. We don't object to sharing your simple fun. That infectious gaiety is the most charming thing about you. And after Roger's killed you, I shall commemorate it in a snappy little epitaph which I've just made up. It's all about "a handsome young hero named Sleat, whose pleasures were simple but sweet. He'd be happy for hours just gathering flowers, or removing his whiskers with Veet." That ought to look well in marble…'

'With a memorial statue over a refuse heap,' added Roger.

Sleat leered and shuffled away.

He went into one corner, and dragged aside a box that stood there. Stooping, he picked up what looked like two ends of black cord, and came a little forward again, trailing them behind him.

'I've been to prison once,' he said, 'and I swore then that I'd never be taken again. I prepared this place so that if the police ever came here I could blow them all to blazes – and myself with them. You see these fuses?'

No one answered.

'This one – marked with a piece of thread – is fast. It burns in about three seconds. The other is slow. It should burn for about eight minutes. And under this floor there are twenty pounds of dynamite. In the next room' – the vacant eyes focused on the girl – 'is your uncle. He is dead. You will soon join him. And there will be no trace – nothing but a crater in the moor – in eight minutes' time. I light the slow fuse, you understand...'

The eyes moved along the short line of bound figures, studied, with a ghastly delight, the girl, sitting numbed with horror, and the two men, sitting erect and unflinching.

'The slow fuse,' said Sleat harshly. 'I don't want to blow myself up as well. So you will have a little leisure in which to meditate your folly. I shall hear the explosion as I drive away, and I shall laugh...'

He laughed then, a short raucous cackle.

'So easy,' he said, 'and so quick, after the first eight minutes. Some matches, Wells... And you may go. You may all go. Find his car, and wait for me with it on the road ... I light the slow fuse–'

The match was sizzling up between his fingers as the men filed out. He touched the match to the fuse, and blew on the glowing end so that it shone like a tiny glow-worm. He held it up.

'You see?' he cackled. 'I've lighted the fuse!'

'Yes,' said Simon mechanically, 'you've lighted the fuse!'

And, now that there was no longer anyone behind him, the Saint was reaching his bound hands down and round behind the chair, twisting them till the cords ate into his wrists. It was impossible to reach the knife on his leg; but if he could only loosen the ropes on his wrists sufficiently – the merest trifle would do – enough to enable the fingers of his right hand to reach the hilt of the little knife on his left forearm...

Sleat dropped the lighted fuse and came over to the Saint. He thrust his face down to within a few inches of Simon's.

'And you die!' he gloated. 'While I go and collect the diamonds for which I gave seven years of my life. You knew about the diamonds?... I thought you did. You know too much, my friend. And you are too funny–'

He lashed out at the Saint's face, but Simon dropped his head and took the blow on his forehead. Sleat did not seem to notice it. He turned to the girl, and took her face between his hands.

'You are beautiful,' he said, and she looked him in the eyes.

'I'm not afraid of you,' she flashed back.

'It is a pity that you should die with your beauty,' said the dwarf, in the same unemotional way. 'But you are like the others – you know too much. So I bid you farewell – like this–'

He bent suddenly and kissed her full on the mouth; and Roger Conway's chair creaked with his mad struggling.

'You disgusting blot! You foul, slimy crawling–'

Sleat let go the girl and shuffled across to him.

'As for you,' he croaked, 'you also know too much. And you also are too funny. I bid *you* farewell – like this–'

His fist struck Roger on the mouth, half stunning him; but through a reeling red haze Roger heard the Saint's voice ring out like the voice of a trumpet.

'Wait, Sleat! You lose!'

Sleat limped round. And the glowing end of the fuse was stealing across the bare floor like the eye of a retreating worm.

'Why do I lose?'

'Because you do,' taunted the Saint. 'Why? I'll tell you in about six minutes – just before the fuse blows up. You'll have the satisfaction of knowing, before you die with us!'

To Roger it was all like a nightmare, from which he could have believed that he would wake up in a moment – if it had not been for the pain which racked his face from brow to chin. He could only guess what the Saint must have been suffering, for Simon had never shown it by the flicker of an eyelid.

The atom of red light seemed to be racing across the floor at lightning speed. Unless Sleat had underestimated the length of his fuse – or unless there was more of it concealed under the boards–

He could see the Saint's hands, behind his chair. The Saint was wrestling with his wrists, but Roger could not see the knife. The Saint's fingers were in his left sleeve, groping and straining, but nothing seemed to happen.

Then Roger saw the Saint's fingers stop moving – saw the Saint's fingers relax and his hands sink limply down behind his back – and understood.

The Saint could not reach his knife.

For once the trick had failed. The ropes had been tied too tightly, or else the knife had slipped round...

And the Saintly smile had never been sweeter.

'Why do I lose?' asked Sleat again.

'Wouldn't you like to know?' jeered the Saint.

Sleat's face convulsed with a spasm of

rage. He stared about him, and saw the discarded piece of rope. He started to move towards it.

'And if you think that'll help you,' came Simon's voice steadily, 'you've got another guess due, sweetheart. Torture doesn't make me whine. You ought to have found that out–'

The smouldering end of the fuse was only a few inches from the hole in the floor. Four inches, at the most … three…

Roger's head swam. The Saint could only be doing one thing. His trump card had been snatched from him, and he was taking the only revenge that was left. To waste time, distract Sleat's attention – to take Sleat with them into eternity…

Roger shouted. He knew he was shouting, because he heard his own voice like the voice of another man across an infinite emptiness. He shouted: 'Betty–'

Her answer came to him as from a vast distance. There was nothing real – nothing. And the glow-worm was slipping into the hole in the floor.

'Why can't you hold me?' sobbed the girl pitifully.

Roger groaned.

'I can't,' he said in a whisper. 'I can't. They've tied me too tight. I can't move. My dear–'

A few feet away, on the other side of the

earth, he saw her. And he saw Spider Sleat, moving with what seemed to be an unbelievable slowness, picking up the rope. And he saw the Saint smiling his indomitable smile.

And again the shaft of sunlight, that was the Saint's voice, leapt through the air. And this time it seemed to fall on a bright banner of triumph.

'You're too late!' cried the Saint. 'It's too late even for torture – because you can't put out the fuse! It's gone. It's been gone for a minute now. You can't reach it unless you tear up the floor – and you haven't the time for that. You've less than four minutes–'

And the Saint's heart was singing with a wild hope.

It was true – Roger's surmise had been right at first. The Saint had been playing for time, fighting to make Sleat forget the lighting of the fuse and the flight of time, with the grim intention of keeping Sleat there to be hurled with his victims into the black sky. He had played for time – but he had won.

He had seen a way out. The wraith of a chance, but–

'About three minutes now, I should say, Sleat. And you'll never see your diamonds. I'll tell you that, dear one!'

Sleat's lips curled back in a dreadful grimace.

'The diamonds–'

'I found them. I dug them up before I came here. Did you think I'd be such a fool as to forget that? They're where you'll never find them – not if you hunt for the rest of your days. And three minutes isn't enough to make me talk – even if you dared stay to try–'

Sleat was at the hole in the floor. His hand was through it. He was trying to force in his arm, but the aperture was far too small. He was scrabbling at the boards with the nails of his other hand, but the boards were fast.

It was a gruesome sight. The man was blubbering and slavering at the mouth like an animal.

'It's no good, Sleat,' the Saint mocked him. 'You've left it too long. You can't reach the fuse – you can't stop the balloon going up – and you'll go with it unless you're quick! But you'll never see those diamonds. Unless…'

Sleat writhed more madly, and then for a moment he lay still, huddled on the floor. Then he drew his hand out of the hole and crawled slowly up on his knees. His eyes seemed blank and sightless.

'Unless what?' he uttered.

Not for a second did the Saint pause, for he recognized the cunning of Sleat's madness. The slightest faltering would have been fatal, but the Saint did not falter. He played his card – the card which had been sent to him out of the blue by whatever beneficent deity guarded him in all his ways – the wildest, most inspired bluff of his career – and played it without batting an eyelid, as casually as he might have gambled a bluff in a poker game with a quarter limit.

'Unless you cut us loose, and get us away from here, in two and a half minutes,' said the Saint steadily.

10

Roger heard the words, and his brain throbbed crazily. He understood – he understood at once – but... Surely the Saint couldn't – the Saint couldn't possibly be betting on such a barefaced bluff! Even if it was their only chance, the Saint couldn't imagine that Sleat would fall for a lie like that!

And an observer with a stop-watch would have noted that there was a silence of fifteen seconds, but to Roger Conway it seemed like fifteen minutes.

Roger thought, in his nightmare: 'He might bring it off. He might bring it off. Only the Saint could do it, but he might bring it off. He's got Sleat half demented.

That was done at the beginning, and the man must be almost insane, anyway. And since he lighted the fuse, the Saint's never stopped baiting him, tantalizing him, making stinging rings round him like a wasp round a mad bull. He might have got Sleat hazed enough to fall. He might bring it off…

And Sleat was getting up.

And again the wasp stung.

'Seven years of your life!' it gibed. 'And a lot of good it's done you, beloved – when you've just arranged to kill the only man who could ever have taken you to your diamonds. Smoke! I'd give a pile for the rest of the boys to be able to hear that funny story. Another two minutes, pretty Sleating, and… Oh, isn't it rich? I ask you – if you've got a sense of humour – isn't it rich?'

And the Saint laughed, as if he hadn't a care in the world – as if they were all a thousand miles away from a land mine that was timed to smithereen them out of life in one hundred and twenty seconds.

Roger thought: 'He might have brought it off, but he's left it too late now. He hasn't a hope in hell–'

Then he saw Sleat's face working, saw it with a startling clarity, as if through a powerful lens, saw the trembling eyelids and the thin trickle of saliva running down from the corner of his mouth, saw–

Saw Sleat jerk a clasp-knife from his pocket and fling himself at the Saint's chair.

Sleat was mad. He must have been. The Saint's barbed taunts, on top of the belief that the Saint had really taken the diamonds and alone knew where they were hidden, must have snapped the last withered shred of reason in his brain. Otherwise Sleat would never have bought the joke. Otherwise Sleat would never have dared take the risk.

If he had been in his senses, he would have known that he hadn't a chance of cutting the Saint free and guarding himself at the same time – even with a gun in his other hand – when his guard had been sent out of hearing. Or did he, in his madness, which the Saint had played on with such a superb touch, think that he could achieve the impossible?

The girl, and Roger, and Simon himself, knew that they would never know.

But the Saint's hands were free, and the Saint's right hand was flying to his left sleeve, and Sleat was freeing the Saint's right foot. And the Saint's right foot was free. And Sleat, on his knees in front of the chair, was hacking wildly at the ropes that held the Saint's left ankle. The Saint's left foot was...

Simon jerked back his right foot, and sent it forward again. The girl gasped.

And, Sleat, overbalanced and almost knocked out by the kick, was groping blindly for his gun, which he had dropped, when the Saint kicked it aside and snatched it up.

Roger's breath came through his teeth in one long sigh.

The Saint's knife was out, and he was beside Conway's chair. Three swift slashes of the razor-keen blade, and Roger rose to his feet, free, as the dwarf came at them with clawing fingers.

'Yours, partner,' drawled the Saint, as if they were playing a friendly game of tennis, and reached the girl's side in two steps.

The cords fell away in a moment; and, as she came stiffly to her feet, the Saint took her arm and hustled her out of the room. The outer door stood open, and the Saint pointed straight ahead across the dark moor.

'Carry on, old dear,' he said. 'We'll catch you up in the dip in about one and a half shakes.'

'But Roger–'

Simon showed his teeth.

'Roger's killing a man,' he said, 'and he never looks his best when he's doing that sort of thing. You oughtn't to see it, for the sake of the romance. But I'll fetch him right along. See you in a minute, kid.'

Then she was gone.

The Saint went back, and went straight through the room they had left to the room that opened off it. There was a man on the bed, and he did not stir when the Saint came in. Simon folded him in a blanket, and carried him out.

Roger was climbing shakily to his feet.

'Who's that?' he asked huskily.

'Uncle Sebastian.' Simon glanced at the thing in the corner. 'Is he–'

Conway passed a hand across his eyes.

'Yes. I killed him.'

Simon looked into Roger's face, and saw the grim reaction there. He spoke for commonplace comfort.

'Careless of you, now I come to think of it,' he remarked lightly. 'It means we'll have to look for the diamonds. Still – we can't stop to weep here. Let's go!'

They went quickly, stumbling over tufts and hummocks in the darkness. Even the Saint, with his instinctive sense of country, tripped once and fell to one knee; but he was up again almost without a check.

A shadow loomed up in the obscurity.

'Is that you?'

Betty's voice.

'This is we,' answered the Saint grammatically, and walked down into the hollow.

Roger was beside him no longer as he laid down his burden.

'If I may interrupt,' said the Saint

apologetically, 'I should advise you to lie down, cover your heads, shut your mouths, and stop your ears. If you can do all that in each other's arms, so much the better; but there's some disturbance about due–'

And as he finished speaking, the earth seemed to billow shudderingly under them, like a giant in torment; and with that the giant roared with pain, with a voice like a hundred thunders. And in front of them the darkness was split with a flash of amethyst fire; and it seemed as if a colossal black mushroom blotted out the cowering stars as the echoes of the detonation rang from end to end of the sky.

Then the black mushroom became a cloud, and the cloud burst in a torrent of pelting black rain.

Some seconds later the Saint scrambled to his feet and tried to shake the earth off his clothes.

'Some balloon, you quiet fellow, some balloon,' he murmured appreciatively. 'If we'd been in that, I reckon we should just about be on our way down.'

They went on with their own thoughts, the Saint with his load, and Roger's arm about the girl's waist.

After a while Simon stopped, and they stopped with him. He was peering into the blackness at something they could not see. Then he bent slowly, and when he straightened up again there was nothing in his arms.

He touched Roger on the shoulder.

'Sorry to interrupt again,' he said softly, 'but between us and the car there are some specimens I promised to take home for Chief Inspector Teal. If you'll just wait here a sec, I'll ripple over and complete the bag.'

He disappeared as silently and swiftly as a hunting panther.

The four men, with Mr Dyson, were standing in a little group by the car, talking in low voices, when the Saint came towards them in the starlight with Sleat's automatic in his hand.

Simon hated firearms, as has been related, but in the circumstances…

'Good evening,' he remarked affably.

Silence fell on the group like a pall. Then, slowly and fearfully, they turned and saw him only a couple of yards away.

Shrilly, one man blasphemed. The others were mute, staring, dumb with a superstitious terror. And the Saint smiled like an angel through the dried blood on his face.

'I am the ghost of Julius Caesar,' he said sepulchrally, 'and unless you all immediately put up your hands, I shall turn you into little frogs.'

He came a little nearer, so that they could see him more plainly. And slowly their hands went up. Whatever doubts they might have had of his reality, the gun he displayed was real enough. But the fear of death was in their faces.

Then the laughter faded from Simon's eyes, leaving them bleak and merciless.

'You were accessories to torture,' he said, 'and you might well have been accessories to murder. Therefore in due course you will go to prison according to the law. But when you come out – in about three years, I should say – you will remember this night, and you will tell your friends. Let it help to teach you that the Saint cannot be beaten. But if I meet you again–'

He paused for a moment.

'If I meet you again,' he said, and waved one hand towards the moor, 'you may go to the place where your leader has already gone. I dislike your kind…

'Meanwhile,' said the Saint, 'you may step forward one by one and take off your coats and braces, keeping up your trousers by faith and hope. Move!'

While his apparently eccentric commands were being carried out, he called Roger and directed him. One by one, the men's braces were used to fasten their hands securely behind their backs, and their coats, knotted by the sleeves, hobbled to their legs.

'Not a bad day's work,' said the Saint, when it was done, 'but–'

Roger shot a quick glance of comprehension at him, and the girl's hand went out.

'I'd forgotten, old boy–'

'A good day's work, but tough,' said the Saint weakly, and leaned against the car.

Conway drove them back.

The prisoners were decanted at the police station in Torquay, there to await the morrow and the pleasure of Inspector Teal. There followed a call on a sympathetic physician on the road to St Marychurch. Finally, they were at the Golden Eagle Hotel, with the Saint clamouring for beer.

The manageress was still waiting up.

'Mr Conway–'

'Miss Cocker.'

'I thought… Why, whatever–'

'No, indeed to goodness,' said Roger. 'If I have to tell that story again tonight, I shall scream.'

'And I shall burst into tears and ask to be taken away,' said the Saint, sinking into the first chair he encountered. 'The blithering idiots at the police station nearly sent me pots with their fool questions. I'm still wondering how we persuaded them not to lock us up as well. Fetch me some beer, somebody, for the love of Mike!'

It took some time to convince the manageress that the Saint had recovered sufficiently to be allowed a drink, but it was done. Simon made a quart look like a gill in hot weather, and then he rose to his feet with a yawn.

'Roger,' he said, 'if you'll hurry up and tuck Betty into bed, we'll go.'

Roger stared. Roger said:

'Go?'

'Go,' said the Saint. 'You know. The opposite of "come". There's something I particularly want to do tonight.'

'As the bishop said to the actress,' murmured the girl.

Gravely the Saint regarded her. Then–

'Betty, old girl,' he said, 'you'll do. I shall allow Roger to fall in love with you if he wants to. Those seven words prove you One of Us. I may say that for a girl who's been through all you've been through tonight–'

'But,' said Roger, 'you don't mean to go on to Newton Abbot now?'

Simon turned.

'When else?' he demanded. 'Teal's due tomorrow. Anyhow, we couldn't assault that garden with spades in broad daylight, looking like retired coalminers on a busman's holiday, when the place is supposed to be closed down. It's tonight or never, son – and I feel we've earned those diamonds. Forty-five thousand to charity, and the odd ten per cent fee for collection – which is one thousand one hundred and fifty pounds apiece – to Dicky Tremayne, Norman Kent, you and me. What pride glory?'

Now, it should be recorded that at exactly 4.17 am that morning, the Saint's spade struck upon something hard yet yielding, and his hail brought Roger across the garden at a run. Together they opened the soft leather bag, and examined the stones in the light of a torch.

At exactly 4.19 am, their own light was eclipsed by another that leapt on them from out of the darkness, and a familiar voice said: 'This is early for you to be up, Mr Templar.'

The Saint closed the bag and rose from the ground with a sigh.

'Late,' he said, 'is what you mean. Teal, you have an admirable faculty for being on the spot.'

'I couldn't wait,' said Chief Inspector Teal slumbrously. 'I was kept awake wondering what you boys were up to. So I got out my car and came right down. Let's go into the house and have a chat.'

'Yes, let's,' said the Saint without enthusiasm.

They went into the house, and Simon had to fight his battle over again. Teal listened – he was a good listener – champing his favourite sweetmeat monotonously. He did not interrupt until the end of the story.

'And what happened to Sleat?'

Simon looked him in the eyes.

'When he saw Roger properly,' he said, 'Sleat was so overcome by Roger's beauty that he had a heart attack, and died all over the place. It was most distressing. However, we hadn't time to remove him, so he went up with the balloon, and all you're likely to find of him is his boots and his back stud. Sorry, I'm sure. It'll be difficult for the coroner.'

Teal nodded like a mandarin.

'I believe you,' he said sleepily. 'Thousands wouldn't, but I will. There's no evidence.'

'No,' said the Saint comfortably. 'There's no evidence.'

Teal got to his feet mountainously, and looked out of the window. The first wan silver of dawn was in the sky.

'I think,' he said, 'we might go over to Mr Conway's hotel and see if we can find some early breakfast.'

And further, as a matter of history, which the Press has had no opportunity to record, it should be noted that Teal himself, in the Saint's company, deposited the bag of diamonds at the police station in Exeter, at the same time as he transferred the Saint's prisoners there to await their trial at the next assizes, the following afternoon.

'You're not going back today?' asked the Saint solicitously.

'Not until tomorrow,' said Teal grimly. 'That's why it occurred to me to leave the diamonds here. If I kept them at the Golden Eagle, you boys might sleepwalk. I'm going to ask your Mr Conway if I can keep my room on for tonight – there's the explosion to investigate, and one or two other details I must get. I hope it won't inconvenience anyone.'

'We shall be delighted,' said the Saint truthfully.

At precisely 9 am the following morning, a man in the uniform of the Metropolitan Police marched smartly into Exeter Police Station.

'Detective-Constable Hawkins, of Scotland Yard,' he reported to the inspector. 'I came down with Mr Teal the night before last on the Policeman case. He's just sent me over to fetch the diamonds he left here and meet him at the railway station.'

'Have you an order?'

The policeman produced a paper. The inspector read it; and then he opened his safe and handed over the bag.

'Better take care of it,' he advised. 'It's supposed to be worth fifty thousand pounds.'

'Blimey!' said the policeman, in understandable awe.

The following morning, Simon Templar was holding a breakfast party when Chief Inspector Teal was admitted.

'Have an egg,' invited the Saint hospitably.

'In fact, have two eggs. Don't go, Orace – we may want you.'

Teal sank into a chair and unwrapped a fresh wafer of gum.

'I'll have some diamonds,' he said.

'Sorry,' said the Saint, 'but Hatton Garden is still where it was, and Brook Street remains free of the sordid commerce. You must have got on the wrong 'bus.'

'Your friend Mr Conway–'

'Has temporarily left us. He's met a girl. You know what these young men are. But if there's any message I can give him–'

'You two are supposed to have come up to London on Friday night, aren't you?' said Teal sluggishly.

Simon raised his eyebrows.

'Why "supposed"?' he demanded innocently.

'Does anyone else know it except yourselves?'

The Saint leaned back in his chair.

'At eight ack emma on Saturday morning, yesterday,' he said, 'a party of us breakfasted here together. That is a ceremony which we observe religiously on every fourth anniversary of the death of Sir Richard Arkwright. After breakfast, we walk out in straw hats and football boots, and go and sail paper boats in the Round Pond. That's part of the ceremony.'

'Yes?' prompted the torpid Mr Teal.

'At this breakfast,' said the Saint, 'there were present Mr Conway and Miss Aldo, who aren't here today to answer for themselves, and also those whom you see repeating the performance this morning – Miss Patricia Holm and Mr Richard Tremayne. Orace served us. You ask them if that isn't true.'

'I see,' said Mr Teal, as if he didn't see at all.

'Therefore,' said the Saint speciously, 'we couldn't possibly have been in Exeter at nine o'clock on Saturday morning, which I understand is the time when the mysterious policeman removed the swag from the police station with a forged order.'

'How did you know about that?' asked Teal, quickly for him.

'About what?'

'About the policeman taking the diamonds.'

'Why,' said the Saint indignantly, 'I never said anything about a policeman or about the diamonds. Did I, Pat?… Did I, Dicky?… Did I, Orace?…'

Solemnly the three persons appealed to shook their heads.

'There!' said the Saint. 'You must be dreaming, Teal!'

Very slowly, Chief Inspector Teal inclined his head.

'I see,' he said, in his monumentally tired

way – 'I see. The technical name for that is an alibi.'

'Do we call it a day, Teal?' said the Saint insinuatingly.

Mr Teal's jaws continued to oscillate rhythmically, and his round head had not stopped nodding. He seemed, as he always did at such moments, on the point of falling off to sleep from sheer boredom.

'It's a day,' said Mr Teal wearily. 'It's a day!'

THE LAWLESS LADY

1

For a lawbreaker, in the midst of his law-breaking, to be attempting at the same time to carry on a feud with a Chief Inspector of Police, might be called heroically quixotic. It might equally well be called pure blame-foolishness of the most suicidal variety – according to the way you look at these things.

Simon Templar found it vastly entertaining.

Chief Inspector Claud Eustace Teal, of the Criminal Investigation Department, New Scotland Yard, that great detective (and he was nearly as great in mere bulk as he was in reputation) found it an interesting novelty.

Teal was reputed to have the longest memory of any man at the Yard. It was said, perhaps with some exaggeration, that if the Records Office happened to be totally destroyed by fire, Teal could personally have rewritten the entire dossier of every criminal therein recorded, methods, habits, haunts, and notable idiosyncrasies completely included – and added thereto a rough but reliable sketch of every set of fingerprints therewith connected. Certainly, he had a long memory.

He distinctly remembered a mysterious Policeman, whom an enterprising journalist called the Policeman with Wings, who was strangely reincarnated some time after the originator and (normal) patentee of the idea had departed to Heaven – or some other place beginning with the same letter – on top of a pile of dynamite, thereby depriving Teal of the pleasure of handing over to his Commissioner fifty thousand pounds' worth of diamonds which had been lost for seven years.

Mr Teal suspected – not without reason – that Simon Templar's fertile brain had given birth to the denouement of that gentle jest. And Mr Teal's memory was long.

Therefore the secret activities of the Saint came to be somewhat hampered by a number of massive gentlemen in bowler hats, who took to patrolling Brook Street in relays like members of a Scottish clan mounting guard over the spot where their chieftain is sure he had dropped a sixpence.

The day arrived when Simon Templar tired of this gloomy spectacle, and, having nothing else to do, armed himself with a stout stick and sallied forth for a walk, looking as furtive and conspiratorial as he knew how.

He was as fit as a fiddle, and shouting for

exercise. He walked westward through London, and crossed the Thames by Putney Bridge. He left Kingston behind him. Continuing south-west, he took Esher and Cobham in his stride. He walked fast, enjoying himself. Not until he reached Ripley did he pause, and there he swung into a convenient hostel towards six o'clock, after twenty-three brisk miles had been spurned by his Veldtschoen.

The afternoon had been sunny and warm. Simon knocked back a couple of pints of beer as if he felt he had earned every drop of them, smoked a couple of cigarettes, and then started back to the road with a refreshed spring in his step.

On his way out, in another bar, he saw a man with a very red face. The man had a bowler hat on the seat beside him, and he appeared to be melting steadily into a large spotted handkerchief.

Simon approached him like an old friend.

'Are you ready to go on?' he asked. 'I'm making for Guildford next. From there, I make for Winchester, where I shall have dinner, and I expect to sleep in Southampton tonight. At six-thirty tomorrow morning I start for Liverpool, via Land's End. Near Manchester, I expect to murder a mulatto gas-fitter with a false nose. After which, if you care to follow me to John o' Groats–'

The rest of the conversation was conducted on one side at least, in language which might have made a New York stevedore feel slightly shocked.

Simon passed on with a pained expression, and went on his way.

A mile further on, he slowed his pace to a stroll, and was satisfied that Red Face was no longer bringing up the rear. Shortly afterwards, a blue sports saloon swept past him with a rush and stopped a few yards away. As he reached it, a girl leaned out, and Simon greeted her with a smile.

'Hullo, Pat darling,' he said. 'Let's go and have a cocktail and some dinner.'

He climbed in, and Patricia Holm let in the clutch.

'How's the market in bowler hats?' she asked.

'Weakening,' murmured the Saint. 'Weakening, old dear. The bulls weren't equal to the strain. Let's change the subject. Why are you so beautiful, Pat?'

She flung him a dazzling smile.

'Probably,' she said, 'because I find I'm still in love with you – after a whole year. And you're still in love with me. The combination's enough to make anyone beautiful.'

It was late when they got back to London.

At the flat in Brook Street, Roger Conway and Dicky Tremayne were drinking the

Saint's beer.

'There was some for you,' said Roger, 'only we drank it in case it went flat.'

'Thoughtful of you,' said the Saint.

He calmly annexed Mr Conway's tankard, and sank into a chair.

'Well, soaks,' he remarked, 'how was the English countryside looking this afternoon?'

'I took the North Road,' said Roger. 'My little Mary's lamb petered out at St Alban's, and Dicky picked me up just beyond. Twenty-one miles by the clock – in five hours forty-five minutes Fahrenheit. How's that?'

'Out,' said the Saint. 'I did twenty-three miles in five and a half hours dead. My sleuth was removed to hospital on an asbestos stretcher, and when they tried to revive him with brandy he burst into flames. We shall hear more of this.'

Nevertheless, the following morning, Orace, bringing in his master's early tea, reported that a fresh detachment of bowler hats had arrived in Brook Street, and the Saint had to devote his ingenuity to thinking out other means of evading their vigilance.

In the next fortnight, the Saint sent £9,000 to charity, and Inspector Teal, who knew that to obtain that money the Saint must have 'persuaded' someone to write him a cheque for £10,000, from which had been deducted the ten per cent commission which the Saint always claimed according to his rules, was annoyed. His squad, interrogated, were unable to make any suggestions as to the source of the gift. No, Simon Templar had done nothing suspicious. No, he had not been seen visiting or associating with any suspicious characters. No, he–

'You're as much use as so many sick headaches,' said Teal unkindly. 'In fact, less use. You can stop watching that house. It's obviously a waste of your time – not,' he added sweetly, 'that the Department has missed you.'

The climax came a few days later, when a cocaine smuggler whom Teal had been watching for months was at last caught with the goods as he stepped ashore at Dover. Teal, 'acting on information received', snapped the bracelets on his wrists in the Customs House, and personally accompanied the prisoner on the train to London, sitting alone in a reserved compartment with his captive.

He did not know that Simon Templar was on the train until they were fifteen minutes out of Victoria Station, when the Saint calmly walked in and hailed him joyfully.

'Can you read?' asked Teal.

'No,' said the Saint.

Teal pointed to the red labels pasted on the windows.

'R-E-S-E-R-V-E-D,' he spelt out. 'Do you know the word?'

'No,' said the Saint.

He sat down, after one curious glance at the man at Teal's side, and produced a gold cigarette-case.

'I believe I owe you an apology for walking one of your men off his feet a while ago,' he said. 'Really, I think you asked for it, but I'm told you're sore. Can't we kiss and be friends?'

'No,' said Teal.

'Have a cigarette?'

'I don't smoke cigarettes.'

'A cigar, then?'

Teal turned warily.

'I've had some of your jokes,' he said. 'Does this one explode, or is it the kind that blows soot all over your face when you light it?'

Simon handed over the weed. It was unmistakably excellent. Teal wavered, and bit off the end absent-mindedly.

'Maybe I was unreasonable,' he conceded, puffing. 'But *you* asked for something before I ever did. And one day you'll get it. See this bright boy?'

He aimed his cigar at the prisoner, and the Saint nodded.

'I've been after him for the best part of a year. And he's had plenty of laughs off me before I got him. Now it's my turn. It'll be the same with you. I can wait. One day you'll go too far, you'll make a mistake, and–'

'I know that man,' said the Saint.

He looked across the compartment with cold eyes.

'He is a blackmailer and a dealer in drugs. His name is Cyril Farrast, and he is thirty-two years old. He had one previous conviction.'

Teal was surprised, but he concealed it by lowering his eyelids sleepily. He always looked most bored when he was most interested.

'I know all that,' he said. 'But how do you know?'

'I've been looking for him,' said the Saint simply, and the man stared. 'Even now, I still want him. Not for the dope business – I see you're going to take care of that – but for a girl in Yorkshire. There are thousands of stories like it, but this one happened to come to my notice. He'll recognize her name – but does he know who I am?'

'I'll introduce you,' said Teal, and turned to his captive. 'Cyril, this is Mr Simon Templar. You've heard of him. He's known as the Saint.'

The man shrank away in horror, and Simon grinned gently.

'Oh, no,' he drawled. 'That's only Teal's nasty suspicious mind... But if I *were* the Saint, I should want you, Cyril Farrast, because of Elsa Gordon, who committed suicide eleven days ago. I ought to kill you, but Teal has told me to be good. So, instead–'

Farrast was white to the lips. His mouth moved, but no sound came. Then–

'It's a lie!' he screamed. 'You can't touch me–'

Teal pushed him roughly back, and faced the Saint.

'Templar, if you think you're going to do anything funny–'

'I'm sure of it.' Simon glanced at his watch. 'That cigar, for instance, is due to function about now. No explosives, no soot. A much better joke than that…'

Teal was holding the cigar, staring at it. He felt very weak. His head seemed to have been aching for a long time.

With a sudden convulsive effort he pitched the cigar through the window, and his hand began to reach round to his hip pocket. Then he sprawled limply sideways.

A porter woke him at Victoria.

That night there were warrants out for the arrest of Simon Templar and all his friends. But the flat in Brook Street was shut up, and the janitor stated that the owners had gone away for a week – destination unknown.

The Press was not informed. Teal had his pride.

Three days later, a large coffin, labelled

FRAGILE – HANDLE CARELESSLY – ANY OLD SIDE UP, was delivered at New Scotland Yard, addressed to Chief Inspector Teal. When examined, it was heard to tick loudly, and the explosives experts opened it at dead of night in some trepidation in the middle of Hyde Park.

They found a large alarm clock – and Cyril Farrast.

He was bound hand and foot, and gagged. And his bare back showed that he had been terribly flogged.

Also in the coffin was a slip of paper bearing the sign of the Saint. And in a box, carefully preserved in tissue paper and corrugated cardboard, was a cigar.

When Teal arrived home that night he found Simon Templar patiently waiting on his doorstep.

'I got your cigar,' Teal said grimly.

'Smoke it,' said the Saint. 'It's a good one. If you fancy the brand, I'll mail you the rest of the box tomorrow.'

'Come in,' said Teal.

He led the way, and the Saint followed. In the tiny sitting-room, Teal unwrapped the cigar, and the Saint lighted a cigarette.

'Also,' said Teal, 'I've got a warrant for your arrest.'

'And no case to use it on,' said Simon. 'You've got your man back.'

'You flogged him.'

'He's the only man who can bring that charge against me. You can't.'

'If you steal something and send it back, that doesn't dispose of the charge of theft – if we care to prosecute.'

'But you wouldn't,' smiled the Saint, watching Teal light the cigar. 'Frankly, now, between ourselves, would it be worth it? I notice the papers haven't said anything about the affair. That was wise of you. But if you charged me, you couldn't keep it out of the papers. And all England would be laughing over the story of how the great Claud Eustace Teal' – the detective winced – 'was caught on the bend with the old, old doped cigar. Honestly – wouldn't it be better to call it a day?'

Teal frowned, looking straight at the smiling young man before him.

From the hour of his first meeting with the Saint, Teal had recognized an indefinable superiority. It lay in nothing that the Saint did or said. It was simply there. Simon Templar was not common clay; and Teal, who was of the good red earth earthy, realized the fact without resentment.

'Seriously, then, Templar,' said Teal, 'don't you see the hole you put me in? You took Farrast away and flogged him – that remains. And he saw you talking to me in the train. If he liked, he could say in Court that we were secretly aiding and abetting you. The police are in the limelight just now, and a lot of mud would stick.'

'Farrast is dumb,' answered Simon. 'I promise you that. Because I told him that if he breathed a word of what had happened, I should find him and kill him. And he believes it. You see, I appreciated your difficulty.'

Teal could think fast. He nodded.

'You win again,' he said. 'I think the Commissioner'll pass it – this once – since you've sent the man back. But another time–'

'I never repeat myself,' said the Saint. 'That's why you'll never catch me. But thanks, all the same.'

He picked up his hat; but he turned back at the door.

'By the way – has this affair, on top of the diamonds, put you in bad with the Commissioner?'

'I won't deny it.'

The Saint looked at the ceiling.

'I'd like to put that right,' he said. 'Now, there's a receiver of stolen goods living in Notting Hill, named Albert Handers. Most of the big stuff passes through his hands, and I know you've been wanting him for a longish while.'

Teal started.

'How the deuce–'

'Never mind that. If you really want to smooth down the Commissioner, you'll wait for Handers at Croydon Aerodrome tomorrow morning, when he proposes to fly to Amsterdam with the proceeds of the Asheton robbery. The diamonds will be sewn into the carrying handle of his valise. I wonder you've never thought of that, the times you've stopped him and searched him… Night-night, sonny boy!'

He was gone before the plump detective could stop him; and that night the Saint slept again in Brook Street.

But the information which the Saint had given came from Dicky Tremayne, another of the gang, and it signalled the beginning of the end of a coup to which Tremayne had devoted a year of patient preparation.

2

Dicky Tremayne walked into the Saint's flat late one night, and found the Saint in pyjamas. Dicky Tremayne was able to walk in at any hour, because, like Roger Conway, he had his own key. Dicky Tremayne said: 'Saint, I feel I'm going to fall in love.'

The Saint slewed round, raising his eyes to heaven.

'What – not again?' he protested.

'Again,' snapped Dicky. 'It's an infernal

nuisance, but there you are. A man must do something.'

Simon put away his book and reached for a cigarette from the box that stood conveniently open on the table at his elbow.

'Burn it,' said Simon. 'I always thought Archie Sheridan was bad enough. Till he went and got married, I used to spend my spare time wondering why he never got landed. But since you came out of your hermitage, and we let you go and live unchaperoned in Paris–'

'I know,' snapped Dicky. 'I can't help it. But it may be serious this time.'

Match in hand, Simon regarded him.

Norman Kent was the most darkly attractive of the Saints; Archie Sheridan had been the most delightfully irresponsible; Roger Conway was the most good-looking; but Dicky–

Dicky Tremayne was dark and handsome in the clean keen-faced way which is the despairing envy of the Latin, and with it Dicky's elegance had a Continental polish and his eye a wicked Continental gleam. Dicky was what romantic maidens call a sheik – and yet he was unspoiled. Also he had a courage and a cheerfulness which never failed him. The Saint had a very real affection for Dicky.

'Who is it this time, son?' he asked.

Tremayne walked to the window and

stared out.

'Her house in Park Lane was taken in the name of the Countess Anusia Marova,' he said. 'So was the yacht she's chartered for the season. But she was born in Boston, Mass, twenty-three years ago, and her parents called her Audrey Perowne. She's had a lot of names since then, but the Amsterdam police knew her best as "Straight" Audrey. You know who I mean.'

'And you–'

'You know what I've done. I spent all my time in Paris working in with Hilloran, who was her right-hand man in the States, because we were sure they'd get together sooner or later, and then we'd make one killing of the pair. And they *are* together again, and I'm in London as a fully accredited member of the gang. Everything's ready. And now I want to know why we ever bothered.

Simon shrugged.

'Hilloran's name is bad enough, and she's made more money–'

'Why do they call her "Straight" Audrey?'

'Because she's never touched or dealt in dope, which is considered eccentric in a woman crook. And because it's said to be unhealthy to get fresh with her. Apart from that, she's dabbled in pretty well everything–'

Dicky nodded helplessly.

'I know, old man,' he said. 'I know it all. You're going to say that she and Hilloran, to us, were just a pair of crooks who'd made so much out of the game that we decided to make them contribute. We'd never met her. And it isn't as if she were a man–'

'And yet,' said the Saint, 'I remember a woman whom you wanted to kill. And I expect you'd have done it, if she hadn't died of her own accord.'

'She was a–'

'Quite. But you'd've treated her exactly the same as you'd've treated a man engaged in the same traffic.'

'There's nothing like that about Audrey Perowne.'

'You're trying to argue that she's really hardly more of a crook than we are. Her crime record's pretty clean, and the men she's robbed could afford to lose.'

'Isn't that so?'

Simon studied his cigarette-end.

'Once upon a time,' he observed, 'there was a rich man named John L. Morganheim. He died at Palm Beach – mysteriously. And Audrey Perowne was – er – keeping him company. You understand? It had to be hushed up, of course. His family couldn't have a scandal. Still–'

Tremayne went pale.

'We don't know the whole of that story,' he said.

'We don't,' admitted the Saint. 'We only know certain facts. And they mayn't be such thundering good facts, anyhow. But they're there – till we know something better.'

He got to his feet, and laid a hand on Dicky's shoulder.

'Let's have some straight talk, Dicky,' he suggested. 'You're beginning to feel you can't go through with the job. Am I right?'

Tremayne spread out his hands.

'That's about the strength of it. We've got to be sure–'

'Let's be sure, then,' agreed the Saint. 'But meanwhile, what's the harm in carrying on? You can't object to the thrashing of Farrast. You can't feel cut up about the shopping of Handers. And you can't mind what sort of a rise we take out of Hilloran. What we do about the girl can be decided later – when we're sure. Till then, where's the point in chucking in your hand?'

Tremayne looked at him.

'There's sense in that.'

'Of course there's sense in it!' cried the Saint. 'There's more in the gang than one girl. We want the rest. We want them like I want the mug of beer you're going to fetch me in a minute. Why shouldn't we have 'em?'

Dicky nodded slowly.

'I knew you'd say that. But I felt you ought to know…'

Simon clapped him on the back.

'You're a great lad,' he said. 'And now, what about that beer?'

Beer was brought, and tasted with a fitting reverence. The discussion was closed.

With the Saint, momentous things could be brought up, argued, and dismissed like that. With Roger Conway, perhaps, the argument would have been pursued all night – but that was only because Roger and the Saint loved arguing. Dicky was reserved. Rarely did he throw off his reserve and talk long and seriously. The Saint understood, and respected his reticence. Dicky understood also. By passing on so light-heartedly to a cry for beer, the Saint did not lose one iota of the effect of sympathy; rather, he showed that his sympathy was complete.

Dicky could have asked for nothing more; and when he put down his tankard and helped himself to a cigarette, the discussion might never have raised its head between them.

'To resume,' he said, 'we leave on the twenty-ninth.'

Simon glanced at the calendar on the wall.

'Three days,' he murmured. 'And the cargo of billionaires?'

'Complete.' Dicky grinned. 'Saint, you've got to hand it to that girl. Seven of 'em – with their wives. Of course, she's spent a year dry-nursing them. Sir Esdras Levy –

George Y. Ulrig – Matthew Sankin–'

He named four others whose names could be conjured with in the world of high finance.

'It's a peach of an idea.'

'I can't think of anything like it,' said the Saint. 'Seven bloated perambulating gold-mines with diamond studs, and their wives loaded up with enough jewellery to sink a battleship. She gets them off on the rolling wave – knowing they'll have all their sparklers ready to make a show at the ports they touch – on a motor yacht maintained by her own crew–'

'Chief Steward, J. Hilloran–'

'And the first thing the world'll know of it will be when the cargo is found marooned on the Barbary coast, and the *Corsican Maid* has sailed off into the blue with the which-nots... Oh, boy! As a philosophic student, I call that the elephant's tonsils.'

Dicky nodded.

'The day after tomorrow,' he said, 'we leave by special train to join the yacht at Marseilles. You've got to say that girl does her jobs in style.'

'How do you go?'

'As her secretary. But – how do you go?'

'I haven't quite made up my mind yet. Roger's taking a holiday – I guess he deserves it. Norman and Pat are still cruising the Mediterranean. I'll handle this one from the outside alone. I leave the inside to you – and that's the most important part.'

'I mayn't be able to see you again before we leave.'

'Then you'll have to take a chance. But I think I shall also be somewhere on the ocean. If you have to communicate, signal in Morse out of a porthole, with an electric torch, either at midnight or four in the morning. I'll be on the look-out at those times. If…'

They talked for two hours before Tremayne rose to go. He did so at last.

'It's the first real job I've had,' he said. 'I'd like to make it a good one. Wish me luck, Saint!'

Simon held out his hand.

'Sure – you'll pull it off, Dicky. All the best, son. And about that girl–'

'Yes, about that girl,' said Dicky shortly. Then he grinned ruefully. 'Goodnight, old man.'

He went, with a crisp handshake and a frantic smile. He went as he had come, by way of the fire escape at the back of the building, for the Saint's friends had caution thrust upon them in those days.

The Saint watched him go in silence, and remembered that frantic smile after he had gone. Then he lighted another cigarette and smoked it thoughtfully, sitting on the table in the centre of the room. Presently he went to bed.

Dicky Tremayne did not go home to bed at once. He walked round to the side street where he had left his car, and drove to Park Lane.

The lights were still on in an upper window of the house outside which he stopped; and Tremayne entered without hesitation, despite the lateness of the hour, using his own key. The room in which he had seen the lights was on the first floor; it was used as a study and communicated with the Countess Anusia Marova's bedroom. Dicky knocked, and walked in.

'Hullo, Audrey,' he said.

'Make yourself at home,' she said, without looking up.

She was in a rich blue silk kimono and brocade slippers, writing at a desk. The reading lamp at her elbow struck gold from her hair.

There was a cut-glass decanter on the side table, glasses, a siphon, an inlaid cigarette-box. Dicky helped himself to a drink and a cigarette, and sat down where he could see her.

The enthusiastic compilers of the gossip columns in the daily and weekly Press had called her the most beautiful hostess of the season. That in itself would have meant little, seeing that fashionable hostesses are always described as 'beautiful' – like fashionable brides, bridesmaids and débutantes. What, therefore, can it mean to be the most beautiful of such a galaxy?

But in this case something like the truth might well have been told. Audrey Perowne had grave grey eyes and an enchanting mouth. Her skin was soft and fine without the help of beauty parlours. Her colour was her own. And she was tall, with the healthy grace of her kind; and you saw pearls when she smiled.

Dicky feasted his eyes.

She wrote. She stopped writing. She read what she had written, placed the sheet in an envelope, and addressed it. Then she turned.

'Well?'

'I just thought I'd drop in,' said Dicky. 'I saw the lights were on as I came past, so I knew you were up.'

'Did you enjoy your golf?'

Golf was Dicky's alibi. From time to time he went out in the afternoon, saying that he was going to play a round at Sunningdale. Nearly always, he came back late, saying that he had stayed late playing cards at the club. Those were the times when he saw the Saint.

Dicky said that he had enjoyed his golf.

'Give me a cigarette,' she commanded.

He obeyed.

'And a match... Thanks... What's the matter with you, Dicky? I shouldn't have had to ask for that.'

He brought her an ashtray and returned to his seat.

'I'm hanged if I know,' he said. 'Too many late nights, I should think. I feel tired.'

'Hilloran's only just left,' she said, with deceptive inconsequence.

'Has he?'

She nodded.

'I've taken back his key. In future, you'll be the only man who can stroll in here when and how he likes.' Dicky shrugged, not knowing what to say. She added: 'Would you like to live here?'

He was surprised.

'Why? We leave in a couple of days. Even then, it hadn't occurred to me–'

'It's still occurring to Hilloran,' she said, 'even if we are leaving in a couple of days. But you live in a poky little flat in Bayswater, while there are a dozen rooms going to waste here. And it's never occurred to you to suggest moving in?'

'It never entered my head.'

She smiled.

'That's why I like you, Dicky,' she said. 'And it's why I let you keep your key. I'm glad you came tonight.'

'Apart from your natural pleasure at seeing me again – why?'

The girl studied a slim ankle.

'It's my turn to ask questions,' she said. 'And I ask you – why are you a crook, Dicky Tremayne?'

She looked up at him quickly as she spoke, and he met her eyes with an effort.

The blow had fallen. He had seen it coming for months – the day when he would have to account for himself. And he had dreaded it, thought he had his story perfectly prepared. Hilloran had tried to deliver the blow; but Hilloran, shrewd as he was, had been easy. The girl was not easy.

She had never broached the subject before, and Dicky had begun to think that Hilloran's introduction had sufficiently disposed of questions. He had begun to think that the girl was satisfied, without making inquiries of her own. And that delusion was now rudely shattered.

He made a vague gesture.

'I thought you knew,' he said. 'A little trouble in the Guards, followed by the OBE. You know. Order of the Boot – Everywhere. I could either accept the licking, or fight back. I chose to fight back. On the whole it's paid me.'

'What's your name?' she asked suddenly.

He raised his eyebrows.

'Dicky Tremayne.'

'I meant – your real name.'

'Dicky is real enough.'

'And the other?'

'Need we go into that?'

She was still looking at him. Tremayne felt that the grim way in which he was returning her stare was becoming as open to suspicion as shiftiness would have been. He glanced away, but she called him back peremptorily.

'Look at me – I want to see you.'

Brown eyes met grey steadily for an intolerable minute. Dicky felt his pulse throbbing faster, but the thin straight line of smoke that went up from his cigarette never wavered.

Then, to his amazement, she smiled.

'Is this a joke?' he asked evenly.

She shook her head.

'I'm sorry,' she said. 'I wanted to make sure if you were straight – straight as far as I'm concerned, I mean. You see, Dicky, I'm worried.'

'You don't trust me?'

She returned his gaze.

'I had my doubts. That's why I had to make sure – in my own way. I feel sure now. It's only a feeling, but I go by feelings. I feel that you wouldn't let me down – now. But I'm still worried.'

'What about?'

'There's a squealer in the camp,' she said. 'Somebody's selling us. Until this moment, I was prepared to believe it was you.'

3

Tremayne sat like an image, mechanically flicking the ash from his cigarette. Every word had gone through him like a knife, but never by a twitch of a muscle had he shown it.

He said calmly enough: 'I don't think anyone could blame you.'

'Listen,' she said. 'You ask for it – from anyone like me. Hilloran's easy to fool. He's cleverer than most, but you could bamboozle him any day. I'm more inquisitive – and you're too secretive. You don't say anything about your respectable past. Perhaps that's natural. But you don't say anything about your disreputable past, either – and that's extraordinary. If it comes to the point, we've only got your word for it that you're a crook at all.'

He shook his head.

'Not good enough,' he replied. 'If I were a dick, sneaking into your gang in order to shop you – first, I'd have been smart enough to get Headquarters to fix me up with a convincing list of previous convictions, with the co-operation of the Press, and, second, we'd have pulled in the lot of you weeks ago.'

She had taken a chair beside him. With an utterly natural gesture, that nevertheless came strangely and unexpectedly from her, she laid a hand on his arm.

'I know, Dicky,' she said. 'I told you I trusted you – now. Not for any logical reasons, but because my hunch says you're not that sort. But I'll let you know that if I hadn't decided I could trust you – I'd be afraid of you.'

'Am I so frightening?'

'You were.'

He stirred uncomfortably, frowning.

'This is queer talk from you, Audrey,' he said, rather brusquely. 'Somehow, one doesn't expect any sign of weakness – or fear – from you. Let's be practical. What makes you so sure there's a squeaker?'

'Handers. You saw he was taken yesterday?' Dicky nodded. 'It wasn't a fluke. I'll swear Teal would never have tumbled to that valise-handle trick. Besides, the papers said he was "acting on information received". You know what that means?'

'It sounds like a squeal, but–'

'The loss doesn't matter so much – ten thousand pounds and three weeks' work – when we're set to pull down twenty times that amount in a few days. But it makes me rather wonder what's going to happen to the big job.'

Tremayne looked at her straightly.

'If you don't think I'm the squeaker,' he said, 'who do you think it is?'

'There's only one other man, as far as I know, who was in a position to shop Handers.'

'Namely?'

'Hilloran.'

Dicky stared.

The situation was grotesque. If it had been less grotesque, it would have been laughable; but it was too grotesque even for laughter. And Dicky didn't feel like laughing.

The second cut was overwhelming. First she had half accused him of being the traitor; and then, somehow, he had convinced her of a lie without speaking a word, and she had declared that she trusted him. And now, making him her confident, she was turning the eye of her suspicion upon the man who had been her chief lieutenant on the other side of the Atlantic.

'Hilloran,' objected Dicky lamely, 'worked for you–'

'Certainly. And then I fired him – with some home truths in lieu of notice. I patched it up and took him back for this job because he's a darned useful man. But that doesn't say he's forgiven and forgotten.'

'You think he's out to double-cross you, and get his own back and salve his vanity?'

'It's not impossible.'

'But–'

She interrupted with an impatient movement.

'You don't get the point. I thought I'd made it plain. Apart from anything else, Hilloran seems to think I'd make a handsome ornament for his home. He's been out for that lay ever since I first met him. He was particularly pressing tonight, and I sent him away with several large fleas in each ear. I'll admit he was well oiled, and I had to show him a gun.'

Dicky's face darkened.

'As bad as that?'

She laughed shortly.

'You needn't be heroic about it, Dicky. The ordinary conventions aren't expected to apply in our world. Being outside the pale, we're reckoned to be frankly ruddy, and we usually are. However, I just happen to be funny that way – Heaven knows why. The point is that Hilloran's as sore and spiteful as a coyote on hot tiles, and if he didn't know it was worth a quarter of a million dollars to keep in with me–'

'He might try to sell you?'

'Even now,' said the girl, 'when the time comes, he mightn't be content with his quarter share.'

Dicky's brain was seething with this new spate of ideas. On top of everything else, then, Hilloran was playing a game of his own. That game might lead him to laying information before the police on his own account, or, far more probably, to the conception of a scheme for turning the entire proceeds of the 'big job' into his own pocket.

It was a factor which Tremayne had never considered. He hadn't yet absorbed it properly. And he had to get the main lines of it hard and clear, get the map of the situation nailed out in his mind in a strong light, before–

Zzzzzzzz ... zzzzzzzz...

'What's that?'

'The front door,' said the girl, and pointed. 'There's a buzzer in my bedroom. See who it is.'

Dicky went to a window and peered out from behind the curtains. He came back soberly.

'Hilloran's back again,' he said. 'Whatever he's come about, he must have seen my car standing outside. And it's nearly four o'clock in the morning.' She met his eyes. 'Shall we say it's difficult?'

She understood. It was obvious, anyway.

'What would you like me to do?' asked Dicky.

The buzzer sounded again – a long, insistent summons. Then the smaller of the two telephones on the desk tinkled.

The girl picked up the receiver.

'Hullo... Yes. He can come up.'

She put down the instrument and returned to her armchair.

'Another cigarette, Dicky.'

He passed her the box, and struck a match.

'What would you like me to do?' he repeated.

'Anything you like,' she said coolly. 'If I didn't think your gentlemanly instincts would be offended, I'd suggest that you took off your coat and tried to look abandoned, draping yourself artistically on the arm of this chair. In any case you can be as objectionable as Hilloran will be. If you can help him to lose his temper, he may show some of his hand.'

Dicky came thoughtfully to his feet, his glass in his hand.

Then the girl raised her voice, clearly and sweetly.

'Dicky – darling–'

Hilloran stood in the doorway, a red-faced giant of a man, swaying perceptibly. His dinner jacket was crumpled, his tie askew, his hair tousled. It was plain that he had had more to drink since he left the house.

'Audrey–'

'It is usual,' said the girl coldly, 'to knock.'

Hilloran lurched forward. In his hand he held something which he flung down into her lap.

'Look at that!'

'I didn't know you were a proud father,' she remarked. 'Or have you been taking up art yourself?'

'Two of 'em!' blurted Hilloran thickly. 'I found one pinned to my door when I got home. The other I found here – pinned to your front door – since I left! Don't you recognize it – the warning? It means that the Saint has been here tonight!'

The girl's face had changed colour. She held the cards out to Dicky.

Hilloran snatched them viciously away.

'No, you don't!' he snarled. 'I want to know what you're doing here at all, in this room, at this hour in the morning.'

Audrey Perowne rose.

'Hilloran,' she said icily, 'I'll thank you not to insult my friend in my own house.'

The man leered at her.

'You will, will you? You'd like to be left alone with him, when you know the Saint's sitting round waiting to smash us. If you don't value your own skin, I value mine. You're supposed to be the leader–'

'I am the leader.'

'Are you?... Yes, you lead. You've led me on enough. Now you're leading him on. You little–'

Tremayne's fist smashed the word back into Hilloran's teeth.

As the man crashed to the floor, Dicky

whipped off his coat.

Hilloran put a hand to his mouth, and the same came away wet and red. Then he shot out a shaky forefinger.

'You – you skunk – I know you! You're here making love to Audrey, crawling in like a snake – and all the time you're planning to squeal on us. Ask him, Audrey!' The pointing finger stiffened, and the light of drunken hate in the man's eyes was bestial. *'Ask him what he knows about the Saint!'*

Dicky Tremayne stood perfectly still.

He knew that the girl was looking at him. He knew that Hilloran could have no possible means of substantiating his accusations. He knew also how a seed sown in a bed of panic could grow, and realized that he was very near death.

And he never moved.

'Get up, Hilloran,' he said quietly. 'Get up and have the rest of your teeth knocked out.'

Hilloran was scrambling to his feet.

'Yes, I'll get up!' he rasped, and his hand was making for his pocket. 'But I've my own way of dealing with rats–'

And there was an automatic in his hand. His finger was trembling over the trigger. Dicky saw it distinctly.

Then, in a flash, the girl was between them.

'If you want the police here,' she said, 'you'll shoot. But I shan't be here to be arrested with you.'

Hilloran raved: 'Out of the way, you–'

'Leave him to me,' said Dicky.

He put her aside, and the muzzle of the automatic touched his chest. He smiled into the flaming eyes.

'May I smoke a cigarette?' he asked politely. His right hand reached to his breast pocket in the most natural way in the world.

Hilloran's scream of agony shattered the silence.

Like lightening, Dicky's right hand had dropped and gripped Hilloran's right hand, at the same instant as Dicky's left hand fastened paralysingly on Hilloran's right arm just above the elbow. The wrench that almost broke Hilloran's wrist was made almost in the same movement.

The gun thuddered into the carpet at their feet, but Tremayne took no notice. Retaining and strengthening his grip, he turned Hilloran round and forced him irresistibly to his knees. Tremayne held him there with one hand.

'We can talk more comfortably now,' he remarked.

He looked at the girl, and saw that she had picked up the fallen automatic.

'Before we go any further, Audrey,' he said, 'I should like to know what you think of the suggestion – that I might be a friend of the Saint's. I needn't remind you that this object is jealous as well as drunk. I won't deny the charge, because that wouldn't cut any ice. I'd just like your opinion.'

'Let him go first.'

'Certainly.'

With a twist of his hand, Dicky released the man and sent him toppling over on to his face.

'Hilloran, get up!'

'If you–'

'Get up!'

Hilloran stumbled to his feet. There was murder in his eyes, but he obeyed. No man of his calibre could have challenged that command. Dicky thought, 'A crook – and she can wear power like a queen...'

'I want to know, Hilloran,' observed the girl frostily, 'why you said what you said just now.'

The man glared.

'He can't account for himself, and he doesn't look or behave like one of us. We know there's a squealer somewhere – someone who squealed on Handers – and he's the only one–'

'I see.' The contempt in the girl's voice had the quality of concentrated acid. 'What I see most is that because I prefer his company to yours, you're ready to trump up any wild charge against him that comes into your head – in the hope of putting him out of favour.'

'And *I* see,' sneered Hilloran, 'that *I'm* the one who's out of favour – because he's taken my place. He's–'

'Either,' said the girl, 'you can walk out on your own flat feet, or you can be thrown out. Take your choice. And whichever way you go, don't come back till you're sober and ready to apologize.'

Hilloran's fists clenched.

'You're supposed to be bossing this gang–'

'I am,' said Audrey Perowne. 'And if you don't like it, you can cut out as soon as you like.'

Hilloran swallowed.

'All right–'

'Yes?' prompted Audrey silkily.

'One day,' said Hilloran, staring from under black brows, 'you're going to be sorry for this. We know where we are. You don't want to fire me before the big job, because I'm useful. And I'll take everything lying down for the same time, because there's a heap of money in it for me. Yes, I'm drunk, but I'm not too drunk to be able to see that.'

'That,' said the girl sweetly, 'is good news. Have you finished?'

Hilloran's mouth opened, and closed again deliberately. The knuckles showed whitely in his hands.

He looked at the girl for a long time. Then, for a long time, in exactly the same way, he looked at Tremayne, without speaking.

At last–

'Goodnight,' he said, and left the room without another word.

From the window, Tremayne watched him walk slowly up the street, his handkerchief to his mouth. Then Dicky turned, and found Audrey Perowne beside him. There was something in her eyes which he could not interpret.

He said: 'You've proved that you trust me–'

'He's crazy,' she said.

'He's mad,' said Dicky. 'Like a mad dog. We haven't heard the last of this evening. From the moment you step on board the yacht, you'll have to watch him night and day. You understand that, don't you?'

'And what about you?'

'A knowledge of ju-jitsu is invaluable.'

'Even against a knife in the back?'

Dicky laughed.

'Why worry?' he asked. 'It doesn't help us.'

The grey eyes were still holding his.

'Before you go,' she said, 'I'd like your own answer – from your own mouth.'

'To what question?'

'To what Hilloran said.'

He was picking up his coat. He put it down, and came towards her. A madness was upon him. He knew it, felt everything in him rebelling against it; yet he was swept before it out of reason, like a leaf before the wind. He held out his hand.

'Audrey,' he said, 'I give you my word of honour that I'd be burnt alive sooner than let you down.'

The words were spoken quite simply and calmly. The madness in him could only prompt them. He could still keep his face impassive and school the intensest meaning out of his voice.

Her cool fingers touched his, and he put them to his lips with a smile that might have meant anything – or nothing.

A few minutes later he was driving home with the first streaks of dawn in the sky, and his mouth felt as if it had been seared with a hot iron.

He did not see the Saint again before they left for Marseilles.

4

Three days later, Dicky Tremayne, in white trousers, blue reefer, and peaked cap, stood at the starboard rail of the *Corsican Maid* and stared moodily over the water.

The sun shone high overhead, turning the water into a sea of quicksilver, and making of the Château d'If a fairy castle. The *Corsican Maid* lay in the open roadstead, two miles from Marseilles Harbour; for the Countess Anusia Marova, ever thoughtful for her guests, had decided that the docks, with their grime and noise and bustle, were no place for holiday-making millionaires and their wives to loiter, even for a few hours. But over the water, from the direction of the harbour, approached a fussy little tender. Dicky recognized it as the tender that had been engaged to bring the millionaires, with their wives and other baggage, to the Countess's yacht, and watched it morosely.

That is to say that his eyes followed it intently; but his mind was in a dozen different places.

The situation was rapidly becoming intolerable – far too rapidly. That, in fact, was the only reflection which was seriously concerned with the approach of the tender. For every yard of that approach seemed, in a way, to entangle him ten times more firmly in the web that he had woven for himself.

The last time he had seen the Saint, Dicky hadn't told him the half of it. One very cogent reason was that Dicky himself, at the time, hadn't even known the half well enough to call it Dear Sir or Madam. Now, he knew it much too well. He called it by its first name now – and others – and it sat back and grinned all over its ugly face at him. Curse it…

When he said that he *might* fall in love with Audrey Perowne, he was underestimating the case by a mile. He *had* fallen in love with her, and there it was. He'd done his level best not to; and, when it was done, he'd fought for all he was worth against admitting it even to himself. By this time, he was beginning to see that the struggle was hopeless.

And if you want to ask why the pink parakeets he should put up a fight at all, the answer is that that's the sort of thing men of Dicky Tremayne's stamp do. If everything had been different – if the Saint had never been heard of – or, at least, if Tremayne had only known him through his morning newspaper – the problem would never have arisen. Say that the problem, having arisen, remains a simple one – and you're wrong. Wrong by the first principles of psychological arithmetic.

The Saint might have been a joke. The Press, at first, had suggested that he must be a joke – that he couldn't, reasonably, be anything else. Later, with grim demonstrations thrust under their bleary eyes, the Press admitted that it was no joke. In spite of which, the jest might have stood, had the men carrying it out been less under the Saint's spell.

There exists a loyalty among men of a

certain type which defies instinct, and which on occasion can rise above the limitations of mere logic. Dicky Tremayne was of that breed. And he didn't find the problem simple at all.

He figured it out in his own way.

'She's a crook. On the other hand, as far as that goes, so am I – though not the way she thinks of it. She's robbing people who can afford to stand the racket. Their records, if you came to examine them closely, probably wouldn't show up any too clean. In fact, she's on much the same ground as we are ourselves. Except that she doesn't pass on ninety per cent of the profits to charity. But that's only a private sentimentality of our own. It doesn't affect the main issue.

'Hilloran isn't the same proposition. He's a real bad *hombre*. I'd be glad to see him go down.

'The snag with the girl is the late John L. Morganheim. She probably murdered him. But then, there's not one of our crowd that hasn't got blood on his hands. What matters is why the blood was shed. We don't know anything about Morganheim, and action's going to be forced on me before I've time to find out.

'In a story, the girl's always innocent. Or, if she's guilty, she's always got a cast-iron reason to be. But I'm not going to be led away. I've seen enough to know that that kind of story is mostly based on vintage boloney, according to the recipe. I'm going to look at it coldly and sanely, till I find an answer or my brain busts. Because–

'Because, in fact, things being as they are, I've as good as sworn to the Saint that I'd bring home the bacon. Not in so many words, but that's what he assumes. And he's got every right to assume it. He gave me the chance to cry off if I wanted to – and I turned it down. I refused to quit. I dug this perishing pitfall, and it's up to me to fight my own way out – and no whining...'

Thus Dicky Tremayne had balanced the ledger, over and over again, without satisfying himself.

The days since the discomfiture of Hilloran had not made the account any simpler.

Hilloran had come round the next morning, and apologized. Tremayne had been there – of course. Hilloran had shaken his hand heartily, boisterously disclaimed the least animosity, declared that it had been his own silly fault for getting canned, and taken Dicky and Audrey out to lunch. Dicky would have had every excuse for being deceived – but he wasn't. That he pretended to be was nobody's business.

But he watched Hilloran when he was not being watched himself; and from time to time he surprised in Hilloran's eyes a curiously abstracted intentness that confirmed his misgivings. It lasted only for a rare second here and there; and it was swallowed up again in a fresh flood of open-handed good humour so quickly that a less prejudiced observer might have put it down to imagination. But Dicky understood, and knew that there was going to be trouble with Hilloran.

Over the lunch, the intrusion of the Saint had been discussed, and a decision had been reached – by Audrey Perowne.

'Whoever he is, and whatever he's done,' she said. 'I'm not going to be scared off by any comic-opera threats. We've spent six thousand pounds on ground bait, and we'd be a cheap lot of pikers to leave the pitch without a fight. Besides, sooner or later, this Saint's going to bite off more than he can chew, and this may very well be the time. We're going to be on the broad Mediterranean, with a picked crew, and not more than twenty per cent of them can be double-crossing us. That gives us an advantage of four to one. Short of pulling out a ship of their own and making a pitched battle of it, I don't see what the Saint can do. I say we go on – with our eyes twice skinned.'

The argument was incontestable.

Tremayne, Hilloran and Audrey had left London quietly so as to arrive twelve hours before their guests were due. Dicky had spent another evening alone with the girl before the departure.

'Do you believe in Hilloran's apology?' he had asked.

She had answered, at once: 'I don't.'

'Then why are you keeping him on?'

'Because I'm a woman. Sometimes, I think, you boys are liable to forget that. I've got the brain, but it takes a man to run a show like this, with a crew like mine to handle. You're the only other man I'd trust it to, but you – well, Dicky, honestly, you haven't the experience, have you?'

It had amazed him that she could discuss a crime so calmly. Lovely to look upon, exquisitely dressed, lounging at her ease in a deep chair, with a cigarette between white fingers that would have served the most fastidious sculptor for a model, she looked as if she should have been discussing, delightfully – anything but that.

Of his own feelings he had said nothing. He kept them out of his face, out of his eyes, out of his voice and manner. His dispassionate calm rivalled her own.

He dared hold no other pose. The reeling tumult of his thoughts could only be masked by the most stony stolidness. Some of the turmoil would inevitably have broken through any less sphinx-like disguise.

He was trying to get her in her right place – and, in the attempt, he was floundering deeper and deeper in the mire of mystification. There was about her none of the hard flashiness traditionally supposed to brand the woman criminal. For all her command, she remained completely feminine, gentle of voice, perfectly gracious. The part of the Countess Anusia Marova, created by herself, she played without effort; and, when she was alone, there was no travesty to take off. The charmingly broken English disappeared – that was all. But the same woman moved and spoke.

If he had not known, he would not have believed. But he knew – and it had rocked his creed to its foundations.

There had only been one moment, that evening, when he had been in danger of stumbling.

'If we bring this off,' she had said, 'you'll get your quarter share, of course. Two hundred and fifty thousand dollars. Fifty thousand pounds of your money. You need never do another job as long as you live. What will you do?'

'What will you do with yours?' he countered.

She hesitated, gazed dreamily into a shadowy corner as though she saw something there. Then:

'Probably,' she said lightly, 'I'll buy a husband.'

'I might buy a few wives,' said Dicky, and the moment was past.

Now he looked down into the blue Mediterranean and meditated that specimen of repartee with unspeakable contempt. But it had been the only thing that had come into his head, and he'd had to say something promptly.

'Blast it all,' thought Dicky, and straightened up with a sigh.

The tender had nosed up to the gangway, and Sir Esdras Levy, in the lead, was helping Lady Levy to the grating.

Mr George Y. Ulrig stood close behind. Dicky caught their eyes. He smiled with his mouth, and saluted cheerily.

He ought to have known them, for he himself had been the means of introducing them to the house in Park Lane. That had been his job, on the Continent, under Hilloran, for the past three months – to travel about the fashionable resorts, armed with plenty of money, an unimpeachable wardrobe, and his natural charm of manner, and approach the Unapproachables when they were to be found in holiday moods with their armour laid aside.

It had been almost boringly simple. A man who would blow up high in the air if addressed by a perfect stranger in the lounge of the Savoy Hotel, London, may be addressed by the same stranger with perfect impunity in the lounge of the Helipolis Hotel, Biarritz. After which, to a man of

Dicky Tremayne's polished worldliness, the improvement of the shining hour came automatically.

Jerking himself back to the realities of immediate importance, he went down to help to shepherd his own selected sheep to the slaughter.

Audrey Perowne stood at the head of the gangway, superbly gowned in a simple white skirt and coloured jumper – superbly gowned because she wore them. She was welcoming her guests inimitably, with an intimate word for each, while Hilloran, in uniform, stood respectfully ready to conduct them to their cabins.

'Ah, sir Esdras, ve 'ardly dare expec' you. I say, "'E vill not com to my seely leetle boat." But 'e is nize, and 'e come to be oncomfortable to please me... And Lady Levy. My dear, each day you are more beautiful.' Lady Levy, who was a fat fifty, glowed audibly. 'And Mrs Ulrig. Beefore I let you off my boat, you shall tell me 'ow eet iss you keep zo sleem.' The scrawny and faded Mrs George Y. Ulrig squirmed with pleasure. 'George Y,' said the Countess, 'I see you are vhat zey call a sheek. Ozairvize you could not 'ave marry 'er. And Mrs Sankin...'

Dicky's task was comparatively childish. He had only to detach Sir Esdras Levy, Mr George Y. Ulrig, and Matthew Sankin from their respective spouses, taking them confidentially by the arm, and murmur that there were cocktails set out in the saloon.

Luncheon, with Audrey Perowne for hostess, could not have been anything but a success.

The afternoon passed quickly. It seemed no time before the bell rung by the obsequious Hilloran indicated that it was time to dress for dinner.

Tremayne went below with the rest to dress. It was done quickly; but the girl was already in the saloon when he arrived. Hilloran was also there, pretending to inspect the table.

'When?' Hilloran was asking.

'Tomorrow night. I've told them we're due at Monaco about half past six. We shan't be near the place, but that doesn't matter. We'll take them in their cabins when they go below to change.'

'And afterwards?' questioned Dicky.

'We make straight across to Corsica during the night, and land them near Calvi the next morning. Then we make round the south of Sicily, and lose ourselves in the Greek Archipelago. We should arrive eventually at Constantinople – repainted, rechristened, and generally altered. There we separate. I'll give the immediate orders tomorrow afternoon. Come to my cabin about three.'

Hilloran turned to Dicky.

'By the way,' he said, 'this letter came with the tender. I'm afraid I forgot to give it to you before.'

Dicky held the man's eyes for a moment, and then took the envelope. It was postmarked in London. With a glance at the flap, he slit it open.

The letter was written in a round feminine hand.

Darling,

This is just a line to wish you a jolly good time on your cruise.

You'll know I'll miss you terribly. Six weeks seems such a long time for you to be away. Never mind. I'm going to drown my sorrows in barley wine.

I refuse to be lonely. Simple Simon, the man I told you about, says he'll console me. He wants me to go with a party he's taking to the Aegean Islands. I don't know yet if I shall accept, but it sounds awfully thrilling. He's got a big aeroplane, and wants us to fly all the way.

If I go, I shall have to leave on Saturday. Won't you be jealous?

Darling, I mustn't pull your leg any more. You know I'm always thinking of you, and I shan't be really happy till I get you back again.

Here come all my best wishes, then. Be

good, and take care of yourself.

It's eleven o'clock, and I'm tired. I'm going to bed to dream of you. It'll be twelve by the time I'm there. My eyes are red from weeping for you.

You have all my love. I trust you.

PATRICIA.

Tremayne folded the letter, replaced it in its envelope, and put it in his pocket.

'Does she still love you?' mocked Audrey Perowne, and Dicky shrugged.

'So she says,' he replied carelessly. 'So she says.'

5

Much later that night, in the privacy of his cabin, Dicky read the letter again.

The meaning to him was perfectly obvious.

The Saint had decided to work his end of the business by aeroplane. The reference to the Aegean Islands, Tremayne decided, had no bearing on the matter – the Saint could have had no notion that the *Corsican Maid's* flight would take her to that quarter. But Saturday – the next day – was mentioned, and Dicky took that to mean that the Saint would be on the look-out for signals from Saturday onwards.

'Take care of yourself,' was plain enough.

The references to 'eleven o'clock' and 'twelve' were ambiguous. 'It'll be twelve by the time I'm there' might mean that, since the aeroplane would have to watch for signals from a considerable distance, to avoid being betrayed by the noise of the engines, it would be an hour from the time of the giving of the signal before the Saint could arrive on the scene. But why 'eleven o'clock' and 'twelve' instead of 'twelve o'clock' and 'one' – since they had previously arranged that signals were to be made either at midnight or four o'clock in the morning?

Dicky pondered for an hour; and decided that either he was trying to read too much between the lines, or that a signal given an hour before the appointed time, at eleven o'clock instead of twelve, would not be missed.

'My eyes are red from weeping for you.' He interpreted that to mean that he was to signal with a red light if there seemed to be any likelihood of their having cause to weep for him. He had a pocket flashlamp fitted with colour screens, and that code would be easy to adopt.

It was the last sentence that hit him fairly between the eyes.

'I trust you.'

A shrewd blow – very shrewd. Just an outside reminder of what he'd been telling himself for the past three days.

Simon couldn't possibly understand. He'd never met Audrey Perowne. And, naturally, he'd do his level best to keep Dicky on the lines.

Dicky crumpled the paper slowly into a ball, rolling it thoughtfully between his two palms. He had picked up the envelope, and rolled that into the ball also. Hilloran had steamed open that envelope and sealed it again before delivering the letter – Dicky was sure of that.

He went to the porthole and pitched the ball far out into the dark waters.

He undressed and lay down in his bunk, but he could not compose his mind to sleep. The night was close and sultry. The air that came through the open porthole seemed to strike warm on his face, and to circulate that torrid atmosphere with the electric fan was pointless. He tried it, but it brought no relief.

For an hour and a half he lay stifling; and then he rose, pulled on his slippers and a thin silk dressing-gown, and made his way to the deck.

He sprawled in a long cane chair, and lighted a cigarette. Up there it was cooler. The ghost of a breeze whispered in the rigging and fanned his face. The soft hiss and wash of the sea cleft by the passage of their bows was very soothing. After a time, he dozed.

He awoke with a curious sensation forcing itself through his drowsiness. It seemed as if the sea was rising, for the chair in which he lay was lurching and creaking under him. Yet the wind had not risen, and he could hear none of the thrash of curling waves which he should have been able to hear.

All this he appreciated hazily, roused but still half asleep. Then he opened one eye, and saw no rail before him, but only the steely glint of waters under the moon. Looking upwards and behind him he saw the foremast light riding serenely among the stars of a cloudless sky.

The convulsive leap he made actually spread-eagled him across the rail; and he heard his chair splash into the sea below as he tumbled over on to the deck.

Rolling on his shoulder, he glimpsed a sea-boot lashing at his head. He ducked wildly, grabbed, and kept his hold. All the strength he could muster went into the wrench that followed, and he heard the owner of the boot fall heavily with a strangled oath. An instant later he was on his feet – to find Hilloran's face two inches from his own.

'Would you!' snapped Dicky.

He slipped the answering punch over his

left shoulder, changed his feet, and crammed every ounce of his weight into a retaliatory jolt that smacked over Hilloran's heart and dropped the man as if his legs had been cut away from beneath him.

Dicky turned like a whirlwind as the man he had tripped up rose from the ground and leapt at him with flailing fists.

Scientific boxing, in that light, was hopeless. Dicky tried it, and stopped a right swing with the side of his head. Three inches lower, and it would probably have put an end to the fight. As it was, it sent him staggering back against the rail, momentarily dazed, and it was more by luck than judgment that his shoulder hunched in the way of the next blow. He hit back blindly, felt his knuckles make contact, and heard the man grunt with pain.

Then his sight cleared.

He saw the seaman recover his balance and gather himself for a renewed onslaught. He saw Hilloran coming unsteadily off the deck, with the moonlight striking a silvery gleam from something in his right hand. And he understood the issue quite plainly.

They had tried to dump him overboard, chair and all, while he slept. A quiet and gentle method of disposing of a nuisance – and no fuss or mess. That having failed, however, the execution of the project had boiled down to a free fight for the same end.

Dicky had a temporary advantage, but the odds were sticky. With the cold grim clarity of vision that comes to a man at such moments, Dicky Tremayne realized that the odds were very sticky indeed.

But not for a second could he consider raising his voice for help. Apart from the fact that the battle was more or less a duel of honour between Hilloran and himself – even if Hilloran didn't choose to fight his side single-handed – it remained to be assumed that, if Hilloran had one ally among the crew, he was just as likely to have half a dozen. The whole crew, finally, were just as likely to be on Hilloran's side as one. The agreement had been that Audrey, Hilloran and Dicky were to divide equally three-quarters of the spoil, and the crew were to divide the last quarter. Knowing exactly the type of man of which the crew was composed, Tremayne could easily reckon the chance of their falling for a bait of a half share to divide instead of a quarter, when the difference would amount to a matter of about four thousand pounds per man.

And that, Tremayne realized, would be a pretty accurate guess at the position. He himself was to be eliminated, as Audrey Perowne's one loyal supporter and a thorn in Hilloran's side. The quarter share thus saved would go to bribe the crew. As for

Hilloran's own benefit, Audrey Perowne's quarter share...

Dicky saw the whole stark idea staring him in the face, and wondered dimly why he'd never thought of it before. Audrey Perowne's only use, for Hilloran, had been to get the millionaires on board the yacht and out to sea. After that, he could take his own peculiar revenge on her for the way she had treated him, revenge himself also on Tremayne for similar things, and make himself master of the situation and half a million dollars instead of a quarter. A charming inspiration...

But Dicky didn't have to think it all out like that. He saw it in a flash, more by intuition than by logic, in the instance of rest that he had while he saw also the seaman returning to the attack and Hilloran rising rockily from the ground with a knife in his hand.

And therefore he fought in silence.

The darkness was against him. Dicky Tremayne was a strong and clever boxer, quicker than most men, and he knew more than a little about ju-jitsu; but those are arts for which one needs the speed of vision that can only come with a clear light. The light he had was meagre and deceptive – a light that was all on the side of sheer strength and bulk, and all against mere speed and skill.

He was pretty well cornered. His back was

against the rail. Hilloran was on his left front, the huge seaman on his right. There was no room to pass between them, no room to escape past either of them along the rail. There was only one way to fight: their own way.

The seaman was nearest, and Dicky braced himself. It had to be a matter of give and take, the only question being that of who was to take the most. As the seaman closed in, Tremayne judged his distance, dropped his chin, and drove with a long left.

The sailor's fist connected with Dicky's forehead, knocking back his head with a jar that ricked his neck. Dicky's left met something hard that seemed to snap under the impact. Teeth. But Dicky reeled, hazed by the sickening power of the two tremendous blows he had taken; and he could hardly see for the red and black clouds that swam before his eyes.

But he saw Hilloran and dropped instinctively to one knee. He rose again immediately under Hilloran's knife arm, taking the man about the waist. Summoning all his strength, he heaved upwards, with some mad idea of treating Hilloran to some of his own pleasant medicine – or hurling the man over the rail into the glimmering black sea. And almost at once he realized that he could not do it – Hilloran was too heavy, and Dicky was already weakened. Nor was there time to struggle, for in another moment Hilloran would lift his right arm again and drive the knife into Dicky's back.

But Tremayne, in that desperate effort, had Hilloran off his feet for a second. He smashed him bodily against the rail, hoping to slam the breath out of him for a momentary respite, and broke away.

As he turned, the seaman's hands fastened on his throat, and Dicky felt a sudden surge of joy.

Against a man who knows his ju-jitsu, that grip is more than futile; it is more than likely to prove fatal to the man who employs it. Particularly was this fact proven then. For most of the holds in ju-jitsu depend on getting a grip on a wrist or hand – which, of course, are the hardest parts of the body to get a grip on, being the smallest and most swift-moving. Dicky had been hampered all along by being unable to trust himself to get his hold in that light, when the faintest error of judgment would have been fatal. But now there could be no mistake.

Dicky's hands went up on each side of his head, and closed on the seaman's little fingers. He pulled and twisted at the same time, and the man screamed as one finger at least was dislocated. But Dicky went on, and the man was forced sobbing to his knees.

The surge of joy in Dicky's heart rose to

something like a shout of triumph – and died.

Out of the tail of his eye, he saw Hilloran coming in again.

Tremayne felt that he must be living a nightmare. There were two of them, both far above his weight, and they were wearing him down, gradually, relentlessly. As fast as he gained an advantage over one, the other came to nullify it. As fast as he was able temporarily to disable one, the other came back refreshed to renew the struggle. It was his own stamina against their combined consecutive staminas – and either of them individually was superior in brute strength to himself, even if one left the knife out of the audit.

Dicky knew the beginning of despair.

He threw the seaman from him, sideways, across Hilloran's very knees, and leapt away.

Hilloran stumbled, and Dicky's hand shot out for the man's knife wrist, found its mark, twisted savagely. The knife tinkled into the scuppers.

If Dicky could have made a grip with both hands, he would have had the mastery, but he could only make it with one. His other hand, following the right, missed. A moment later he was forced to release his hold. He swung back only just in time to avoid the left cross that Hilloran lashed out at his jaw.

Then both Hilloran and the sailor came at him simultaneously, almost shoulder to shoulder.

Dicky's strength was spent. He was going groggy at the knees, his arms felt like lead, his chest heaved terribly to every panting breath he took, his head swirled and throbbed dizzily. He was taking his licking.

He could not counter the blows they both hurled at him at once. Somehow, he managed to duck under their arms, with some hazy notion of driving between them and breaking away into the open, but he could not do it. They had him cold.

He felt himself flung against the rail. The sailor's arms pinioned his own arms to his sides; Hilloran's hands were locked about his throat, strangling him to silence, crushing out life. His back was bent over the rail like a bow. His feet were off the ground.

The stars had gone out, and the moon had fallen from the sky. His chest was bound with ever-tightening iron bands. He seemed to be suspended in a vast void of utter blackness, and, though he could feel no wind, there was the roaring of a mighty wind in his ears.

And then, through the infinite distances of the dark gulf in which he hung, above even the great howling of that breathless wind, a voice spoke as a silver bell, saying: 'What's this, Hilloran?'

6

Dicky seemed to awake from a hideous dream.

The fingers loosened from his throat, the iron cage that tortured his chest relaxed, the rushing wind in his ears died down to a murmur. He saw a star in the sky; and, as he saw it, a moon that had not been there before seemed to swim out of the infinite dark, back to its place in the heavens. And he breathed.

Also, he suddenly felt very sick.

These things happened almost immediately. He knew that they must have been almost immediate, though they seemed to follow one another with the maddening slowness of the minute hand's pursuit of the hour hand round the face of a clock. He tried to whip them to a greater speed.

He could not pause to savour the sensations of this return to life. His brain had never lost consciousness. Only his body was dead, and that had to be forced back to activity without a pause.

One idea stood out distinctly from the clearing fog that blurred his vision. Audrey Perowne was there, and she had caused an interruption that was saving him; but he was not safe yet. Neither was she.

She slept, he remembered, in a cabin whose porthole looked out on to the very stretch of deck where they had been fighting, and the noise must have roused her. But, in that light, she could have seen little but a struggling group of men, unless she had watched for a time before deciding to intervene – and that was unlikely. *And she must not be allowed to know the true reason for the disturbance.*

Tremayne now understood exactly how things were.

If Hilloran was prepared to dispose of him, he was prepared to dispose of the girl as well – Dicky had no doubt of that. But that would require some determination. The habit of obedience would remain, and to break it would require a conscious effort. And that effort, at all costs, must not be stimulated by any provocation while Hilloran was able to feel that he had things mostly his own way. All this Dick Tremayne understood, and acted upon it in an instant, before his senses had fully returned.

His feet touched the deck; and he twisted and held the seaman in his arms as he himself had been held a moment earlier. Then he looked across and saw Audrey Perowne.

She stood by a bulkhead light, where they

could see her clearly, and the light glinted on an automatic in her hand. She said again: 'Hilloran–'

And by the impatient way she said it, Dicky knew that she could not have been waiting long for her first question to be answered.

'It's all right,' said Dicky swiftly. 'One of the men's gone rather off his rocker. Hilloran and I stopped him, and he fought. That's all.'

The girl came closer, and neither Hilloran or the seaman spoke. Now it was all a gamble. Would they take the lead he had offered them, and attest the lie? Or, rather, would Hilloran? – for the other man would take the cue from him.

It was a pure toss-up – with Audrey's automatic on Dicky's side. If Hilloran had a weapon – which he probably had – he would not dare to try and reach it when he was already covered, unless he had a supreme contempt for the girl's intelligence and straight shooting. And Dicky had surmised that the man was not yet prepared for open defiance.

But there was a perceptible pause before Hilloran said:

'That's so, Audrey.'

She turned to the sailor.

'Why did you want to throw yourself overboard?'

Sullenly, the man said: 'I don't know, miss.'

She looked closely at him.

'They seem to have been handling you pretty roughly.'

'You should have seen the way he struggled,' said Dicky. 'I've never seen anyone so anxious to die. I'm afraid I did most of the damage. Here–'

He took the man's hand.

'I'm going to put your finger back,' he said. 'It'll hurt. Are you ready?'

Her performed the operation with a sure touch; and then he actually managed a smile.

'I should take him below and lock him up, Hilloran,' he remarked. 'He'll feel better in the morning. It must have been the heat…'

Leaning against the rail, he watched Hilloran, without a word, take the man by the arm and lead him away. He felt curiously weak, now that the crisis was past and he hadn't got to fight any more. The blessing was that the girl couldn't see the bruises that must have been rising on his forehead and the side of his head.

But something must have shown in his face that he didn't know was showing, or the way he leaned against the rail must have been rather limp, for suddenly he found her hand on his shoulder.

'It strikes me,' she said softly, 'that that man wasn't the only onc who was roughly handled.'

Dicky grinned.

'I got some of the knocks, of course,' he said.

'Did Hilloran?' she asked quietly.

He met her eyes, and knew then that she was not deceived. But he glanced quickly up and down the deck before he answered.

'Hilloran took some knocks, too,' he answered, 'but it was a near thing.'

'Thcy tried to bump you off?'

'That, I believe, was the general idea.'

'I see.' She was thoughtful. 'Then–'

'I was trying to sleep on deck,' said Dicky suddenly. 'Hilloran was here when I arrived. We saw the man come along and try to climb over the rail–'

He broke off as Hilloran's shadow fell between them.

'I've locked him up,' said Hilloran, 'but he seems quite sensible now.'

'Good,' said the girl casually. 'I suppose you'd got the better of him by the time I came out. We'll discuss what's to be done with him in the morning. Dicky, you might take a turn round the deck with me before we go back to bed.'

She carried off the situation with such an utter naturalness that Hilloran was left with no answer. Her arm slipped through

Dicky's, and they strolled away.

They went forward, rounded the deck-house, and continued aft, saying nothing; but when they came to the stern she stopped and leaned over the taffrail, gazing absorbedly down into the creaming wake.

Dicky stopped beside her. Where they stood, no one could approach within hearing distance without being seen.

He took cigarettes and matches from his dressing-gown pocket. They smoked. He saw her face by the light of the match as he held it to her cigarette, and she seemed rather pale. But that might have been the light.

'Go on telling me about it,' she ordered.

He shrugged.

'You've heard most of it. I woke up when they were about to tip me over the side. There was some trouble. I did my best, but I'd have been done if you hadn't turned up when you did.'

'Why did you lie to save them?'

He explained the instinctive reasoning which had guided him.

'Not that I had time to figure it out as elaborately as that,' he said, 'but I'm still certain that it was a darned good guess.'

'It's easily settled,' she said. 'We'll put Hilloran in irons – and you'll have to do the best you can in his place.'

'You're an optimist,' said Dicky sardonically. 'Haven't I shown you every necessary reason why he should have the crew behind him to a man? They aren't the kind that started the story about honour among thieves.'

She turned her head.

'Are you suggesting that I should quit?'

He seemed to see his way clearly.

'I am. We haven't an earthly – short of out-bribing Hilloran, which'ud mean sacrificing most of our own shares. We aren't strong enough to fight. And we needn't bank on Hilloran's coming back into the fold like a repentant sheep, because we'd lose our bets. He's got nothing to lose, and everything to gain. We'd served our purpose. He can handle the hold-up just as well without us, and earn another quarter of a million dollars for the shade of extra work. I don't say I wouldn't fight it out if I were alone. I would. But I'm not alone, and I suspect that Hilloran's got a nasty mind. If he's only thinking of taking your *money* – I'll be surprised.'

She said coolly: 'In that case, it doesn't look as if we'd gain anything by quitting.'

'I could guarantee to get you away.'

'How?'

'Don't ask me, Audrey. But I know how.'

She appeared to contemplate the glowing end of her cigarette as though it were a crystal in which she could see the solution of all problems.

Then she faced him.

She said: 'I don't quit.'

'I suppose,' said Dicky roughly, 'you think that's clever. Let me tell you that it isn't. If you know that the decision's been framed against you right from the first gong, you don't lose caste by saving yourself the trouble of fighting.'

'The decision on points may have been framed against you,' she said, 'but you can get round that one. You can win on a knock-out.'

'Possibly – if that were the whole of it. But you're forgetting something else, aren't you?'

'What's that?'

'The Saint.'

He saw the exaggerated shrug of kimono'd shoulders.

'I should worry about him. I'll stake anything he isn't among the passengers. I've had the ship searched from end to end, so he isn't here as a stowaway. And I haven't taken many chances with the crew. What is he going to do?'

'I don't know. But if the people he's beaten before now had known what the Saint was going to do – they wouldn't have been beaten. We aren't the first people who've been perfectly certain they were safe. We aren't the only clever crooks in the world.'

Then she said again: 'I've told you – I

don't quit.'

'All right–'

'This is the biggest game I've ever played!' she said, with a kind of savage enthusiasm. 'It's more – it's one of the biggest games that ever *has* been played. I've spent months preparing the ground. I've sat up night after night planning everything out to the smallest detail, down to the last item of our getaways. It's a perfect machine. I've only got to press the button, and it'll run from tomorrow night to safety – as smoothly as any human machine ever ran. And you ask me to give that up!'

A kind of madness came over Dicky Tremayne. He turned, and his hands fell on her shoulders, and he forced her round with unnecessary violence.

'All right!' he snapped. 'You insist on keeping up this pose that you think's so brave and clever. You're damned pleased with yourself about it. Now listen to what I think. You're just a spoilt, silly little fool–'

'Take your hands off me!'

'When I've finished. You're just a spoilt, silly little fool that I've a good mind to spank here and now, as I'd spank any other child–'

The moonlight gleamed on something blue-black and metallic between them.

'Will you let me go?' she asked dangerously.

'No. Go ahead and shoot. I say you ought to be slapped, and, by the Lord … Audrey, Audrey, why are you crying?'

'Damn you,' she said. 'I'm not crying.'

'I can see your eyes.'

'Some smoke–'

'You dropped your cigarette minutes ago.'

His fierce grip had slackened. She moved swiftly, and flung off his hands.

'I don't want to get sentimental,' she said shakily. 'If I'm crying, it's my own business, and I've got my own good reasons for it. You're quite right. I *am* spoilt. I *am* a fool. I want that quarter of a million dollars, and I'm going to have it – in spite of Hilloran – in spite of you, too, if you want to take Hilloran's side–'

'I'm not taking Hilloran's side. I'm–'

'Whose side are you taking, then? There's only two sides to this.'

The moment had passed. He had chanced his arm on a show of strength – and failed. He wasn't used to bullying a girl. And through the dispersal of that shell-burst of madness he was aware again of the weakness of his position.

A barefaced bluffer like the Saint might still have carried it off, but Dicky Tremayne couldn't. He dared not go too far. He was tied hand and foot. It had been on the tip of his tongue to throw up the game, then – to tell the truth, present his ultimatum, and damn the consequences. Prudence – perhaps too great a prudence – had stopped him. In that, in a way, he was like Hilloran. Hilloran was in the habit of obedience; Tremayne was in the habit of loyalty; neither of them could break his habit on the spur of the moment.

'I'm taking your side,' said Dicky.

And he wondered, at the same time, whether he oughtn't to have given way to the impulse of that moment's loss of temper.

'Then what's the point of all this?' she demanded.

'I'm taking your side,' said Dicky, 'better than you know. But we won't go into that any more – not just now, anyway. Let it pass. Since you're so clever – what's your idea for dealing with the situation?'

'Another cigarette.'

He gave her one, lighted it, and turned to stare moodily over the sea. It was a hopeless dilemma. 'I wonder,' he thought bitterly, 'why a man should cling so fanatically to his word of honour? It's sheer unnatural lunacy, that's what it is.' He knew that was what it was. But he was on parole, and he would have no chance to take back his parole until the following night at the earliest.

'What do you think Hilloran'll do now?' she asked. 'Will he try again tonight, or will he wait till tomorrow?'

The moment was very much past. It might never have been.

Dicky tried to concentrate, but his brain seemed to have gone flabby.

'I don't know,' he said vaguely. 'In his place, I'd probably try again tonight. Whether Hilloran has that type of mind is another matter. You know him better than I do.'

'I don't think he has. He's had one chance tonight to make the stand against me, and he funked it. That's a setback, psychologically, that'll take him some time to get over. I'll bet he doesn't try again till tomorrow. He'll be glad to be able to do some thinking, and there's nothing to make him rush it.'

'Will you have any better answer tomorrow than you have now?'

She smiled.

'I shall have slept on it,' she said carelessly. 'That always helps… Goodnight, Dicky. I'm tired.'

He stopped her.

'Will you promise me one thing?'

'What is it?'

'Lock your door tonight. Don't open to anyone – on any excuse.'

'Yes,' she said. 'I should do that, in any case. You'd better do the same.'

He walked back with her to her cabin. Her hair stirred in the breeze, and the moon silvered it. She was beautiful. As they passed by a bulkhead light, he was observing the serenity of her proud lovely face. He found that he had not lost all his madness.

They reached the door.

'Goodnight, Dicky,' she said again.

'Goodnight,' he said.

And then he said, in a strange strained voice: 'I love you, Audrey. Goodnight, my dear.'

He was gone before she could answer.

7

Dicky dreamed that he was sitting on Hilloran's chest, with his fingers round Hilloran's throat, banging Hilloran's head on the deck. Every time Hilloran's head hit the deck, it made a lot of noise. Dicky knew that this was absurd. He woke up lazily, and traced the noise to his cabin door. Opening one eye, he saw the morning sunlight streaming in through his porthole.

Yawning, he rolled out of the bunk, slipped his automatic from under the pillow, and went to open the door.

It was a white-coated steward, bearing a cup of tea. Dicky thanked the man, took the cup, and closed the door on him, locking it again.

He sat on the edge of the bunk, stirring the tea thoughtfully. He looked at it thoughtfully, smelt it thoughtfully, and poured it thoughtfully out of the porthole. Then he lighted a cigarette.

He went to his bath with the automatic in his dressing-gown pocket and his hand on the automatic. He finished off with a cold shower, and returned to his cabin to dress, with similar caution, but feeling better.

The night before, he had fallen asleep almost at once. Dicky Tremayne had an almost Saintly faculty for carrying into practice the ancient adage that the evil of the day is sufficient thereto; and, since he reckoned that he would need all his wits about him on the morrow, he had slept. But now the morrow had arrived, he was thoughtful.

Not that the proposition in front of him appeared any more hopeful in the clear light of day. Such things have a useful knack of losing many of their terrors overnight, in the ordinary way – but this particular specimen didn't follow the rules.

It was true that Dicky had slept peacefully, and, apart from the perils that might have lurked in the cup of tea which he had not drunk, no attempt had been made to follow up the previous night's effort. That fact might have been used to argue that Hilloran hadn't yet found his confidence. In a determined counter-attack, such trifles as locked doors would not for long have stemmed his march; but the counter-attack had not been made. Yet this argument gave Dicky little reassurance.

An estimated value of one million dollars' worth of jewellery was jay-walking over the Mediterranean in that yacht, and every single dollar of that value was an argument for Hilloran – and others. Audrey Perowne had described her scheme as a foolproof machine. So it was – granted the trustworthiness of the various cogs and bearings. And that was the very snag on which it was liable to take it into its head to seize up.

The plot would have been excellent if its object had been monkey-nuts or hot dogs – things of no irresistible interest to anyone but an incorrigible collector. Jewels that were readily convertible into real live dollars were another matter. Even then, they might have been dealt with in comparative safety on dry land. But when they and their owners were more or less marooned in the open sea, far beyond the interference of the policeman at the street corner, with a crew like that of the *Corsican Maid*, each of those dollars became not only an argument but also a very unstable charge of high explosive.

Thus mused Dicky Tremayne while he

dressed, while he breakfasted, and while he strolled around the deck afterwards with Sir Esdras Levy and Mr Matthew Sankin. And the question that was uppermost in his mind was how he could possibly stall off the impending explosion until eleven or twelve o'clock that night.

He avoided Audrey Perowne. He saw her at breakfast, greeted her curtly, and plunged immediately into a discussion with Mr George Y. Ulrig on the future of the American negro – a point of abstract speculation which interested Dicky Tremayne rather less than the future of the Patagonian paluka. Walking round the deck, he had to pass and re-pass the girl, who was holding court in a shady space under an awning. He did not meet her eye, and was glad that she did not challenge him. If she had, she could easily have made him feel intolerably foolish.

The madness of the night before was over, and he wondered what had weakened him into betraying himself. He watched her out of the tail of his eye each time he passed. She chatted volubly, joked, laughed delightfully at each of her guests' clumsy sallies. It was amazing – her impudent nerve, her unshakable self-possession. Who would have imagined, he asked himself, that before the next dawn she was proposing that those same guests that she was then entertaining so charmingly should see her cold and masterful behind a loaded gun?

And so to lunch. Afterwards–

It was hot. The sun, a globe of eye-aching fire, swung naked over the yard-arm in a burnished sky. It made the tar bubble between the planks of the open deck, and turned the scarcely rippling waters to a sheet of steel. With one consent, guests and their wives, replete, sought long chairs and the shade. Conversation suffocated – died.

At three o'clock, Dicky went grimly to the rendezvous. He saw Hilloran entering as he arrived, and was glad that he had not to face the girl alone.

They sat down on either side of the table, with one measured exchange of inscrutable glances. Hilloran was smoking a cigar. Dicky lighted a cigarette.

'What have you done about that sailor?' asked Audrey.

'I let him out,' said Hilloran. 'He's quite all right now.'

She took an armchair between them.

'Then we'll get to business,' she said. 'I've got it all down to a timetable. We want as little fuss as possible, and there's going to be no need for any shooting. While we're at dinner, Hilloran, you'll go through all the cabins and clean them out. Do it thoroughly. No one will interrupt you. Then you'll go down to the galley and serve out – this.'

She held up a tiny flask of a yellowish liquid.

'Butyl,' she said, 'and it's strong. Don't overdo it. Two drops in each cup of coffee, with the last two good ones for Dicky and me. And there you are. It's too easy – and far less trouble than a gun hold-up. By the time they come to, they'll be tied hand and foot. We'll drop anchor off the Corsican coast near Calvi at eleven, and put them ashore. That's all.'

Dicky arose.

'Very neat,' he murmured. 'You don't waste time.'

'We haven't to do anything. It all rests with Hilloran, and his job's easy enough.'

Hilloran took the flask and slipped it into his pocket.

'You can leave it to me,' he said; and that reminder of the favourite expression of Dicky's friend, Roger Conway, would have made Dicky wince if his face hadn't been set so sternly.

'If that's everything,' said Dicky, 'I'll go. There's no point in anyone having a chance to notice that we're both absent together.'

It was a ridiculous excuse, but it was an excuse. She didn't try to stop him.

Hilloran watched the door close without making any move to follow. He was carefully framing a speech in his mind, but the opportunity to use it was taken from him.

'Do you trust Dicky?' asked the girl.

It was so exactly the point he had himself been hoping to lead up to that Hilloran could have gasped. As it was, some seconds passed before he could trust himself to answer.

'It's funny you should say that now,' he remarked. 'Because I remember that when *I* suggested it, you gave me the air.'

'I've changed my mind since last night. As I saw it – mind you, I couldn't see very well because it was so dark – but it seemed to me that the situation was quite different from the way you both described it. It seemed,' said the girl bluntly, 'as if Dicky was trying to throw *you* overboard, and the sailor was trying to stop him.'

'That's the truth,' said Hilloran blindly.

'Then why did you lie to save him?'

'Because I didn't think you'd believe me if I told the truth.'

'Why did the sailor lie?'

'He'd take his tip from me. If I chose to say nothing, it wasn't worth his while to contradict me.'

The girl's slender fingers drummed on the table.

'Why do you think Dicky should try to kill you?'

Hilloran had an inspiration. He couldn't stop to give thanks for the marvellous coincidence that had made the girl play straight into his hands. The thanksgiving could come later. The immediate thing was to leap for the heaven-sent opening.

He took a sheet of paper from his pocket and leaned forward.

'You remember me giving Dicky a letter yesterday evening, before dinner?' he asked. 'I opened it first and took a copy. Here it is. It looks innocent enough, but–'

'Did you test it for invisible ink?'

'I made every test I knew. Nothing showed up. But just read the letter. Almost every sentence in it might be a hint to anyone who knew how to take it.'

The girl read, with a furrow deepening between her brows. When she looked up, she was frowning.

'What's your idea?'

'What I told you before. I think Dicky Tremayne is one of the Saint's gang.'

'An arrangement–'

'That can't be right. I don't know much about the Saint, but I don't imagine he'd be the sort to send a man off on a job like this and leave his instructions to a letter delivered at the last minute. The least delay in the post, and he mightn't have received the letter at all.'

'That's all very well, but–'

'Besides, whoever sent this letter, if it's what you think it is, must have guessed that it might be opened and read. Otherwise the instructions would have been written in plain language. Now, these people are clever. The hints may be good ones. They may just as probably be phoney. I wouldn't put it above them to use some kind of code that anyone might tumble to – and hide another code behind it. You think you've found the solution – in the hints, if you can interpret them – but I say that's too easy. It's probably a trap.'

'Can you find any other code?'

'I'm not a code expert. But that doesn't say there isn't one.'

Hilloran scowled.

'I don't see that that makes any difference,' he said. 'I say that that letter's suspicious. If you agree with me, there's only one thing to be done.'

'Certainly.'

'He can't go over the side, where he might have put me last night.'

She shook her head.

'I don't like killing, Hilloran. You know that. And it isn't necessary.' She pointed to his pocket. 'You have the stuff. Suppose there was only *one* coffee without it after dinner tonight?'

Hilloran's face lighted up with a brutal eagerness. He had a struggle to conceal his delight. It was too simple – too utterly, utterly sitting. Verily, his enemies were delivered into his hands... But he tried to make his acknowledgment of the idea restrained and calculating.

'It'd be safer,' he conceded. 'I must say I'm relieved to find you're coming round to my way of thinking, Audrey.'

She shrugged, with a crooked little smile.

'The more I know you,' she said, 'the more I realize that you're usually right.'

Hilloran stood up. His face was like the thin crust of a volcano, under which fires and horrible forces boil and batter for release.

'Audrey–'

'Not now, Hilloran–'

'I've got a first name,' he said slowly. 'It's John. Why don't you ever use it?'

'All right – John. But please ... I want to rest this afternoon. When all the work's done, I'll – I'll talk to you.'

He came closer.

'You wouldn't try to double-cross John Hilloran, would you?'

'You know I wouldn't!'

'I want you!' he burst out incoherently. 'I've wanted you for years. You've always put me off. When I found you were getting on too well with that twister Tremayne, I went mad. But he's not taking you in any more, is he?'

'No–'

'And there's no one else?'

'How could there be?'

'You little beauty!'

'Afterwards, Hilloran. I'm so tired. I want to rest. Go away now–'

He sprang at her and caught her in his arms, and his mouth found her lips. For a moment she stood passively in his embrace. Then she pushed him back, and dragged herself away.

'I'll go now,' he said unsteadily.

She stood like a statue, with her eyes riveted on the closing door, till the click of the latch snapping home seemed to snap also the taut coil that held her rigid and erect. Then she sank limply back into her chair.

For a second she sat still. Then she fell forward across the table, and buried her face in her arms.

8

'Ve vere suppose,' said the Countess Anusia Marova, 'to come to Monaco at none o'clock. But ve are delay, and ze captayne tell me ve do nod zere arrive teel ten o'clock. So ve do nod af to urry past dinair to see ourselves come in ze port.'

Dicky Tremayne heard the soft accents across the saloon, above the bull-voiced drawl of Mr George Y. Ulrig, who was holding him down with a discourse on the future of the Japanese colony in California. Dicky was rather less interested in this than he would have been in a discourse on the future of the Walloon colony in Cincinnati. A scrap of paper crumpled in the pocket of his dinner-jacket – or Tuxedo (George Y. Ulrig) – seemed to be burning his side.

The paper had come under his cabin door while he dressed. He had been at the mirror, fidgeting with his tie, and he had seen the scrap sliding on to the carpet. He had watched it, half-hypnotized, and it had been some time before he moved to pick it up. When he had read it, and jerked open the door, the alleyway outside was deserted. Only, at the end, he had seen Hilloran, in his uniform, pass across by the alley athwartships without looking to right or to left.

The paper had carried one line of writing, in block letters.

DON'T DRINK YOUR COFFEE.

Nothing else. No signature, or even an initial. Not a word of explanation. Just that. But he knew that there was only one person on board who could have written it.

He had hurried over the rest of his toilet in the hope of finding Audrey Perowne in the saloon before the other guests arrived, but she had been the last to appear. He had not been able to summon up the courage to knock on the door of her cabin. His desire to see her and speak to her again alone, on any pretext, was tempered by an equal desire to avoid giving her any chance to refer to his last words of the previous night.

'The Jap is a good citizen,' George Y. Ulrig droned on, holding up his cocktail glass like a sceptre. 'He has few vices, he's clean, and he doesn't make trouble. On the other hand, he's too clever to trust. He... Say, boy, what's eatin' you?'

'Nothing,' denied Dicky hastily. 'What makes you think the Jap's too clever to trust?'

'Now the Chinaman's the honestest man in this world, whatever they say about him,' resumed the drone. 'I'll tell you a story to illustrate that...'

He told his story at leisure, and Dicky forced himself to look interested. It wasn't easy.

He was glad when they sat down to dinner. His partner was the less eagle-eyed Mrs George Y. Ulrig, who was incapable of noticing the absent-minded way in which he listened to her detailed description of her last illness.

But half-way through the meal he was recalled to attention by a challenge, and for some reason he was glad of it.

'Deeky,' said the girl at the end of the table.

Dicky looked up.

'Ve are in ze middle of an argument,' she said.

'Id iss this,' interrupted Sir Esdras Levy. 'Der Gountess asks, if for insdance you vos a friendt off mine, ant I hat made a business teal mit odder friendts off mine, ant bromised to tell nobody nothing, ant I see you vill be ruined if you don't know off der teal, ant I know der teal vill ruined be if you know off it – vot shoot I to?'

This lucid exposition was greeted with a suppressed titter which made Sir Esdras whiffle impatiently through his beard. He waved his hands excitedly.

'I say,' he proclaimed magisterially, 'dot a man's vort iss his pond. I am sorry for you, bud I must my vort keep.'

''Owever,' chipped in Mr Matthew Sankin, and, catching his wife's basilisk eye upon him, choked redly. '*How*-ever,' said Mr Matthew Sankin, 'I 'old by the British principle that a man oughter stick by his mates – friends – an' he ain't – asn't – *hasn't* got no right to let 'em down. None of 'em. That's wot.'

'Matthew, deah,' said Mrs Sankin silkily, 'the Countess was esking Mr Tremayne the question, Ay believe. Kaindly give us a chance to heah his opinion.'

'What about a show of hands?' suggested Dicky. 'How many of you say that a man should stand by his word – whatever it costs him?'

Six hands went up. Sankin and Ulrig were alone among the male dissenters.

'Lost by one,' said Dicky.

'No,' said the Countess. 'I do not vote. I make you ze chairman, Deeky, and you 'ave ze last vord. 'Ow do you say?'

'In this problem, there's no chance of a compromise? The man couldn't find a way to tell his friend so that it wouldn't spoil the deal for his other friends?'

'Ve hof no gompromises,' said Sir Esdras sternly.

Dicky looked down the table and met the girl's eyes steadily.

'Then,' he remarked, 'I should first see my partners and warn them that I was going to break my word, and then I should go and do it. But the first condition is essential.'

'A gompromise,' protested Sir Esdras. 'Subbose you hof nod der dime or der obbortunity?'

'How great is this friend?'

'Der greatest friendt you hof,' insisted the honourable man vehemently. 'Id mags no tifference.'

'Come orf it,' urged Mr Sankin. 'A Britisher doesn't let 'is best pal dahn.'

'Wall,' drawled George Y. Ulrig, 'does an American?'

'You say I am nod Briddish?' fumed Sir Esdras Levy, whiffling. 'You hof der imberdinence–'

'Deeky,' said the girl sweetly, 'you should make up your mind more queekly. Ozairvise ve shall 'ave a quarrel. Now, 'ow do you vote?'

Dicky looked round the table. He wondered who had started that fatuous argument. He could have believed that the girl had done it deliberately, judging by the way she was thrusting the casting vote upon him so insistently. But, if that were so, it could only mean…

But it didn't matter. With zero hour only a few minutes away, a strange mood of recklessness was upon him. It had started as simple impatience – impatience with the theories of George Y. Ulrig, impatience with the ailments of Mrs Ulrig. And now it had grown suddenly to a hell-for-leather desperation.

Audrey Perowne had said it. 'You should make up your mind more quickly.' And Dicky knew that it was true. He realized that he had squandered all his hours of grace on fruitless shilly-shallying which had taken him nowhere. Now he answered in a kind of panic.

'No,' he said. 'I'm against the motion. I'd

let down any partners, and smash the most colossal deal under the sun, rather than hurt anyone I loved. Now you know – and I hope you're satisfied.'

And he knew, as the last plates were removed, that he was fairly and squarely in the cart. He was certain then that Audrey Perowne had engineered the discussion, with intent to trap him into a statement. Well, she'd got what she wanted.

He was suspect. Hilloran and Audrey must have decided *that* after he'd left her cabin that afternoon. Then why the message before dinner?' They'd decided to eliminate him along with the rest. That message must have been a weakness on her part. She must have been banking on his humanity – and she'd inaugurated the argument, and brought him into it, simply to satisfy herself that her shirt was on a stone-cold certainty.

All right…

That was just where she'd wrecked her own bet. A grim, vindictive resentment was freezing his heart. She chose to trade on the love he'd confessed – and thereby she lost it. He hated her now, with an increasing hatred. She'd almost taken him in. Almost she'd made him ready to sacrifice his honour and the respect of his friends to save her. And now she was laughing at him.

When he'd answered, she'd smiled. He'd seen it – too late – and even then the meaning of that smile hadn't dawned on him immediately. But he understood it all now.

'Fool! Fool! Fool!' he cursed himself savagely, and the knowledge that he'd so nearly been seduced from his self-respect by such a waster was like a worm in his heart.

'But she doesn't get away with it,' he swore savagely to himself. 'By God, she doesn't get away with it!'

And savagely that vindictive determination lashed down his first fury to an intensely simmering malevolence. Savagely he cursed the moment's panic that had made him betray himself – speaking from his heart without having fully reckoned all that might be behind the question. And then suddenly he was very cold and watchful.

The steward was bringing in the tray of coffee.

As if from a great distance, Dicky Tremayne watched the cups being set before the guests. As each guest accepted his cup, Dicky shifted his eyes to the face above it. He hated nearly all of them. Of the women, Mrs Ulrig was the only one he could tolerate – for all her preoccupation with the diseases which she imagined afflicted her. Of the men, there were only two whom he found human: Matthew Sankin, the henpecked Cockney who had, somehow, come to be cursed rather than blessed with more money than he knew how to spend, and George Y. Ulrig, the didactic millionaire from the Middle West. The others he would have been delighted to rob at any convenient opportunity – particularly Sir Esdras Levy, an ill-chosen advertisement for a frequently noble race.

Dicky received his cup disinterestedly. His right hand was returning from his hip pocket. Of the two things which it brought with it, he hid one under his napkin: the cigarette-case he produced, and offered.

The girl caught his eye, but his face was expressionless.

An eternity seemed to pass before the first cup was lifted.

The others followed. Dicky counted them, stirring his own coffee mechanically. Three more to go … two more…

Matthew Sankin drank last. He alone dared to comment.

'Funny taste in this cawfy,' he said.

'It tastes good to me,' said Audrey Perowne, having tasted.

And Dicky Tremayne, watching her, saw something in her eyes which he could not interpret. It seemed to be meant for him but he hadn't the least idea what it was meant to be. A veiled mockery? A challenge? A gleam of triumph? Or what? It was a curious look. Blind…

Then he saw Lady Levy half rise from her

chair, clutch at her head, and fall sprawling across the table.

'Fainted,' said Matthew Sankin, on his feet. 'It's a bit stuffy in here – I've just noticed...'

Dicky sat still, and watched the man's eyes glaze over with a state of comical perplexity – watched, his mouth open, and saw him fall before he could speak again.

They fell one by one, while Dicky sat motionless, watching, with the sensation of being a spectator at a play. Dimly he appreciated the strangeness of the scene; dimly he heard the voices, and the smash of crockery swept from the table; but he himself was aloof, alone with his thoughts, and his right hand held his automatic pistol hidden under his napkin. He was aware that Ulrig was shaking him by the shoulder, babbling again and again: 'Doped – that coffee was doped – some goldurned son of a coot!' – until the American in his turn crumbled to the floor. And then Dicky and the girl were alone, she standing at her end of the table, and Dicky sitting at his end with the gun on his knee.

That queer blind look was still in her eyes. She said, in a hushed voice: 'Dicky–'

'I should laugh now,' said Dicky. 'You needn't bother to try and keep a straight face any longer. And in a few minutes you'll have nothing to laugh about – so I should laugh now.'

'I only took a sip,' she said.

'I see the rest was spilt,' said Dicky. 'Have some of mine.'

She was working round the table towards him, holding on to the backs of the swivel chairs. He never moved.

'Dicky, did you mean what you answered – just now?'

'I *did.* I suppose I might mean it still, if the conditions were fulfilled. You'll remember that I said – *Anyone I loved.* That doesn't apply here. Last night, I said I loved you. I apologise for the lie. I don't love you. I never could. But I thought–' He paused, and then drove home the taunt with all the stony contempt that was in him: 'I thought it would amuse me to make a fool of you.'

He might have struck her across the face. But he was without remorse. He still sat and watched her, with the impassivity of a graven image, till she spoke again.

'I sent you that note–'

'Because you thought you had a sufficient weapon in my love. Exactly. I understand that.'

She seemed to be keeping her feet by an effort of will. Her eyelids were drooping, and he saw tears under them.

'Who are you?' she asked.

'Dicky Tremayne is my real name,' he said, 'and I am one of the Saint's friends.'

She nodded so that her chin touched her chest.

'An – I – suppose – you – doped – my coffee,' she said, foolishly, childishly, in that small hushed voice that he had to strain to hear; and she slid down beside the chair she was holding, and fell on her face without another word.

Dicky Tremayne looked down at her in a kind of numb perplexity, with the ice of a merciless vengefulness holding him chilled and unnaturally calm. He looked down at her, at her crumpled dress, at her bare white arms, at the tousled crop of golden hair tumbled disorderly over her head by the fall, and he was like a figure of stone.

But within him something stirred and grew and fought with the foundations of his calm. He fought back at it, hating it, but it brought him slowly up from his chair at last, till he stood erect, still looking down at her, with his napkin fallen to his feet and the gun naked in his right hand.

'Audrey!' he cried suddenly.

His back was to the door. He heard the step behind him, but he could not move quicker than Hilloran's tongue.

'Stand still!' rapped Hilloran.

Dicky moved only his eyes.

These he raised to the clock in front of him, and saw that it was twenty minutes past nine.

9

'Drop that gun,' said Hilloran.

Dicky dropped the gun.

'Kick it away.'

Dicky kicked it away.

'Now you can turn round.'

Dicky turned slowly.

Hilloran, with his own gun in one hand and Dicky's gun in the other, was leaning back against the bulkhead by the door with a sneer of triumph on his face. Outside the door waited a file of seamen. Hilloran motioned them in.

'Of course, I was expecting this,' said Dicky.

'Mother's Bright Boy, you are,' said Hilloran.

He turned to the seamen, pointing with his gun.

'Frisk him and tie him up.'

'I'm not fighting,' said Dicky.

He submitted to the search imperturbably. The scrap of paper in his pocket was found and taken to Hilloran, who waved it aside after one glance at it.

'I guessed it was something like that,' he said. 'Dicky, you'll be glad to hear that I saw her slip it under your door. Lucky for me!'

'Very,' agreed Dicky dispassionately. 'She must have come as near fooling you as she was to fooling me. We ought to get on well together after this.'

'Fooling *you!*'

Dicky raised his eyebrows.

'How much did you hear outside that door?'

'Everything.'

'Then you must have understood – unless you're a born fool.'

'I understand that she double-crossed me, and warned you about the coffee.'

'Why d'you think she did that? Because she thought she'd got me under her thumb. Because she thought I was so crazy about her that I was as soundly doped that way as I could have been doped by a gallon of "knock-out". And she was right – then.'

The men were moving about with lengths of rope, binding wrists and ankles with methodical efficiency. Already pinioned himself, Dicky witnessed the guests being treated one by one in similar fashion, and remained outwardly unmoved. But his brain was working like lightning.

'When they're all safe,' said Hilloran, with a jerk of one gun, 'I'm going to ask you some questions – Mr Dicky Tremayne! You'd better get ready to answer right now, because I shan't be kind to you if you give trouble.'

Dicky stood in listless submission. He seemed to be in a kind of stupor. He had been like that ever since Hilloran had disarmed him. Except for the movements of his mouth, and the fact that he remained standing, there might have been no life in him. Everything about him pointed to a paralysed and fatalistic resignation.

'I shan't give any trouble,' he said tonelessly. 'Can't you understand that I've no further interest in anything – after what I've found out about her?'

Hilloran looked at him narrowly, but the words, and Dicky's slack pose, carried complete conviction. Tremayne might have been half-chloroformed. His apathetic, benumbed indifference was beyond dispute. It hung on him like a cloak of lead.

'Have you any friends on board?' asked Hilloran.

'No,' said Dicky flatly. 'I'm quite alone.'

'Is that the truth?'

For a moment Tremayne seemed stung to life.

'Don't be so damned dumb!' he snapped. 'I say I'm telling you the truth. Whether you believe me or not, you're getting just as good results this way as you would by torture. You've no way of proving my statements – however you obtain them.'

'Are you expecting any help from outside?'
'It was all in the letter you read.'
'By aeroplane?'
'Seaplane.'
'How many of your gang?'
'Possibly two. Possibly only one.'
'At what time?'
'Between eleven and twelve, any night from tonight on. Or at four o'clock any morning. I should have called them by flashing – a red light.'
'Any particular signal?'
'No. Just a regular intermittent flash,' said Dicky inertly. 'There's no catch in it.'
Hilloran studied his face curiously.
'I'd believe you – if the way you're surrendering wasn't the very opposite of everything that's ever been said about the Saint's gang.'
Tremayne's mouth twitched.
'For heaven's sake!' he burst out seethingly. 'Haven't I told you, you poor blamed boob? I'm fed up with the Saint. I'm fed up with everything. I don't give another lonely damn for anything anyone does. I tell you, I was mad about that double-crossing little slut. And now I see what she's really worth, I don't care what happens to her or to me. You can do what you like. Get on with it!'
Hilloran looked round the saloon. By then, everyone had been securely bound

except the girl, and the seamen were standing about uncertainly, waiting for further instructions.

Hilloran jerked his head in the direction of the door.

'Get out,' he ordered. 'There's two people here I want to interview – alone.'

Nevertheless, when the last man had left the room, closing the door behind him, Hilloran did not immediately proceed with the interview. Instead, he pocketed one gun, and produced a large bag of soft leather. With this he went round the room, collecting necklaces, ear-rings, brooches, rings, studs, bracelets, wallets – till the bag bulged and weighed heavy.

Then he added to it the contents of his pockets. More and more jewels slipped into the bag like a stream of glittering hailstones. When he had finished, he had some difficulty in tightening the cords that closed the mouth of it.

He balanced it appreciatively on the palm of his hand.

'One million dollars,' he said.

'You're welcome,' said Dicky.

'Now I'll talk,' said Hilloran.

He talked unemotionally, and Dicky listened without the least sign of feeling. At the end, he shrugged.

'You might shoot me first,' he suggested.

'I'll consider it.'

No sentence of death could ever have been given or received more calmly. It was a revelation to Dicky, in its way, for he would have expected Hilloran to bluster and threaten luridly. Hilloran, after all, had a good deal to be vindictive about. But the man's restraint was inhuman.

Tremayne's stoicism matched it. Hilloran promised death as he might have promised a drink: Dicky accepted the promise as he might have accepted a drink. Yet he never doubted that it was meant. The very unreality of Hilloran's command of temper made his sincerity more real than any theatrical elaboration could have done.

'I should like to ask a last favour,' said Dicky calmly.

'A cigarette?'

'I shouldn't refuse that. But what I should appreciate most would be the chance to finish telling – her – what I was telling her when you came in.'

Hilloran hesitated.

'If you agree,' added Dicky callously, 'I'd advise you to have her tied up first. Otherwise, she might try to untie me in the hope of saving her own skin. Seriously – we haven't been melodramatic about this tonight, so you might go on in the same way.'

'You're plucky,' said Hilloran.

Tremayne shrugged.

'When you've no further interest in life, death loses its terror.'

Hilloran went and picked up a length of rope that had been left over. He tied the girl's wrists behind her back; then he went to the door and called, and two men appeared.

'Take these two to my cabin,' he said. 'You'll remain on guard outside the door.' He turned back to Dicky. 'I shall signal at eleven. At any time after that, you may expect me to call you out on deck.'

'Thank you,' said Dicky quietly.

The first seaman had picked up Audrey Perowne, and Dicky followed him out of the saloon. The second brought up the rear.

The girl was laid down on the bunk in Hilloran's cabin. Dicky kicked down the folding seat and made himself as comfortable as he could. The men withdrew, closing the door.

Dicky looked out of the porthole and waited placidly. It was getting dark. The cabin was in twilight; and, beyond the porthole, a faintly luminous blue-grey dusk was deepening over the sea.

Sometimes he could hear the tramp of footsteps passing over the deck above. Apart from that, there was no sound but the murmuring undertone of slithering waters slipping past the hull, and the vibration, felt rather than heard, of the auxiliary engines.

It was all strangely peaceful. And Dicky waited.

After a long time, the girl sighed and moved. Then she lay still again. It was getting so dark that he could hardly see her face as anything but a pale blur in the shadow.

But presently she said, softly: 'So it worked.'

'What worked?'

'The coffee.'

He said: 'I had nothing to do with that.'

'Almost neat butyl, it was,' she said. 'That was clever. I guessed my own coffee would be doped, of course. I put the idea into Hilloran's head, because it's always helpful to know how you're going to be attacked. But I didn't think it'd be as strong as that. I thought it'd be safe to sip it.'

'Won't you believe that I didn't do it, Audrey?'

'I don't care. It was somebody clever who thought of catching me out with my own idea.'

He said: 'I didn't do it, Audrey.'

Then for a time there was a silence.

Then she said: 'My hands are tied.'

'So are mine.'

'He got you as well?'

'Easily. Audrey, how awake are you?'

'I'm quite awake now,' she said. 'Just very tired. And my head's splitting. But that doesn't matter. Have you got anything else to say?'

'Audrey, do you know who I am?'

'I know. You're one of the Saint's gang. You told me. But I knew it before.'

'You knew it before?'

'I've known it for a long time. As soon as I noticed that you weren't quite an ordinary crook, I made inquiries – on my own, without anyone knowing. It took a long time, but I did it. Didn't you meet at a flat in Brook Street?'

Dicky paused.

'Yes,' he said slowly. 'That's true. Then why did you keep it quiet?'

'That,' she said, 'is my very own business.'

'All the time I was with you, you were in danger – yet you deliberately kept me with you.'

'I chose to take the chance. That was because I loved you.'

'You what?'

'I loved you,' she said wearily. 'Oh, I can say it quite safely now. And I will, for my own private satisfaction. You hear me, Dicky Tremayne? I loved you. I suppose you never thought I could have the feelings of an ordinary woman. But I did. I had it worse than an ordinary woman has it. I've always lived recklessly, and I loved recklessly. The risk was worth it – as long as you were with me. But I never thought you cared for me, till last night…'

'Audrey, you tell me that!'

'Why not? It makes no difference now. We can say what we like – and there are no consequences. What exactly is going to happen to us?'

'My friends are coming in a seaplane. I told Hilloran, and he proposes to double-cross the crew. He's got all the jewels. He's going to give my signal. When the seaplane arrives, he's going to row out with me in a boat. My friends will be told that I'll be shot if they don't obey. Naturally, they'll obey – they'll put themselves in his hands, because they're that sort of fool. And Hilloran will board the seaplane and fly away – with you. He knows how to handle an aeroplane.'

'Couldn't you have told the crew that?'

'What for? One devil's better than twenty.'

'And what happens to you?'

'I go over the side with a lump of lead tied to each foot. Hilloran's got a grudge to settle – and he's going to settle it. He was so calm about it when he told me that I knew he meant every word. He's a curious type,' said Dicky meditatively. 'I wish I'd studied him more. Your ordinary crook would have been noisy and nasty about it, but there's nothing like that about Hilloran. You'd have thought it was the same thing to him as squashing a fly.'

There was another silence, while the cabin

grew darker still. Then she said: 'What are you thinking, Dicky?'

'I'm thinking,' he said, 'how suddenly things can change. I loved you. Then, when I thought you were trading on my love, and laughing at me up your sleeve all the time, I hated you. And then, when you fell down in the saloon, and you lay so still, I knew nothing but that I loved you whatever you did, and that all the hell you could give me was nothing because I had touched your hand and heard your blessed voice and seen you smile.'

She did not ask.

'But I lied to Hilloran,' he said. 'I told him nothing more than that my love had turned to hate, and not that my hate had turned back to love again. He believed me. I asked to be left alone with you before the end, to hurl my dying contempt on you – and he consented. That again makes him a curious type – but I knew he'd do it. That's why we're here now.'

'Why did you do that?'

'So that I could tell you the truth, and try to make you tell me the truth – and, perhaps, find some way out with you.'

The darkness had become almost the darkness of night.

She said, far away: 'I couldn't make up my mind. I kept on putting myself off and putting myself off, and in order to do that I *had* to trade on your love. But I forced you into that argument at dinner to find out how great your love could be. That was a woman's vanity – and I've paid for it. And I told Hilloran to dope your coffee, and told you not to drink it, so that you'd be ready to surprise him and hold him up when he thought you were doped. I was going to double-cross him, and then leave the rest in your hands, because I couldn't make up my mind.'

'It's a queer story, isn't it?' said Dicky Tremayne.

'But I've told you the truth now,' she said. 'And I tell you that if I can find the chance to throw myself out of the boat, or out of the seaplane, I'm going to take it. Because I love you.'

He was silent.

'I killed Morganheim,' she said, 'because I had a sister – once.'

He was very quiet.

'Dicky Tremayne,' she said, 'didn't you say you loved me – once?'

He was on his feet. She could see him.

'That was the truth.'

'Is it – still – true?'

'It will always be true,' he answered; and he was close beside her, on his knees beside the bunk. He was so close beside her that he could kiss her on the lips.

10

Simon Templar sat at the controls of the tiny seaplane, and stared thoughtfully across the water.

The moon had not yet risen, and the parachute flares he had thrown out to land by had been swallowed up into extinction by the sea. But he could see, a cable's length away, the lights of the yacht riding sulkily on a slight swell; and the lamp in the stern of the boat that was stealing darkly across the intervening stretch of water was reflected a thousand times by a thousand ripples, making a smear of dancing luminance across the deep.

He was alone. And he was glad to be alone, for undoubtedly something funny was going to happen.

He had himself, after much thought, written Patricia's letter to Dicky Tremayne, and he was satisfied that it had been explicit enough. 'My eyes are red from weeping for you.' It couldn't have been plainer. Red light – danger. A babe in arms couldn't have missed it.

And yet, when he had flown nearer, he had seen that the yacht was not moving; and his floats had hardly licked the first flurry of spray from the sea before the boat he was watching had put off from the ship's side.

He could not know that Dicky had given away that red signal deliberately, hoping that it would keep him on his guard and that the inspiration of the moment might provide for the rest. All the same, the Saint was a good guesser, and he was certainly on his guard. He knew that something very fishy was coming towards him across that piece of fishpond, and the only question was – what?

Thoughtfully the Saint fingered the butt of the Lewis gun that was mounted on the fuselage behind him. It had not been mounted there when he left San Remo that evening; for the sight of private seaplanes equipped with Lewis guns is admittedly unusual, and may legitimately cause comment. But it was there now. The Saint had locked it on to its special mounting as soon as his machine had come to rest. The tail of the seaplane was turned towards the yacht; and, twisting round in the roomy cockpit, the Saint could comfortably swivel the gun round and keep the sights on the approaching boat.

The boat, by that time, was only twenty yards away.

'Is that you, sonny boy?' called the Saint sharply.

The answering hail came clearly over the water:

'That's me, Saint.'

In the dark, the cigarette between the Saint's lips glowed with the steady redness of intense concentration. Then he took his cigarette from his mouth and sighted carefully.

'In that case,' he said, 'you can tell your pals to heave to, Dicky Tremayne. Because, if they come much nearer, they're going to get a lead shower-bath.'

The sentence ended in a stuttering burst from the gun; and five tracer bullets hissed through the night like fireflies and cut the water in a straight line directly across the boat's course. The Saint heard a barked command, and the boat lost way; but a laugh followed at once, and another voice spoke.

'Is that the Saint?'

The Saint only hesitated an instant.

'Present and correct,' he said, 'complete with halo. What do your friends call you, honeybunch?'

'This is John Hilloran speaking.'

'Good evening, John,' said the Saint politely.

The boat was close enough for him to be able to make out the figure standing up in the stern, and he drew a very thoughtful bead upon it. A Lewis gun is not the easiest weapon in the world to handle with a microscopic accuracy, but his sights had been picked out with luminous paint, and the standing figure was silhouetted clearly against the reflection in the water of one of the lights along the yacht's deck.

'I'll tell you,' said Hilloran, 'that I've got your friend at the end of my gun – so don't shoot any more.'

'Shoot, and be damned to him!' snapped in Dicky's voice. 'I don't care. But Audrey Perowne's here as well, and I'd like her to get away.'

'My future wife,' said Hilloran, and again his throaty chuckle drifted through the gloom.

Simon Templar took a long pull at his cigarette, and tapped some ash fastidiously into the water.

'Well – what's the idea, big boy?'

'I'm coming alongside. When I'm there, you're going to step quietly down into this boat. If you resist, or try any funny business, your friend will pass in his checks.'

'Is – that – so?' drawled Simon.

'That's so. I want to meet you – Mr Saint!'

'Well, well, *well!*' mocked the Saint alertly.

And there and then he had thrust upon him one of the most desperate decisions of a career that continued to exist only by the cool swift making of desperate decisions.

Dicky Tremayne was in that boat, and

Dicky Tremayne had somehow or other been stung. That had been fairly obvious ever since the flashing of that red signal. Only the actual details of the stinging had been waiting to be disclosed. Now the Saint knew.

And, although the Saint would willingly have stepped into a burning fiery furnace if he thought that by so doing he could help Dicky's getaway, he couldn't see how the principle applied at that moment. Once the Saint stepped down into that boat, there would be two of them in the *consommé* instead of one – and what would have been gained?

What, more important, would Hilloran have gained? Why should J. Hilloran be so anxious to increase his collection of Saints?

The Saint thoughtfully rolled his cigarette end between his finger and thumb, and dropped it into the water.

'Why,' ruminated the Saint – 'because the dear soul wants this blinkin' bus what I'm sitting in. He wants to take it and fly away into the wide world. Now, again – why? Well, there were supposed to be a million dollars' worth of jools in that there hooker. It's quite certain that their original owners haven't got them any longer – it's equally apparent that Audrey Perowne hasn't got them, or Dicky wouldn't have said that he wanted her to get away – and, clearly, Dicky hasn't got them. Therefore, Hilloran's got them. And the crew will want some of them. We don't imagine Hilloran proposes to load up the whole crew on this airyplane for their getaway: therefore, he only wants to load up himself and Audrey Perowne – leaving the ancient mariners behind to whistle for their share. Ha! Joke…'

And there seemed to be just one solitary way of circumventing the opposition.

Now, Hilloran wasn't expecting any fight at all. He'd had several drinks, for one thing, since the hold-up, and he was very sure of himself. He'd got everyone cold – Tremayne, Audrey, the crew, the Saint, and the jewels. He didn't see how anyone could get out of it.

He wasn't shaking with the anticipation of triumph, because he wasn't that sort of crook. He simply felt rather satisfied with his own ingenuity. Not that he was preening himself. He found it as natural to win that game as he would have found it natural to win a game of stud poker from a deaf, dumb, and blind imbecile child. That was all.

Of course, he didn't know the Saint except by reputation, and mere word-of-mouth reputations never cut much ice with Hilloran. He wasn't figuring on the Saint's uncanny intuition of the psychology of the crook, nor on the Saint's power of lightning logic and lightning decision. Nor had he reckoned on that quality of reckless audacity which lifted the Saint as far above the rut of ordinary adventures as Walter Hagen is above the man who has taken up golf to amuse himself in his old age – a quality which infected and inspired also the men whom the Saint led.

There was one desperate solution to the problem, and Hilloran ought to have seen it. But he hadn't seen it – or, if he had, he'd called it too desperate to be seriously considered. Which was where he was wrong to all eternity.

He stood up in the stern of the boat, a broad dominant figure in black relief against the shimmering waters, and called out again: 'I'm coming alongside now, Saint, if you're ready.'

'I'm ready,' said the Saint; and the butt of the Lewis gun was cuddled in to his shoulder as steadily as if it had lain on a rock.

Hilloran gave an order, and the sweeps dipped again. Hilloran remained standing.

If he knew what happened next, he had no time to co-ordinate his impressions. For the harsh stammer of the Lewis gun must have merged and mazed his brain with the sharp tearing agony that ripped through his chest, and the numbing darkness that blinded his eyes must have been confused with the numbing weakness that sapped all the strength from his body, and he could not have heard the choking of the breath in his throat, and the cold clutch of the waters that closed over him and dragged him down could have meant nothing to him at all…

But Dicky Tremayne, staring stupidly at the widening ripples that marked the spot where Hilloran had been swallowed up by the sea, heard the Saint's hail.

'Stand by for the mermaids!'

And at once there was a splash such as a seal makes in plunging from a high rock, and there followed the churning sounds of a strong swimmer racing through the water.

The two men who were the boat's crew seemed for a moment to sit in a trance; then, with a curse, one of them bent to his oars. The other followed suit.

Dicky knew that it was his turn.

He came to his feet and hurled himself forward, throwing himself anyhow across the back of the man nearest to him. The man was flung sideways and over on to his knees, so that the boat lurched perilously. Then Dicky had scrambled up again, somehow, with bruised shins, and feet that seemed to weigh a ton, and launched himself at the back of the next man in the same way.

The first man whom he had knocked over struck at him, with an oath, but Dicky didn't care. His hands were tied behind his back, but he kicked out, swung his shoulders, butted with his head – fought like a madman. His only object was to keep the men from any effective rowing until the Saint could reach them.

And then, hardly a foot from Dicky's eyes, a hand came over the gunwale, and he lay still, panting. A moment later the Saint had hauled himself over the side, almost overturning the boat as he did so.

'OK, sonny boy!' said the Saint, in that inimitable cheerful way that was like new life to those who heard it on their side, and drove his fist into the face of the nearest man.

Then the other man felt the point of a knife prick his throat.

'You heard your boss telling you to row over to the seaplane,' remarked the Saint gently, 'and I'm very hot on carrying out the wishes of the dead. Put your back into it!'

He held the knife in place with one hand, with the other hand he reached for the second little knife which he carried strapped to his calf.

'This way, Dicky boy, and we'll have you loose in no time.'

It was so. And then the boat was alongside the seaplane, and Dicky had freed the girl.

The Saint helped them up, and then went down to the stern of the boat and picked up the bag which lay fallen there. He tossed it into the cockpit, and followed it himself.

From that point of vantage he leaned over to address the crew of the boat.

'You've heard all you need to know,' he said. 'I am the Saint. Remember me in your prayers. And when you've got the yacht to a port, and you're faced with the problem of accounting for all that's happened to your passengers – remember me again. Because tomorrow morning every port in the Mediterranean will be watching for you, and on every quay there'll be detectives waiting to take you away to the place where you belong. So remember the Saint!'

And Simon Templar roused the engine of the seaplane and began to taxi over the water as the first shot spat out from the yacht's deck and went whining over the sea.

A week later, Chief Inspector Teal paid another visit to Brook Street.

'I'm very much obliged to you, Mr Templar,' he said. 'You'll be interested to hear that *Indomitable* picked up the *Corsican Maid* as she was trying to slip through the Straits of Gibraltar last night. They didn't put up much of a scrap.'

'You don't say!' murmured the Saint mockingly. 'But have some beer.'

Mr Teal sank ponderously into the chair.

'Fat men,' he declined, 'didn't ought to

drink – if you won't be offended. But listen, sir – what happened to the girl who was the leader of the gang? And what happened to the jewels?'

'You'll hear today,' said the Saint happily, 'that the jewels have been received by a certain London hospital. The owners will be able to get them back from there, and I leave the reward they'll contribute to the hospital to their own consciences. But I don't think public opinion will let them be stingy. As for the money that was collected in cash, some twenty-five thousand dollars. I – er – well, that's difficult to trace, isn't it?'

Mr Teal nodded sleepily.

'And Audrey Perowne, *alias* the Countess Anusia Marova?'

'Were you wanting to arrest her?'

'There's a warrant–'

The Saint shook his head sadly.

'What a waste of time, energy, paper, and ink! You ought to have told me that before. As it is, I'm afraid I – er – that is, she was packed off three days ago to a country where extradition doesn't work – I'm afraid I shouldn't know how to intercept her. Isn't that a shame?'

Teal grimaced.

'However,' said the Saint, 'I understand that she's going to reform and marry and settle down, so you needn't worry about what she'll do next.'

'How do you know that?' asked Teal suspiciously.

The Saint's smile was wholly angelic.

He flung out his hand.

'A little Dicky bird,' he answered musically, 'a little Dicky bird told me so this morning.'

The publishers hope that this book has given you enjoyable reading. Large Print Books are especially designed to be as easy to see and hold as possible. If you wish a complete list of our books please ask at your local library or write directly to:

Dales Large Print Books
Magna House, Long Preston,
Skipton, North Yorkshire.
BD23 4ND

This Large Print Book, for people
who cannot read normal print,
is published under the auspices of

THE ULVERSCROFT FOUNDATION

... we hope you have enjoyed this book.
Please think for a moment about those
who have worse eyesight than you ...
and are unable to even read or enjoy
Large Print without great difficulty.

You can help them by sending a
donation, large or small, to:

The Ulverscroft Foundation,
1, The Green, Bradgate Road,
Anstey, Leicestershire, LE7 7FU,
England.
or request a copy of our brochure for
more details.

The Foundation will use all donations
to assist those people who are visually
impaired and need special attention
with medical research, diagnosis
and treatment.

Thank you very much for your help.